Phantom Rustlers

Phantom Rustlers

Francis W. Hilton

SAGEBRUSH
Large Print Westerns

First published in Great Britain by Bles
First published in the United States by Kinsey

Published in Large Print 2009 by ISIS Publishing Ltd.,
7 Centremead, Osney Mead, Oxford OX2 0ES
United Kingdom
by arrangement with
Golden West Literary Agency

British Library Cataloguing in Publication Data
Hilton, Francis W.
    Phantom rustlers. – Large print ed. –
    (Sagebrush western series)
    1. Western stories
    2. Large type books
    I. Title
    813.5'4 [F]

ISBN 978–0–7531–8251–2 (hb)

Printed and bound in Great Britain by
T. J. International Ltd., Padstow, Cornwall

TO THE MEMORY OF MY FATHER,
one of the old West, who played the
game high, wide and handsome,
and never sold his saddle, is this
book affectionately dedicated.

CHAPTER
ONE

"Tokee! Tokee! Tokee!"

The shrill, eery cry, half human, half bestial, split the prairie stillness, echoed through the seared brush and died in the void of the night-wrapped Colorado wastes.

Big, raw boned Ed Maken, owner of the K-Spear ranch, dozing with his spur rowels hooked over the railing of the porch, brought his tilted chair down with a bang.

"There's that damned thing screeching again, Cochita. Sounds like it's up yonder in those breaks around Buck Riley's."

Dragging his ponderous bulk to his feet, he strained forward to catch the distant cry above a raucous medley of cowboy ballads arising lustily from the bunk house.

"Wish to God we could bury some of that noise on the lone prairie," he growled, nervously fingering the .45 slung at his angular hip. "Got so's you can hardly hear yourself think around this place with those bronc-peeling nightingales bawling fit to burst their wind-pipes."

His restless glance swept past the ranch buildings clustered in sharp silhouette against a soft June moon, wandered across the adobe flats dotted with chico brush and sage looming like misshapen sentinels in the effulgent glow, and on to the north where the filmy peaks of the Sangre de Cristos seemed to melt into the star-lit sky.

"Not getting anywhere standing here listening," he muttered presently. "Reckon it's up to us to run this 'tokee' down instead of depending on John Dawson. I'm betting if Joe Cline was still sporting that sheriff's badge we'd get action *pronto*, but this Dawson — hell!"

"Tokee! Tokee! Tokee!"

The flaxen-haired, blue-eyed girl at his side, staring dreamily out over the silver-tinted prairies toward the black, ugly gashes that marked the foothill breaks, shivered and drew the wrap closer about her shoulders as the unearthly cry again wavered through the night even above the dolorous strains of "Bury Me Not on the Lone Prairie", still emanating from the bunk house.

"Something must be done, daddy," she said in a tense, musical voice, "but I don't think it's fair to blame John Dawson. He has no clew to work on. You know way down in your heart it isn't the way he's handled this mystery that you hold against him — it's because you two disagreed over arresting that Double-Spear-Box bunch for rustling on the barest kind of suspicion. You're getting soured on everybody lately. Why don't you sell the ranch, and if Ramon and I —"

"You're not hooked up with that foreigner yet," he interrupted harshly. "Always was against it and always will be, else he turns up a hole card that shows me he's got more'n I think he has in his hand. Go on in the house!" In spite of the gruffness there was a note of tenderness in the big fellow's voice as he slipped his arm about her. "It's bad enough having this 'tokee' to worry about without getting all riled up over Spaniards. We ought to be riding those breaks right now trying to get a shot at that thing. Dawson'll come loping along *pronto* aiming to organize a posse and I want to beat him to it. I'm laying odds though it'll be just like it's always been — we'll find nothing."

"Can't I go with you?" she asked quickly.

He hesitated, watching her with loving eyes as she stood, slender and graceful, in the path of light from the open door. The rays, playing in the loose strands of her hair, seemed to bathe her in an aura of gold which brought out her profile with startling clearness.

"Go get your duds," he granted huskily. "Reckon I would feel a mite easier with you along instead of staying here by yourself. 'Low you can take care of yourself in a pinch as well as any of us anyhow. I'll hoof down and rout out those punchers. They can't hear anything with all that bellowing." He swung on his heel as she disappeared within.

"Aren't you Rocky Mountain canaries about all brayed out?" he demanded of the warbling cowhands as he stuck his head in at the door of the bunk house. "If you'd keep quiet once in a while you might hear that thing tokeeing again up in those breaks. Let's see if we can't find out what it is. One of you climb on the night horse and haze in the *cave*." Without waiting for an answer, he strode on to the barns.

The mention of the "tokee" roused the cowboys to instant action. The raucous song ceased abruptly. Faces that but a moment before were wreathed in pleasant grins and twisted awry in attempts to reach harmonious high notes, became set with seriousness. A silent, grim-mouthed group suddenly busy twirling the cylinders of six-guns and slipping cartridges into empty belt loops replaced the chorus that since sundown had tormented the soothing quiet of the night with lusty melody.

The snorting, blazing-eyed *cave* thundered in; the corral was transformed into an arena of choking, fighting horseflesh and grumbling humanity as the punchers singled out their mounts from the milling bunch. In an incredibly short time the horses were saddled and led from the enclosure into the lane where Maken and Cochita stood waiting.

"It's no use of me telling you fellows we're gunning for bear," said the cowman quietly, helping the girl up and swinging aboard his own mount. "We'll ride those breaks sharp. Ought to be easy to see anything with this moon. Won't anybody be prowling around up yonder this time of night that's got any business. Don't hold your fire for nothing. Shoot at a shadow and be damned sure you hit it."

With grim nods the punchers galloped into the night, the rancher and the girl setting the breakneck pace.

Outside the home ranch gate they struck a course for the foothills, misleadingly near, which loomed almost above them in the moonlight, the tops seemingly detached from the murky-streaked bottoms. Crossing

4

the flats they loped into the breaks in silence, the "clop-clop" of the horses' hoofs on the adobe sounding a pulsating, throbbing alarm against the mountain walls.

"Cochita." In a guarded tone Maken gave voice to the thing that had been on his mind for weeks. "What do you want with that Spaniard? He's got nothing except those skinny-looking long-horns and that half-wit peon following him around like a dog. Haven't seen him for a couple of days. What's become of him? Look out for this washout, fellows," he warned the posse as he detoured sharply to avoid a chasm-like ravine.

"Ramon was called to town," she replied stiffly, jerking up her pony at the very brink of the draw and wheeling in behind her father. "Some kind of legal business concerning an estate in old Mexico."

"Legal business?" he snorted disgustedly. "All the estate that hombre's got or ever will have is that choice section he squatted on down yonder in my home pasture."

"It wasn't yours anyway," she flashed, jabbing her pony angrily with the silver spurs tinkling on her booted heels and riding alongside him. "It belonged to the government."

"But those north water holes are mine," he snapped, "and those Double-Spear-Box dogies are going to get powerful gaunt before they get a drink, I'm telling you. Your homesteader's too friendly with that bunch to suit me."

"Why do you continually link Ramon's name with that gang?" she demanded. "You know he's not one of them. They're his nearest neighbors. Why shouldn't he be friendly?"

"Scatter boys!" Maken suddenly ordered, bringing up the silent men with a sweep of the hand. "Ride those gullies in pairs. If you see anything suspicious, open up. If you need help fire three times. Meet me and Cochita at Buck Riley's cabin in an hour."

He turned back to the girl as the men paired off, spread out and faded from sight in the haze-drenched breaks.

"Maybe so," he answered her, picking up the thread of their conversation, "but there's too many cows missing. Your Spaniard, or whatever he is, dresses too foxy, does no work and is always hanging around that Double-Spear-Box."

"Daddy!" she gasped. "You don't believe Ramon —"

"I'm saying nothing," he interrupted evasively, "but I'm doing some tall thinking. One thing I do know. Everytime anybody gets anything on the cow thieves he ups and croaks and this thing begins tokeeing."

"Well, you needn't accuse him!" she flared. "You seem to doubt everyone else lately, and now —"

"There, there," he consoled her. "Don't take on that way, I'm not intimating your billy boy's swinging a long rope, but I've got no use for him. His señors and meesters make me so all-fired hot I'd like to bust him on the jaw. Let's forget it now. We'd better keep our mouths shut and our eyes peeled. Watch sharp and if anything moves, holler."

Silence fell between them as they picked their way, knee to knee, through the ravine-gashed breaks.

Ed Maken and Cochita were not the only ones who had heard the bestial cry, which, during the few weeks since it first had screamed through the Sangre foot-hills, had instilled in the minds of the range folk a dread terror of some fabulous monster, some unknown, eery thing that dealt mysterious death at night. A mile to the south of the K-Spear, Sheriff John Dawson, riding back to Cibola, the county-seat, after a day of fruitless search for the rustlers whose depredations were driving the big cattlemen to desperation, jerked his pony to a halt in the trail and strained forward, listening.

"That damn thing's screechin' agin up toward Buck Riley's," he muttered aloud after the manner of men of the open spaces who talk constantly with their horses to pass the long, silent hours. "I'd sure like to get a shot at it, whatever it is. Reckon I'd better mosey over an' see if ol' Buck's alright."

Pulling his unwilling mount about, he started north at a gallop.

Still another horseman heard the cry. Jack Larimore, top rope for the Lazy-T outfit, picking his way through the cactus beds two miles ahead of the sheriff, drew rein and stood up in his stirrups, muscular body taut, as the "tokee" wavered across the prairie.

"Sounds like singing lizards!" he exclaimed. "Funny I never heard any in the range country before. Reminds me more of chasing old Aguinaldo in the Philippines than hunting grazing land for a bunch of dogies."

Sighting a light twinkling through the silver mist laying over the flats, he dismissed the incident as trivial in comparison to finding food and drink after a sweltering, endless day in the saddle, and urged his weary pony ahead.

Three miles of stiff riding brought him to a slabsided homestead shack.

"What's the chance of bedding down?" he shouted, pulling up and dismounting.

No answer save the night cries of the prairies.

"Queer anybody'd go away and leave a lamp burning," he mused aloud as he tied his horse at the corral and stamped toward the house. "Reckon even if I am a stranger I'll nose around and find me a bite of grub."

Entering the open door, he stood casually surveying the barely furnished interior of the cabin. A rough board table was littered with dirty tin plates and the remnants of an unfinished meal. A sadly battered chair, its rungs lying about the floor as though broken in a scuffle, and an upended box tilted against the side of the sap-streaked wall, were the only seats the shack boasted. Heat still radiated from a camp stove at his left, from which came the sickening fumes of burning grease.

A throbbing, ominous silence which aroused vague misgivings, beat down on him and tightened his nerves. The very atmosphere of the place seemed charged by the foreboding, sinister quiet. He experienced an unexplainable sensation of being watched by unseen eyes, yet a hasty glance at the one dirt-smeared window and back along the path to the corral revealed nothing.

"Hi, there!" he yelled, sighting a man stretched on a tarpaulin roll in the farthest corner. "Wake up and let's rustle some grub . . . Well, I'm damned!" The exclamation burst from lips that had drawn tight over even teeth. He bounded across the room and stood above the motionless figure.

The man was dead!

CHAPTER
TWO

"Eet ees better that yuh make the surrender!"

Startled, Larimore wheeled toward the open door to confront a .45 in the hands of a tall, swarthy-faced man with small, glittering black eyes shaded by an ornate sombrero. "I 'ave caught the señor weeth thees goods."

"Don't know what you're driving at," snapped the puncher, "but if you're connecting me with this hombre's dying you're sure all tangled up in your own throw-rope." He coolly sized up the good-looking stranger who had stepped within.

The fellow's chaparejos of soft, brown leather stamped with flowers, were fringed with short strings of white buckskin tied in the center of glistening metal discs. A gaudy, red silk shirt, thrown open at the neck, flamed violently beneath a brilliant vest checkerboarded with vivid colors. A well-filled cartridge belt sagged at his waist, the gun holster being notched away from the trigger guard to facilitate the draw. Inlaid spurs, set with large rowels and adorned with pear-shaped "danglers" which tinkled even above the scraping of the rowels when he walked, completed the costume.

Considering the noise made by the "grappling hooks" it struck Larimore as odd that he had not heard the fellow approach.

"So, the meester Riley 'e ees dead?" The stranger arched his eyebrows in question. "Eet ees as I 'spose. Therefore, I stop." His thin upper lip, set off by a sleek, pointed mustache, skinned back over his teeth in a smile that reminded Jack of a collie dog grinning under a caress. "Yore gun, señor. I weel now take 'eem *pronto*."

"What did you want me to surrender for if you didn't know this hombre was dead?" demanded the puncher suspiciously. "I'm not giving my iron to you or anybody like you. I just rode up to this place and asked for some grub."

The swarthy-faced man flushed dully and stared into the cowboy's cool, gray eyes. His gaze swept the lithe figure garbed in dun-colored chaps and dark shirt powdered with alkali dust, which presented a sharp contrast to his own flashy apparel. The broad shoulders, slightly stooped from riding, gave an impression of their real breadth and a powerful chest expansion when squared. The .45, well forward at the slender hips, suggested a cat-like speed, while the easy grace and calm assurance told of a latent energy and prodigious strength.

"What ees the name of the señor an' from where did 'e come?"

Larimore thought he could detect just a trace of uneasiness in the smooth, oily voice.

"None of your damn business." His quiet, deadly tone was a challenge. "I'm from a country where they plug hombres like you for getting heavy. If you're going to shoot, why don't you hop to it? Haven't you got nerve enough?" The taunt came from lips that were smiling, but the bloodless lines at the corners of the firm mouth gave the pleasant, almost boyish face, a look of determination which held the newcomer tense, the firearm steadied at his side, silent.

Again master of himself after the first shock of finding the body and the sudden appearance of the stranger, the cowboy scrutinized him in a superior, aggravating way as though deliberately trying to force gunplay. Then easing his weight on one leg he fearlessly dropped his hand to the butt of his Colt.

They stood glaring at one another like two strange bulls about to settle in mortal combat the supremacy of a wandering range herd. Both faces were expressionless. While the newcomer had the advantage of the draw, his finger hung loosely on the trigger. He started perceptibly as a shadow fell across the room. Aside from a shifting glance, however, Larimore gave no sign that he had seen the sheriff enter stealthily, gun in hand. Seconds of tense, nerve-racking stillness dragged by.

John Dawson was far from being a coward. His forty years on the trail were pregnant with recollections of fatal gunplay. His own .45 had exacted its toll of human life in the name of the law. Yet it occurred to him as he hesitated in the doorway that never before had he seen

12

eyes so utterly devoid of fear as the steady, gray orbs of the Texan, smiling a defiance at the threatening guns.

Sizing up the situation with a precision born of many desperate encounters where one false move meant death, his voice was little more than a whisper, yet it seemed to boom through the room. The tension snapped.

"What's goin' on here, Vasquale? Where's ol' Buck?"

The shrug of the Spaniard's shoulders, meant to be careless, fell short of its mark. The grin he essayed froze in a snarl across his flashing teeth.

"I fin' 'eem 'ere when the meester Riley 'e ees dead." He jerked his head toward Larimore.

"So ol' Buck's cashed in?" There was real concern in the officer's voice. "Kinda expected it though, when I heard that 'tokee'."

"Thees ees those 'ombre for which yuh search, Señor Dawson, si?"

The officer sized up the puncher who stood watching them unperturbed.

"I'm sheriff a this here county," he said quietly. "Who are yuh an' what's yore bus'ness, young feller?"

"Name's Jack Larimore of the Lazy-T, down on the Rio Grande. Riding through to the Yellowstone hunting range. Drought hit Texas and we 'lowed to trail some dogies north. Loped in here and found this stranger dead." He pointed to the still figure on the tarpaulin in the corner toward which the man the officer had called Vasquale had not even glanced. "Don't know who he is or what killed him. You can see for yourself all the chambers of my gun are full."

"That don't cut no ice. Mebbyso yuh plugged him an' filled 'em up agin." The officer's voice was colder as he became more certain of his ground. "Didn't hear no shootin', though," he conceded. "Le's take a look at him, but be damn shore yuh don't start nothin'."

Still under cover of the guns of the two, Larimore turned over the body.

"Same as all the resta 'em," growled Dawson after a cursory examination of the body which was clad in sadly-patched overalls, black shirt and heavy undergarments. "I've seen two others jes like him in the las' month. Daid without a way a tellin' how come. There ain't nothin' we can do. It's another case fer the coroner. Yore under arrest. Take his gun, Vasquale!"

"Aren't you going to try and find out what croaked him?" demanded Larimore, backing off. "When anybody dies it's a cinch there's some cause for it."

"Reckon yuh orter know enough 'bout it to tell us somethin'," snapped the officer testily.

Ignoring the accusation, and smiling almost pleasantly at Vasquale, who after the first start had made no attempt to execute the sheriff's command, the Texan stooped over the body.

A close examination failed to reveal any powder marks or bullet wounds. The throat he found to be bruised as though the man had been choked with a thong. Mentally putting the case down as one of strangulation, he straightened up, casting about for the rope which had been used by the slayer. Puzzled by his failure to locate it, and wondering why the assassin should have been so cautious about removing it unless it was a particular piece which might have furnished a clew, he stood thoughtfully, allowing his gaze to rove over the figure.

The buttons, he noted, were missing from the shirt and undergarments. They had been torn away violently, along with bits of the material, which seemed to indicate that the rancher had been attacked from behind, choked and dragged to the tarpaulin. This accounted for the smoking grease on the stove and the unfinished meal. Riley had been eating with his back to the open door, he reasoned quickly, the killer had entered stealthily and had seized him about the throat. The struggle had been brief. The victim had been choked into unconsciousness, but not before the rungs had been broken from the chair and the box kicked across the room.

He glanced at Vasquale. The noise made by the spur rowels and danglers weighed heavily in his favor as far as the murder was concerned. He could not well have approached Riley without having been heard.

Paying no heed to his captors, the puncher again bent over the body. Opening the clothing, he discovered two tiny flesh punctures in a discolored bruise directly over the heart. With his eye he traced the purple streaks radiating under the skin from the swelling. They bore the appearance of having been made with a hypodermic needle.

Puzzled by the methods employed by the slayer to make doubly certain that his victim was dead, he raised up, cudgeling his brain for a solution to the perplexing problem. He gazed idly about the room. Suddenly the unearthly cry he had heard on the trail seemed to ring in his ears.

He stooped hastily and re-examined the marks. They had a peculiar likeness to the mutilation of fetishism he had heard of among the savage tribes of the Philippines. And that scream!

" 'Tokee!' " he mused aloud, staring down at the body. "I'm damned!"

He wheeled back to the sheriff who was watching him with hawk-like intensity, and started to voice his suspicion, but the hostile attitude of the two, who seemed to resent his attempt to fathom the mystery, stayed his words.

"Well?" Dawson's voice had lost every vestige of friendliness. Convinced that the cowboy knew something of the murder and was sparring for time while casting about for an avenue of escape, he had determined to disarm him without gunplay, if possible, and thus prevent a recurrence of the tense scene into which he had walked. But the coldness of his tone, calculated to put him in command of the situation, failed utterly to impress Larimore.

"Figure it out for yourself," said the puncher coolly. "You've made up your mind I'm guilty. Reckon you don't want to know —"

"Shut up!" barked the officer. "I'm goin' to run yuh in. Get his gun, Ramon!"

"Feel like you just got to take somebody, do you?" parried Jack. "Why don't you arrest this other hombre?" He indicated Vasquale who had not moved, apparently having little stomach for the job. "He came

16

single-footing in here 'lowing I'd better surrender and then was surprised as the devil when he found out somebody was dead. He must have been here when I rode up because he pops right in and he didn't come from the corrals either or I'd a heard those fancy spurs of his. He's got a shifty eye —"

"'Ave a care, señor," grated the swarthy-faced man. "I weel —"

"You'll play hell!" challenged the cowboy. "If you think you're going to take me for this killing," he hurled at Dawson, meanwhile watching from the corner of his eye every move of Vasquale who had flushed and stepped forward threateningly, "you've got another think a-coming. I'm a plumb stranger in these parts and I'm not going to trust myself being tried for murder in one of your kangaroo courts. There's a thousand head of dogies at the Lazy-I' depending on me for range. They'd all die while I was laying in your calaboose. Howsomever, I'll make you a proposition if you'll forget this arresting business and talk sense."

"Don't know any kinda deal yuh could make," snorted the sheriff, now thoroughly angered by the puncher's aggravating calm and even voice, "but play yore cards."

"Got a hunch after looking at this body that may or may not amount to something. Along with a noise I heard coming up the trail a while back it set me to thinking."

"A holler that sounded like 'tokee'!?"

"Yep."

"Don't reckon that takes much heavy figgerin' on yore part." The officer was determined to force a showdown. "Yuh probably know what it is. I've heard it three times in the last few weeks an' it's allus been right after a killin'. Whaddaya goin' to spring?"

"Nothing." Larimore whipped out the word. "I reckon I do know more about this 'tokee' thing than any of you hombres that was raised here in the cow country and never been west of Salt Lake." Vasquale shifted uneasily. Larimore glanced at him quickly, wondered, but the man's face was as expressionless as a death mask. "I'll stick around and see if we can run it down if you'll help me find some range hereabouts and not lock me up."

" 'Low yuh could spill a right smart knowlige 'bout it if yuh'd a mind to," flared Dawson, "but that ain't makin' no diff'rence. Yore under arrest an' I'm goin' to jail yuh. If yuh got anythin' to say the jedge'll be plumb tickled to hear it."

"I'm not afraid of you nor your law nor anything you have up here in this country of rain-beaters," drawled the puncher so quietly that his tone was maddening. "Go ahead and try and take me if you feel lucky. You've got no case against me. I was just offering to help you work this thing out."

"Don't need yore help." Dawson's clasp tightened on the butt of his .45. "Vasquale, get that gun!"

The order created exactly the situation he had hoped to avoid. The smile on Larimore's face broadened and set on bloodless lips. His steady gray eyes were flicked with points of angry flame. In spite of the overwhelming odds against him, his hand fell to his Colt. An almost effortless move, as smooth as a trick of legerdemain, and the .45 rested lightly on his hip.

"Drop your irons!" His tone was metallic, like flint on steel. "I'm not going to jail for something I didn't do."

The sheriff's firearm blazed. The bullet whined past the cowboy's head and struck the side of the shack with a dull thud. Vasquale's trigger finger contracted with deadly, tantalizing slowness.

"Shooting to kill, are you?" grated Larimore between gritting teeth. His six-gun spat, then swung on Vasquale and cracked again. "Two can play at that game. Guess an innocent man can even pot a sheriff in self-defense."

Dawson reeled drunkenly, clutched blindly at the table, dragging the tin plates to the floor with a crash, and slumped weakly into the swaying chair with the broken rungs.

The swarthy-faced man's aim had been too deliberate, he had been too cock-sure of his advantage. His .45 flew from numbed fingers. He shook his tingling hand frantically and backed off, but the snarling smile never left his face.

Larimore stood motionless, wondering, admiring the fellow's courage. The tense, breathless pantomime, broken only by Dawson's groans, seemed endless.

Vasquale's grin broadened. The puncher started for the door. A few steps and he halted, listening.

He turned back, the reason for the other's smile explained. Vasquale's quick ear had caught the sound of pounding hoofs which now drifted to Larimore from without.

CHAPTER
THREE

Even above the dull hammering in his brain which set him swaying to and fro in the creaking chair, the sheriff heard the hoofbeats. He clutched the table dizzily with one hand while with the other he wiped the blood trickling into his eyes from a slight scalp wound which traced the part in his hair.

"That'll like as not be ol' Ed Maken an' his K-Spear punchers," he mumbled jerkily. "Better get that iron a your'n stashed afore they come ridin' in. They'll blow yuh clean off'n this range." He shook himself like a dog coming out of water and stared about in a daze.

"Don't be so damn sure," retorted Larimore. "I'll take care of myself."

In spite of his outward calm, he was uneasy. Paying little attention to Dawson — in his stupefied condition scarcely a dangerous adversary — he kept Vasquale, who stood nursing his pain-shot hand, well within range of his vision as he cast about for a way of escape. The approaching horsemen, he realized, commanded a clear view of the door in the bright moonlight, thus cutting off his retreat in that direction. The dust-covered window was too small for him to squeeze through even had he dared turn his back on the pair within the room.

The sound of hoofs grew louder. The riders were galloping up to the corral. Grimly he faced the fact that he was trapped! Vasquale's tantalizing smile broadened. It kindled a dull rage within him. With an effort he overcame a wild desire to smash the leering, handsome face with the butt of his gun.

Filling the two empty chambers of his .45, and facing the door, he backed from the circle of light and waited in the shadows beside the tarpaulin. His already taut nerves twanged at the sound of stamping, booted feet and jangling spur rowels on the path leading to the house.

"You'd better call 'em off or there's going to be a whole heap of funerals," he warned quietly.

Dawson's reply was unintelligible as he attempted with his foot to work the Colt that had fallen from his nerveless hand within reach of his shaking fingers. He looked up stupidly at Larimore's even drawl:

"Drop those guns!"

Ten K-Spear punchers, headed by Maken, leaped into the room. Taken completely by surprise, they halted dead in their tracks. Their firearms clattered to the floor. Maken's move was typical of the man. Instead of heeding the terse command, he calmly shoved his iron back into its holster.

"Who's doing the shooting?" he demanded.

"I was." The steady voice of the cowboy, obscured to the eyes not yet accustomed to the wan light, set the men to shifting uneasily, peering into the shadows for a glimpse of their dimly outlined opponent. "There's going to be more if you hombres bat an —"

The warning died on his lips. He caught his breath sharply. The most beautiful girl he ever had seen had stepped up beside the tall leader of the party.

"What's the matter, Dawson?" asked Maken, ignoring the threatening Colt which gleamed blue and sinister from the gloom, and advancing fearlessly toward the officer.

"Why, he's wounded, daddy! Look at the blood on his face!" cried the girl, starting forward.

"Hold up, Cochita," snapped her father, pushing her back roughly. "Let's get laid out here before we lose our heads." His strained tone increased the tenseness which hung like a pall over the room.

"Come in here an' found ol' Buck dead jes like Bevens an' Cline," faltered Dawson, his words coming thickly from between teeth clenched with pain. "This stranger was in the cabin." The creasing had taken the fight out of him. He sat nursing his bleeding head, trying to collect his hazy thoughts. "Vasquale —"

A smothered cry from the girl interrupted him. Eluding her father, she leaped to where the swarthy-faced man stood in the shadows.

"Ramon!" she cried. "Are you hurt?"

Larimore followed her movements from the corner of his eye, his .45 trained on the line of punchers.

"Mi hand he ees pain." The fellow shrugged his shoulders carelessly and grinned at Cochita. "Thees 'tokee' ees one fine shot."

He shook his tingling fingers sharply in an attempt to restore circulation. The girl wheeled back to Jack. Her blue eyes blazed a defiance of the steady gun. Her body trembled with anger. She suddenly took on the appearance of a gorgeous leopardess at bay, ready to spring upon him, tearing him to pieces. The angry color playing in her face only seemed to accentuate her beauty, which held him spellbound as his eyes met hers, evenly, unflinchingly.

"You found this hombre in the cabin?" Maken picked up the thread of the sheriff's conversation, cutting in on the mental battle raging between the youth and girl and indicating the Texan, who now was plainly visible as the cowman's eyes became accustomed to the dull light.

"Yep." Dawson dabbed gingerly at his wounded scalp with a red bandanna. "Ramon had the drop on him. He shot me an' threw the fear a God into Vasquale after I'd put him under arrest. Watch him. He's a killer an' chain lightnin' with that .45." Trembling rage had replaced the falter in the officer's voice. "I'm deputizin' yore bunch to take him if yuh hafta shoot him plumb full a holes!"

"Just a minute," interposed Maken. "Like as not he's got a story. What's your name and what are you doing here, young fellow?"

Tearing his gaze from the girl, Larimore met the ranchman's eyes fearlessly. He saw a friendliness and fairness which inspired confidence. The stillness seemed to throb through the room as they sized up one another, attempting to pierce the expressionless masks that veiled each face and peer beyond into the swiftly working minds.

A student of human nature, as was every baron of the old range days, Maken rated men by the steadiness of their eyes and gun-arm and the horse-flesh they chose. Larimore met the test. In addition he possessed a visible dash and vigor which the cowman himself had lost during the latter years. He liked the honesty and determination stamped in the pupils of the puncher's cool, gray orbs, while the youth's easy, nonchalant grace stirred him deeply. He found himself completely won over to the cause of the stranger.

"Jack Larimore," answered the Texan presently. "Hunting range for the Lazy-T outfit of Texas."

"Lazy-T?" queried Maken. "Know a hombre by the name of Peters — Boss Peters?"

Vasquale started perceptibly, but the movement might have passed for a relaxation of his tense body.

"He's my foreman." Larimore's words were colored with suspicion and surprise. "Do you know him?"

Beginning to exercise some sort of control over his spinning head, Dawson stared incredulously as the cowman walked forward to the very muzzle of the puncher's leveled .45, his hand extended. The girl stifled a scream. The K-Spear hands stood rigid, expecting momentarily to hear the gun crack.

"My name's Ed Maken of the K-Spear, and I'm powerful glad to meet you, Larimore." The broad smile on the weather-beaten face showed no trace of fear. "I'll say I know old Boss Peters. He and I hit the trail together for ten years. How's Boss?"

24

Completely nonplussed, Jack's gun wavered for an instant. Shifting it, he grasped the cowman's hand. Then pulling himself up sharply, he recovered his composure and drawled:

"Oh, Boss is all right."

"Glad to hear it," returned Maken. "How did you get into this mess, young fellow?"

The frank, whole-souled friendliness was chipping at the crust of the cowboy's mistrust. Briefly he told his story.

"And this breed," he concluded, pointing to Vasquale who had moved until he was partly concealed behind the girl, "just walks in and gets the drop. We both have been here for quite a spell. I've got no cause to kill him and he's got nerve enough to —"

From the corner of his eye he caught the glint of a knife blade. Again changing his .45 to his left hand, he bounded forward. His fist shot out. Vasquale dropped like a log.

"Let 'em lay!" he snapped, master of the situation before the men, who had taken advantage of the by-play, could close their eager fingers on the butts of the guns at their feet.

"Give him hell even if he is aiming to be my son-in-law!" roared Maken. "Any hombre who packs a knife ought to be worked over."

"Daddy!" cried the girl, burying her face in her hands. "I'll never forgive you for that."

The flush of anger receded from her face, leaving her pale. Dropping to her knees beside the prone man, she raised his head in her arms.

Only stunned by the blow, Vasquale staggered to his feet. He stood glaring at the puncher but made no move to recover the knife that had caromed across the floor and come to a stop beside his gun. A restless movement along the line of cowhands showed plainly that the result of the battle had been to their liking.

"Beg pardon, miss," said Larimore softly. "I plumb forgot myself when I started a scrap in front of a lady. It's not often I do it, but I've stood around here looking into these hombres' guns so long I'm kind of skittish."

"Don't speak to me, you — you — murderer!" she flared. Her voice cut through the room and whipped the color from his face. "If I were a man I'd — I'd —" Words failed her.

"You'd do just like the rest of these fellows have done." His tone was as cold as her own. "You'd talk turkey. I'm right glad you're not a man for —" He checked himself abruptly. "Well, I just wouldn't be called a murderer, that's all. I hope you never get accused of anything like that, for if you ever do you'll know how I feel." Her challenge had aroused him to a fury. His gray eyes were pointed with shafts of livid flame. "Get a way cleared to that door," he barked to the punchers. "I'm going through and the first man that bats an eye gets plugged!"

He started forward. Tearing from her father's grasp, Cochita moved directly into his path. Her fists were clenched tightly. Her bosom heaved with anger. Their eyes met and clashed. Words sprang to her tongue but she held them back, biting her white lips nervously. He fought against a wild desire to throw down his gun and

26

take his chances of proving his innocence in court, but the hot blood drumming in his veins conquered. Brushing past her he sidled along the wall.

"Stop him!" shouted Dawson, swaying to his feet and leaning weakly against the table. "He's that 'tokee'. He killed Buck. It's a clean-cut case — circumstantial if nothin' else. Shut that door!"

"I'll drill the first man that touches that door!" Larimore's voice was as cold as chilled steel.

Breathing a sigh of relief as the fearless, headstrong Cochita shrank from the anger blazing in the Texan's eyes, Maken stepped across the room and looked down at the body of Riley.

"Just like the rest of 'em," he muttered to himself. Turning back he watched the puncher who had almost succeeded in reaching the entrance. His glance roved to the girl. She stood with one hand on her breast, her eyes resting in fascination on the cowboy. Her taut body plainly showed the rage his ease and assurance had aroused.

The K-Spear hands were frozen in their tracks, held motionless by the compelling personality of the man and his steady gun. Their expressions varied from actual fear to the broad grin of "Red" Mowbry, one of Maken's top men, who seemed to be enjoying the proceedings immensely.

As he gazed at the faces, then back to the blood-smeared, fuming Dawson who stood unarmed, powerless to prevent the escape of his prisoner, Maken found himself groping for a way to aid the youth. A man of quick decisions, his mind, once made up, was unalterable. Added to this stubbornness was a contempt for the sheriff which many times had brought them to the point of gunplay. Yet above all the cowman was convinced by the fearless movements and extreme confidence of the puncher that he was innocent.

"Just a minute," he said slowly. "That kid never did this, Dawson. Take a look at him close. If he was to murder it'd be plumb between the eyes with that Colt he's packing. He could have killed you, but only creased you instead. He had a chance to plug Vasquale but laid off because Ramon didn't have a gun, even if he was flashing a knife. He's not this 'tokee' any more'n I am. I know cows and men. He's one of my old side kick's hands and Boss wouldn't have anybody around who wasn't there and over. I'm short of punchers. Let me take him. I'll be responsible for him any time you want him, providing you've really got something to convict him on." His eyes met those of Larimore who had paused and was hanging on to his words. "Give me your pledge you won't try to sneak off the range?"

"What are you doing, trying to stack the deck on me?" demanded the Texan suspiciously.

"I shoot square," snapped the cowman. "I'm offering to help you because I don't think you're guilty. I'm willing to take you down to the K-Spear till things clear up."

"Daddy!" gasped the girl incredulously. "Have you lost your mind?"

"Not near so much as you did a while back by getting in that hombre's way when he was riled up," he threw at her. "I'm talking turkey."

28

The sincerity of his tone was unmistakable.

"Show me your *rancho*," grinned Larimore. "I'm with you till the cows come home."

"Can't do it, Maken," protested the sheriff, pressing his aching head between his hands. "He's my prisoner an' I can't turn him over."

"He don't look like your prisoner or anybody else's to me," snorted the cowman. "But if that's the way you feel about it —" he addressed himself to the punchers — "mosey out to your horses, boys. We're heading home. You want this hombre so damn bad, you take him!" he hurled at Dawson as he started for the door. "If you don't have any more luck than you did before we rode up, I reckon we'll have a double funeral for you and old Buck."

"I'm deputizin' yuh an' yore punchers, Maken!" shouted the sheriff, playing his last card. "Yuh help me make this arrest or I'll have yuh an' yore hull gang yanked into court."

The cowman smiled. "I offered you a proposition. Take it or leave it. I won't lose any sleep over your dragging me and my men into court."

Dawson swallowed the hot retort that hovered on his tongue. While he was convinced of Larimore's guilt and chagrined at his apparent inability at every turn to cope with the Texan, still he did not care to cross Maken, who as one of the big cattle barons on the range was not only a power to be reckoned with, but who as a gunman for years had been the inexorable master along the Sangre trails. It was no time for bravado or threats. He realized that diplomacy was his one chance to bring about the capture which he himself was powerless to make.

"I'll hafta take yore proposition rather than let him get away," he said sullenly. "Yore forcin' me into it, but there'll be a kick back somewheres. I'm givin' yuh fair warnin' though. Yore responsible fer a prisoner that's facin' a murder charge. If I can't send him up fer the killin' a ol' Buck, I allus got his woundin' me while resistin' arrest to fall back on."

"It's a go, then?" asked Maken.

"It'll hafta be," was the surly reply.

Larimore ducked outside as the officer answered. From the door he watched Dawson stoop dizzily, seize his six-gun and ram it viciously into its holster. An almost irresistible force urged him to flee while the opportunity was at hand, but pinning his faith in the integrity stamped on the face of Maken he waited, listening.

"I'm tellin' yuh," the sheriff wheeled on the cowman, "yuh wanna be damn shore an' have him handy when I come fer him, 'cause I'm comin' a-shootin'."

Without glancing to left or right, he strode from the cabin. The K-Spear hands, recovering their own fire-arms, followed. The girl, still angry, head high, brought up the rear with her father and Vasquale.

Suspicious in spite of himself of the almost unbelievable turn of events, and on his guard against trickery, Larimore lingered in the shadow of the shack not yet fully convinced that the cowman's intercession in his behalf had been prompted by other than ulterior motives.

"Put up your gun," said Maken pleasantly, pausing beside him. "There's going to be no more shooting tonight. My word's good as my bond. A man's always innocent with me till he's proved guilty. You wouldn't get a break with Dawson. He'd a nabbed you if he'd had a chance, because he's got to arrest somebody in these killings pretty soon or old Judge Lynch's going to open court. If you didn't croak Buck Riley there's a bed roll waiting for you at the K-Spear till the thing's sifted down. If you did, you'd better start riding, for we'll get you if it takes every man I've got." He waited, his gaze boring into the Texan's.

Calmly Larimorc sheathed his six-gun.

"I didn't kill Riley," he said quietly, extending his hand. "Shake, pard."

In silence he walked beside the cowman back to the corral where he had tied his pony,

CHAPTER
FOUR

Still vaguely uneasy, Larimore hesitated at the enclosure until the others had mounted, then keeping well behind his horse he stooped for his bridle reins. A sound startled him. He leaped back, reaching for his gun.

A figure curled along the bottom pole of the fence, like a huge snake seeking warmth, arose and stood outlined in the moonlight. Jack's .45 swung up, but Maken, spurring forward with a shout, seized the barrel.

"He's all right. It's only Pedro," he laughed.

Larimore stared at the man who was leering through cracked, repulsive lips stretched across toothless gums. Almost bent double with age, the figure reminded him of a mangy coyote humped-back with cold and hunger. Long, withered arms dangling from a ragged shirt many sizes too small, gave the same impression of strength as the listless body of a boa. The seamed face, almost the color of wet buckskin, drew to a peak at the chin that protruded sharply from below the mere slit of a mouth and which was surmounted by a thin, beak-like nose. Small, beady eyes glittered beneath shaggy brows. Unkempt, grayish locks hanging over his

32

shoulders were caught up at the low, furrowed forehead by a dirty ribbon that once had been red. A sash of the same faded material held up the soiled, flare-bottom, cotton trousers which wrapped playfully about his badly bowed legs and moccasined feet when he stepped, and also served as a sheath for a long, wicked-looking knife.

"Much obliged for the information, Maken," said Larimore in a measured voice which plainly showed his nervousness. "He might be all right, but I'd sure hate to meet him alone at night."

"He's Vasquale's shadow," explained the cowman as the Texan swung into the saddle and the crowd started for the K-Spear. "He's so old he's harmless. Not all there. Kind of loco. You know?" He tapped his forehead significantly. "He's a regular dog, though, to that Spaniard, and he thinks Cochita's finer than frog legs. Never feel uneasy when he's round the ranch, because I know anybody'd have to walk over his body to harm my little gal."

With the explanation Maken fell silent, while Jack, sunk in thought, was content to jog along turning the chain of startling occurrences over in his mind.

Vasquale rode ahead with the girl, old Pedro trotting beside his horse like an awkward, hunched animal. The punchers were laughing and poking fun at Dawson who, obviously disgusted with the whole proceedings, answered their jibes with surly grunts. Maken and Larimore brought up the rear of the cavalcade.

The moon, glowing like a huge lantern on the horizon, bathed the prairies in a soft, mellow light.

From the foothills of the Sangre de Cristos came the occasional *yip, yip* of a coyote, followed by a long, quivering wail. The dogs on the neighboring ranches caught up the challenge and hurled it back with throaty, ferocious barks.

Two miles from the K-Spear the sheriff halted on the branch road to Cibola.

"Don't fergit, Maken," he warned, "yore responsible fer this feller. I'm only lettin' yuh have him 'cause I couldn't a-took him without a gun back yonder at Riley's, an' 'cause I ain't carin' to start nothin' with yore hull gang. But I'm tellin' yuh, as soon as I gets the coroner lined up on this case an' we holds an inquest, yuh'd better be ready to turn him over. I'll be wantin' him *pronto*."

"You got my word," snapped the cowman none too pleasantly. "If he tries to give me the slip, I'll come and get you and you can trail him down again."

Without replying to the thrust, Dawson reined into the road and headed south for town, twenty miles distant.

"What do you make of it?" asked Maken presently, breaking the silence that again had fallen between them as they dropped back into the rear of the crowd after the officer's departure.

"Rather not say right now," Larimore tossed his cigarette into the trail and turned from his observation of the peaceful prairies. "Got a hunch I want to play. I believe the sheriff said something about there being two other killings lately? Anything like this one?"

34

"Both of 'em," growled the cowman, rubbing his bristling beard savagely at the recollection of the crimes. "First some cows turn up missing, usually from the Franklin, Brewster or my herds. Then the fellow who's been riding those north brakes, and like as not has seen something, gets killed. This 'tokee' thing begins hollering. When we find the corpse there're those marks around its throat from choking and those little purple dots over the heart.

"There was my foreman, Jim Bevens, as fine a cowhand as ever hit these parts. Then Joe Cline, the deputy sheriff. Now it's Riley. Old Buck's been working for me. Every time it's a fellow who's pushing those rustlers hard. I'm doing that. Maybe they've got me spotted, you can never tell."

The musical laugh of the girl drifted back to them. It struck Larimore as strangely out of place — like a burst of barbaric song during a funeral. He took hold of himself, attempting to shake off the unreasonable depression that had enveloped him since he had walked into Riley's cabin.

"Creepy, all right," he admitted, unconsciously watching old Pedro shuffling along beside Vasquale's horse. "But it shouldn't be very hard to run down."

"Holding a joker?" Maken glanced at him quickly.

"Maybe so. But if you don't mind I'll play my own hand for a spell. First thing I've got to do is find range for a thousand head of dogies —"

"Mind a little roughhousing?"

Larimore eyed the cowman sharply at the interruption. "Do I look like a blushing posey?"

"Well, no, not exactly. Here's my cards, face up. I know the Double-Spear-Box gang's rustling, but I can't hang anything on 'em. I've got a fine piece of range that runs clean past Old Woman creek yonder to the foothills north of Riley's place. Supposing I let you have that, along with the water holes, gratis?"

"Play your joker," cut in Jack. "It isn't Christmas."

Maken leaned over in his saddle. "*Providing* Boss Peters'll send a half dozen men who know their rights and aren't afraid to shoot and who'll keep their eyes peeled for that Double-Spear-Box bunch."

"You're on." The Texan extended his hand. "I'll ride south —"

"Whoa! You're riding nowheres, only on K-Spear range. You gave me your word you'd stay as long as you were suspected of this killing. Don't get it into your head I think you're guilty. If I had I'd shot it out with you back there at Riley's. You need help and I need help. But there's still another thing."

"That 'tokee' business?" Larimore anticipated his thoughts.

"Yep. You see, my foreman, Bevens, was doing a little gum-shoeing when somebody shuffles him off. We found him out near the brakes killed just like old Buck. I'm plumb certain in my own mind Jim knew too much. I'm needing a man to take his place."

"Well?" Jack's tone showed but mild interest.

"I want a bronc peeler who can shoot, rope and raise hell in particular when he has to. The job's open if you can convince me you're pure-bred stuff instead of stray grade."

"How'll I get word to Boss to come on with the Lazy-T dogies?"

"Give me a few days and I'll see what I can do. Are you willing to sit in?"

"What about that gal? She kind of strikes me as having a little something to say about things herself. And I'm sure poison to her."

"Reckon Cochita'll come out of it all right. She's used to having her own way and won't stand for bossing like you did up at that cabin. She's my side-kick. Rides, ropes, shoots with the best of 'em, and the hardest hombre on the range hunts cover when she gets riled, so it isn't surprising you got her sore."

"I don't mind a little gunplay now and then just to liven things up, but I'm plumb yellow when it comes to women," confessed Jack. "If you'll handle the filly, you can just give me a tryout on the rest of it."

At the gate to the lane, winding like a ribbon in the moonlight to the clustered buildings of the ranch, Vasquale, after bidding the girl good night, waited until the two rode up.

"A thousan' pardons, Señor Larimore," he apologized, extending his hand. "Shall we be the so-good frien's an' forgeeve?"

"By the way, Vasquale," cut in the ranchman before the astonished Texan could reply, "I thought you were in town for a couple of days on some estate business?"

"The affair, señor," flashed the fellow, "'e ees take but the so leetle time. I return *pronto* by way of Riley's. I fin' thees señor weetheen. But eef the so beeg meester

Maken say thees 'ombre no keel Riley, then weel I offer mi hand in those frien'sheep."

"Ugh!" grunted Maken.

Fighting against a feeling of revulsion at sight of the toothless Pedro smiling beside his master, Larimore clasped the extended hand. He gazed steadily into Vasquale's eyes, which met his evenly. Something about the handsome face and suave manner of the fellow was impelling, yet try as he would he could not shake off a sense of uneasiness which the sharp, black eyes inspired. The roving orbs reminded him of a wolf slinking through a herd, apparently fearful for its life, yet only waiting a chance to sink its fangs into the throat of some straggling calf. And it took but Pedro to complete the picture in his mind.

"Sure," he said quietly, which was far from the way he felt. "But you remember from now on I'm all-fired skittish when any fellow yanks a gun on me, and I'm plumb dead set against being carved up with a knife."

"Ah, eet ees to be remember, *amigo*," smiled Vasquale, rubbing his jaw which was badly swollen from the blow of the puncher's fist. "Per'aps I was what yuh call thees-een the wrong stall — 'ombre, si? But I shall carry no ill-will. An' señor," he turned to Maken, "I shall be over early to 'elp yore *vaquerors* ride thees snakey 'orses een the mornin'."

"Well, I'm damned!" snorted the cowman disgustedly as the fellow spurred into the night followed by Pedro, who, clinging to a saddle string, shuffled along easily beside the horse. "That's the first time a Spaniard ever shook hands with a hombre who'd shot his gun out of his paw and busted him in the jaw to boot. Keep your eyes peeled. Those fellows pack a smile and a knife at the same time."

"I know 'em," said Larimore. "You want to recollect I come from a country that's lousy with 'em. That fellow is no more Spaniard than you or me. He's a plain Navajo breed who's been educated by the government. They're the most treacherous mess ever thrown together."

"Just what I thought," observed Maken. "And he's stringing the gal plumb ory-eyed with his palavering of estates and castles and pure-bred pedigrees. He's sure got me guessing, though. One day I want to pat him on the back and the next I get a hankering to bust his head wide open. He makes me feel cheap when he offers to ride ten miles over here from his homestead to top off a bunch of outlaws when he knows I'm short of bronc peelers. Then when I see him again he reminds me of maggots. Something tells me he's snakey. I get to watching him and he ups and does me a good turn that makes me plumb ashamed . . .

"Cochita there's got a touch of loco about him. He's such a good-looking devil you can't blame her, and he's nervy, too. Then he's a gent around her and I haven't the heart to run him off the place. God knows she's got no women folks around for company. She had eastern schooling, and I want to keep her contented. Her ma — she — just — couldn't stand the lonesomeness. We buried her yonder at the ranch." The gruff voice broke. He swiped viciously at a tear. "As I was saying, Vasquale'd lay down and let her wipe her feet on him.

And old Pedro's the same way. Rather have him around than a watch-dog anytime. But I haven't a heap of use for foreigners. Cochita's ma named her, or you bet your life she wouldn't be packing her high-faluting monicker. She's only eighteen, and I guess we kind of spoiled her making over her, but she'll come out of it. Reckon it's only a passing fancy for Vasquale, but if she does really get to caring for him — which she's never done yet for any hombre more'n a few months at a time — I'll have to pack her up and ship her back east for a spell."

He changed his line of conversation abruptly. "I can't figure Vasquale. He's always hanging around the Double-Spear-Box ranch. All the hands over there are breeds or something, and near as I can find out, nobody ever sees their boss, who's supposed to be in Mexico City. You take it from me, though, his shaking hands with you after you batted him on the jaw sure is no sign of friendship. He's not the general run of grade stuff. He's got that holster notched, and it isn't to look tough, either. He's quicker'n lightning with that gun and I never saw a yellow streak. Keep your eye peeled, that's all."

Silence again fell between them as they rode up to the corrals and dismounted. Turning their ponies over to the punchers, the girl, Maken and Larimore, at the cowman's request, made their way toward the big ranch house.

Within the large living-room, made homey by the unmistakable touch of a woman's hand, the father, in a voice which seemed pleading for permission, told

Cochita of Larimore's willingness to join the K-Spear force. She smiled coldly, yet could not hide a certain elusive sweetness that set Jack's blood drumming. There was about her a distant reserve, tempered with the anger he had aroused back at Riley's cabin, that made him twirl his hat awkwardly and shift uncomfortably under her steady gaze.

"Congratulations, Mr. Larimore," she said icily. "A man of your ability with a gun should be a decided asset to daddy in running down his phantom rustlers."

"Phantom?" exploded Maken. "Why do you keep harping that there's no cow stealing?"

"Simply because our balance sheets do not show any missing," she replied quickly, as though glad to be done with being pleasant to Larimore. "We're shipping as many cattle now as we did five years ago, in spite of the fact that you estimate we are losing a thousand head a year."

"You want to remember," protested her father, "that yearlings this fall are producers next, and five years should show a heap of difference in the number of steers loaded for market. Somebody's swinging a long rope in my profits — either that or those Double-Spear-Box punchers have got a bunch of critters that has calves faster'n rabbits." While he was talking he was busy scrawling a note with the stub of a pencil.

"What are you doing, daddy?" she asked.

"Your aunt's wedding anniversary tomorrow," he answered shortly, "and I 'lowed to get a message off to her. You kids chew the fat while I start a puncher for

Cibola." Stamping outside, he made his way to the bunk house.

"Take this straight to the telegraph office," he ordered, calling one of the men from the table where the hands already were deep in a game of "stud" for the "makin's", and handing him the message he had written, "and wait in town for an answer. Do you understand?"

Nodding his head, the cowboy started for the corrals. A short time later the thud of hoofs was lost on the trail to town.

Maken returned to the house to find the girl silent and Larimore squirming uneasily.

"What's the matter?" he demanded. "You haven't quit speaking already, have you?"

Cochita arose and started from the room.

"I'm terribly tired and upset, daddy," she explained. "Good night."

"Reckon all of those didoes up to Riley's did kind of get under her hide," apologized Maken as she closed the door behind her. "Then again it never entered my head that she might not feel easy in here all alone with a hombre that the sheriff thinks killed old Buck. But she didn't seem scared. She's riled up about something. What did you say to her?"

"Say?" blurted out Larimore. "I didn't get a chance to say anything. She's sore clean through, about me busting that breed in the jaw. Reckon if I'd a been the dangest gun-toter in seven counties I'd have kept my mouth shut. She just naturally told me where to head

42

in. 'Lowed I didn't need to bother about even speaking to her."

"She sure can tell a fellow," agreed Maken, grinning. "I ought to've wised you up. When Cochita gets riled we hombres quit the flat high, wide, and handsome." Then seriously. "Don't expect it's being done with prisoners, but I reckon you'll be more comfortable in the bunk house instead of up here with me standing guard —" his face again broke into a grin — "or snoring. Besides I'm too tuckered out to night-hawk you. You'll just have to turn in down yonder. Red'll show you a bed roll. Good night."

CHAPTER
FIVE

Daybreak found Larimore shivering as he pulled on his dew-damp boots. Stamping from the bunk house in the chill of the summer dawn, he surveyed the country about the K-Spear. To the north the rock-crowned, pine-clad peaks of the Sangre de Cristos caught up the slanting beams of the sun as it crept over the horizon, hurling them in a rainbow of color among the blues and reds and yellows of cliff and precipice and crag.

To the south, dotted with chaparral and sage, the plains stretched in unbroken expanse, quiet save for the song of the meadow-larks teetering in the tops of the brush and the sharp bark of the prairie dog. Cotton-woods traced the course of the arroyos, writhing like giant, green-backed serpents toward the deep, heavily-timbered cañon of Old Woman creek. From the foot-hills drifted the bleat of a calf or the kingly roar of some sire aroused from a one-eyed nap.

Maken's fences were everywhere. Even to Larimore who was accustomed to boundless range, the extent of the K-Spear holdings was unbelievable.

He turned back to the large, two-story house. It was painted and well kept. Here and there a drooping flower-bed spoke of Cochita. The pretty pieces of flint, the glistening stones that lined the gravel walk to the outbuildings were evidence of an almost childish love for the beautiful, and pricked him sharply with an unexplainable longing for the things he never had been able to know.

The squatty log bunk houses, too, which straggled toward the peeled, cottonwood corrals, gave the appearance of having the attention of an employer who looked to the comfort and welfare of his men. The enormous barn with its yawning mow doors was as inviting as the other buildings. The whole scene was one of peace and contentment which seemed to ease the tumult of the thoughts that had kept him tossing restlessly throughout the night.

The shouts of the wranglers, galloping behind a kicking, frolicking *remuda* through which a bunch of outlaws criss-crossed, their snorts whistling through flaring nostrils, interrupted his observations and brought him back to the somber reality of his situation. With a sigh he stirred himself and made his way toward the kitchen, from the rough, stone chimney of which a thin column of smoke melted to nothing in the gray-blue sky. Filling the battered wash basin with cold water, he sloshed it over his face.

"There they come, chawin' the groun' they're so wild!"

He blinked through dripping fingers at the rotund, bow-legged figure of the cook whose fat body was shaking with mirth at the antics of the *cave* and the outlaws which the jinglers were attempting to throw into the corrals. "Snakey as hell," he admitted, peering at the pitching animals with one eye as he dragged a towel across his face.

"Who asked yuh what yuh thought of 'em?" The chef glowered belligerently and described an arc with a huge butcher knife, to which clung pieces of the steaks he had just cut for breakfast.

"Listen, grub sp'iler," growled Larimore, "I'm no new hand. I've been in this game a long spell. If there's anything I hate worse'n a dough-god hombre that ruins grub in a chuck wagon on a round-up, it's a sourdough Johnny at a home ranch. You and me're going to get on fine if you don't drive me to kill you right off at the start."

The cook sized him up in a leisurely, insulting way.

"Oh, yore one of them Sam Basses from Texas that eats 'em alive, yuh are, are yuh?" he snarled. "Well, yore my bacon. Had a feller up here oncest — yuh make me think a heap a him only he was a hull lot bigger an' I reckon a better man all the way 'roun'. I carved him down like a this —" he made a pass with the knife — "and then thataway." The blade whistled by Larimore's ear.

"Snake up, pard," roared the puncher. "I used to kill me a grub sp'iler every morning to get an appetite. I wallow in blood. I love to chaw —"

He stopped short. A broad grin spread over the face of the cook as it disappeared behind a flour sack apron. Cochita stood in the doorway.

"I really believe you do, Mr. Larimore," she said frigidly. "At least your actions last night struck me that way." She swept past haughtily on her way to the corrals, leaving the speechless cowboy staring after her. A dull flush crept to the roots of his hair. Fighting against the slow anger her words had kindled, he turned back to the chef whose fat sides were quivering with suppressed laughter.

"See, I got frien's, I have, yuh common cowhand," taunted the cook. "Yore a man killer —"

"Shut up!" Larimore's voice had lost its bantering tone. "I've pulled a loco play. That gal doesn't like me nohow. I'll blow the head plumb off of you if you chuckle again, you braying jackass."

"Aw, hell!" The man extended a pudgy, flour-powdered hand. "Yuh win. Shake. I ain't got no bus'ness with a Sam Bass like yuh. But don't let Cochita get under yore hide. She likes yuh fine or she wouldn't even take the trouble to bawl yuh out. That's her."

In spite of the cook's attempt to explain the girl's sharpness, the cowboy was hurt far deeper than even he would admit to himself. He sauntered about restlessly, only nodding at the friendly sallies of the punchers as they trooped, yawning and stretching, from the bunk houses. They seemed to bear no grudge, in fact appeared to have forgotten completely the events of the previous night. The greeting of Red Mowbry, for whom he had taken an instant liking, was typical.

"Jack, ol' companero," the freckle-faced, fiery-topped cowboy had assured him soberly, "it ain't the K-Spear way to pick up strays, but when one comes driftin' in a-needin' shelter the hull gang, even to that loudmouthed cook, turns out to make it feel to home."

Larimore had accepted the offer of friendship as it had been given — wholeheartedly and without reservations — and felt better for it. Yet with the girl's remarks still rankling, he determined to see Maken, withdraw his pledge to stay on the ranch, and if necessary surrender to Dawson or fight his way out of the country. While with the decision came a lighter feeling, he could not rouse himself to answer the good-natured jibes poked at him across the table a short time later, when the big triangle chimed its welcome notes to the hungry punchers.

"Fill up yore bread baskets," laughed Red during the course of the meal. "We're goin' to top off them snake-eyes today fer the beef round-up strings. Yore goin' to need a heap a grub stowed away 'cause it won't take them outlaws very long to digest it for yuh."

The business of breakfast — which to the cowboy is serious and which takes precedent over almost anything else on the ranch, with the possible exception of dinner and supper — having been finished, saddles were lifted from pegs in the barn or rolled from beneath bunks in the adobe houses, spurs were jerked up a notch, and kinks whirled from lariats.

A laughing, jesting crew, the K-Spear hands trooped out, dragging their paraphernalia behind them. One by one they took their turns on the horses cut singly into the round corrals ready for "forkin'".

Aside from those who helped saddle the plunging, bawling cayuses, and Red, astride the "snubbing horse" — on which Maken insisted, as a governor to check the cowboys' failing for deliberately making the animals pitch — the rest of the men, spurs hooked in the fence, were distributed along the top poles, alternately sucking on cigarettes and taunting the reeking, fighting riders.

Topping off the wild bunch was but part of the day's work for Larimore, who lolled on the fence, uninterested. The shouts about him, an occasional grunt knocked from the body of some "peeler" as he hit the hard-packed earth in the corrals, fell on deaf ears. He found himself craning his neck for a sight of the girl who had returned to the house while the men were at breakfast. But she did not put in an appearance.

"You're a fine mark," he mused bitterly. "A forty-dollar cowhand gettin' a kink in your neck trying to sight the boss's gal."

Fully aware of the chasm that yawned between them, he was still determined to talk with Cochita and convince her, if possible, that he knew nothing whatever of the killing of Riley. From that point on he could not reason, but through his mind ran a forlorn hope which the girl's stinging remarks had flayed cruelly and on which he clicked his teeth savagely.

Lost in thought, he started at the cheery: "Hallo!" at his elbow. He turned quickly to face Vasquale, who sat on his horse below, grinning up at him. The ancient Pedro, shuffling his moccasined feet in the dust, smiled in his leering way.

"Now watch 'em duck fer cover!"

Mowbry's shout from within the corrals brought Jack about, watching the horse that had been cut into the yard. His idle glance became a stare of admiration. The great blue-roan gelding, head up, nostrils flaring, circled the enclosure, its legs moving with the precision of a mechanical doll. Terror showed in the depths of the liquid eyes rolled back to the whites, yet a defiance and unconquerable spirit that would test the mettle of any cowboy lurked in the steel-like muscles rippling beneath the sleek hide.

"Vasquale! Vasquale!" bellowed a puncher. "Here's yore chancet to show what yuh can do. Come on, yuh bronc peeler! Yuh ain't never been throwed and Blue ain't never been rid clean. Do yuh want some of it?"

Vasquale, who had climbed to a perch beside Larimore, shrugged his shoulders.

"Eet ees the boys would like to see thees 'orse get 'eemself one vaquero, *si?*" he grinned. "I weel 'ave mucha *gusto* to try for ride your outlaw," he yelled to the waiting men. "*Carajo!* Ees not so what yuh call thees-eat 'em alive. Pedro, my riata!" He dropped lightly into the corrals.

Larimore saw a flash of fear in the faded eyes of the peon as he leaped for the rope that hung at the bow of his master's saddle.

"Got the old badger plumb scared to death," he muttered to himself as Pedro returned quickly and passed the lariat through the poles. "Anybody can handle a dog if they beat him into doing what they say."

He idly watched the scene below. With an easy grace, Vasquale tossed the noose in a back-hand throw, catching the snorting Blue about the neck.

But the big roan was not to be subdued without a battle. As the rope grew taut, it wheeled and charged like a thunderbolt, mouth open, teeth bared, ears laid back hatefully. Up on its hind legs it came, pawing, striking, squealing.

With the speed of a cougar Vasquale leaped aside. A dexterous flip and a half-hitch ran smoothly along the riata, encircling the threshing forefeet. An almost effortless move, that brought a salvo of cheers from the punchers, and the gelding crashed to the ground with a thud that drove the wind from its heaving body.

It lay stunned for a minute, making no fight against the hackamore and the new lariat that was slipped over its front hoofs by another puncher, who braced himself with the rope over his hip. Vasquale's riata was shaken from the fetlocks and the noose, which was bringing the animal's breath in hoarse raspings, was snubbed about the horn of Red's saddle.

The outlaw struggled to its feet, its head high, but the fall had warned it not to attempt another hostile move while the riata burned into its fetlocks. It stood trembling as Vasquale eased the saddle, that old Pedro had brought, into place.

"That hombre sure knows how to use a rope," mused Larimore, his mistrust of the fellow slowly giving way to admiration. "If he can ride like that —"

Vasquale's cat-like grace as he vaulted to the back of Red's horse and slipped into the saddle aboard Blue interrupted his thoughts. The puncher braced with the lariat over his hip flipped it loose from the fetlocks. Mowbry jerked up the snubbing rope around the horn as Vasquale gathered in the reins of the hackamore.

The gelding hesitated for a moment, shaking violently, the swaying back threatening to give under the weight of the rider. The cowboy's foot flew forward to dodge a vicious kick that scraped the stirrup leather. His spurs sank home with a force that brought a bawl of pain from the animal. It catapulted across the corral. Apparently unprepared for the move, Red fought futilely to hold the snubbing rope which burned the horn as it was torn from its moorings. With the choking rope loose about its windpipe, before Vasquale could throw his strength on the hackamore, the horse buried its head, straightened out with the speed of a striking snake and left the ground with all four feet. Its belly curved with the grace of a leaping fish. It hit the adobe with a thud that sent the chunks of earth flying.

"God!" came the voice of Red, who, having lost the lariat, had spurred around to where Larimore sat on the fence. "If the boss'd see us toppin' without snubbin' he'd raise pertic'l'r hell. Aw, I don't reckon he'd shoot off his head much either, seein' it's Vasquale forkin' Blue." Something in the tone brought a quick glance from Jack.

"Did you lose that rope or turn the outlaw loose on purpose?" he asked in an undertone.

"I turned him loose a-purpose," grinned the puncher, "an' I hopes he wipes up the hull range with that damn smart alec."

Larimore smiled. It was plain to be seen that Vasquale rated no higher with the K-Spear men than with Maken himself. Yet as he watched the fellow ride he could not help but admire his easy grace and assurance. Suddenly he felt himself go taut.

"Ride him clean, you kiote!" he shouted, hot anger replacing the admiration Vasquale's exhibition had aroused. "That isn't an Indian pony. If he was my horse I'd pull you off there and break your head. Do you see that, Red?"

Mowbry stared. Vasquale's fancy spurs were locked. The sharp rowels were sunk like grappling hooks into the bleeding sides of the gelding. The rider's quirt was slicing blood from the froth-streaked neck and shoulders.

"By God, yore right!" hissed Red. "He's ridin' with locked spurs."

"We're not going to have horses cut to pieces while I'm around here," snapped Larimore. "Get him, Blue!"

As though hearing the words, the animal reared, walked half-way across the corrals on its hind legs, sending the helpers scrambling to cover from its striking hoofs, then hurled itself over backward.

It struggled to its feet in a choking mass of dirt, its head buried, its bleeding nose scraping the ground. Vasquale was on top and again the merciless rowels were sunk in its sides.

"Ten dollars he can't ride him even with his spurs locked!" shouted Larimore. The punchers glanced at him uneasily. "Are you on, Red?" The tone itself was a challenge. "Ten bucks as says he bites the dust!"

"Lay off'n him," warned the man at his elbow in an undertone. "He ain't got no love fer yuh nohow after las' night, an' he packs a gun-arm that ain't to be monkeyed with."

"No man that ever cut a good horse to pieces with spurs has guts!" blazed Jack. "I'll play my hand. Any you fellows want this money?"

Above the thud of the pounding hoofs and the bawling of the enraged outlaw, Vasquale heard the offer. His lips twisted in a smile.

"Make eet the 'undred an' I weel call yuh!" he panted.

"You're on," bellowed Larimore. "A hundred bucks you're not slung right to fork that horse without pulling leather, even with your spurs locked!" Unconsciously he felt the roll of bills Boss Peters had given him for expense money. It was exactly the size of the wager.

"Get yourself a cowboy, bronc!" he cried. "Get yourself a cowboy!"

CHAPTER
SIX

The challenge Larimore hurled at Vasquale brought the K-Spear hands up expectantly. While the expressions on their faces showed their sympathies were with the Texan, still it was plain that not one of them could foresee a possibility of his winning his bet. To those without the finer instincts of sportsmanship that had caused Jack's outburst, the wager and the warning it carried were pregnant with opportunities for an open break which was to their liking. Knowing Vasquale as they did, they knew that even if by chance he should fail to ride the outlaw, still smarting under the events of the night before, he could do little less than defend his sensitive pride.

His apparently quiet submission to Larimore at Riley's cabin had caused no small comment among the cowboys, who now leaned forward breathlessly, assured of action either way the cards fell. A cloud of apprehension as thick as the blanket of dust raised by the "thumpity, thumpity" of the pitching horse's hoofs hung over the group.

"Get yourself a waddy, horse!" roared Jack, the least nervous of the entire crew.

The words were scarcely out of his mouth when the gelding landed stiff-legged, spun about, and bucked straight away in the opposite direction.

Riding with an abandon designed more to bring cheers from the onlookers than for safety, Vasquale lost a stirrup, grabbed frantically for the horn as it swept past, missed, and shot across the corrals. He was on his feet in an instant.

"Sacre!" he screamed, whipping his six-gun from its holster. As though anticipating a hostile move, the roan reared and started for him, striking and pawing the air viciously. Larimore leaped down from the fence.

"Kill that horse and I'll kill you!" he blazed, his Colt resting on his hip. "You're a fine sport, you are. Tear an animal all to pieces with locked spurs, then expect him to eat out of your hand. Put up that iron before I take it away from you and bust it over your head!"

He sprang aside as the outlaw lunged toward them. Red's rope whistled through the air. The punchers dragged the snorting gelding back.

The two men stood glaring at one another. A tenseness that was electric charged the atmosphere. The cowboys waited with bated breath.

Vasquale was the first to move. The scowl that darkened his face broke into a broad grin. The crew stared incredulously. His .45 slipped back into its holster.

"I'll take the señor another 'undred 'e can't ride thees Blue weethout spurs, or weeth, as 'e shall choose."

56

His even tone, which gave the lie to the yellow he had just displayed in backing down before Larimore's draw, set the men wondering. They made no attempt to conceal their surprise. While it was evident that Vasquale was avoiding an open break with Jack, it was just as obvious that his attitude was not inspired by fear, but rather was a cool, calculating indifference that portended swift and deadly action when the opportunity arrived for him to call the turn. In spite of his offer of friendship, after the Riley episode, the K-Spear men knew that Vasquale did not forget.

"I heard you the first time," returned Jack calmly. "I'm calling your bet and warning you that you're not abusing horses when I'm around." Sheathing his gun, he deliberately turned his back on Vasquale. "Snake up Blue and snub him, Red," he said quietly to Mowbry. "Not so tight, just so's I can handle him easy-like."

Despite the gelding's mistrust, he changed saddles with little difficulty, sliding his own onto the steaming back and tightening the cinch gently.

"Thataboy," he crooned. "We're all through getting hurt now. Your day's gouging with spurs is over."

The horse eyed him savagely; started to strike as he reached out and scratched its forelock. Then, intrigued by the unprecedented tenderness, it nosed forward.

Having broken through the crust of the outlaw's suspicion, Jack climbed up behind Red on the snubbing horse.

"Watch Vasquale," warned Mowbry in an undertone. "He's too damn all-fired handy with that gun. Yuh seem to have throwed the fear a God into him to his face, but that .45 a his'n might go off behind yore back."

"Don't worry," muttered the Texan. "I know those hombres."

"I been achin' to crack down on him fer quite a spell," admitted the snubber, "but I reckon yuh saved me the trouble. I'll keep my eye on him while yore forkin' this cayuse, but you've gotta be yore own bodyguard after that. Them fellers can't stand havin' their pride rassled 'roun' a corral. While I plumb admire to hear yuh call his hand, that bet'll cost yore life if he ever gets a bead on yuh. What yuh goin' to do?" He stared in astonishment as Larimore reached down and stripped off his spurs.

"Going to show that breed you don't have to cut even an outlaw to pieces to ride him; 'lowing to bust me out a top horse and buy him if the old man'll sell him," explained the Texan. "He's the prettiest gelding I ever saw. Ain't he?"

"He shore is," agreed the puncher as Jack gathered up the reins of the hackamore and eased himself from the snubbing horse into the saddle aboard Blue, "but if there's any little chores 'bout windin' up yore estate, yuh better lemme know afore yuh tops him off without diggers."

"Just pay out that snubbing rope and turn him loose," smiled Jack. "If the old man says anythin' tell him the half-hitch slipped again."

"I'm damned!" exclaimed Mowbry, staring at Larimore who had settled himself in the saddle and sat scratching the gelding's ears.

The horse casually looked over the silent crowd on the fence. It shook its head impatiently at the crooning voice of the rider and took one or two mincing steps forward, then turning, gazed studiously at the boot hanging in the stirrup at its side. Bending its body, it sniffed of the foot. Apparently satisfied, it resumed its survey of the waiting, motionless punchers.

The events of the next few minutes probably never would have occurred had not the rider Maken dispatched to town with the message thundered up with a war-whoop. Never pausing at the corrals, he galloped on to the house. Frightened by the shout just when the soothing voice of the man on its back was winning his confidence, Blue cut loose.

Ed Maken looked up from the table where he was breakfasting with Cochita and reached for the telegram the cowboy extended.

"Just as I thought," he chuckled, tossing it to the girl. "You can't go wrong when Boss Peters talks that away." She glanced at the message.

Los Pinos, Tex.

Ed Maken,
Cibola, Colo.

Jack Larimore is my top hand. He is a bronc peeler from who laid the chunk. Handles a gun as if it was part of him. When he tells you anything you can bet your life on it. If he is in trouble the old man will sell the Lazy-T to help him. Wire me.

Boss Peters.

59

"So that's the telegram you sent auntie on her wedding anniversary?" she sniffed. "It doesn't alter the fact —"

"Stop right there, gal," he cautioned. "I gave this kid a chance because I couldn't figure him pulling that Riley killing an' then checked up on his word. It's plumb good. I'm not the one that's getting soured. It's you."

"Forgive me, daddy!" she cried, throwing her arms about his neck. "But you know he struck Ramon."

"Why?" he flashed. "Because that hombre pulled a knife on him. You can say anything about Larimore you want to. I like him and he's going to stay. I know a man when I see one." He stopped, listening. From without came a mighty cheer. "Now what's happened?" he demanded, springing to his feet. With the girl at his heels, he started for the corrals.

Jack Larimore's ride that day became history at the K-Spear and won the friendship of every cowboy on the ranch with the possible exception of Vasquale, who watched him through narrowed eyes, and old Pedro, stretched on the ground blinking through the poles at the bawling outlaw.

As Maken and Cochita came up, the gelding, bellowing like a terrified calf, blood streaming from its nose, was sun-fishing, dodging and plunging. Twice it reared and started to fall backward, but the quirt that hung at Larimore's wrist brought it down shaking its head savagely.

When it seemed that the foam-flecked animal was about to surrender to the fearless rider glued to the saddle, it gathered its steel-knotted muscles and pitched blindly into the cottonwood pole gate. A splintering crash! The corrals gave under the impact. The ragged edges of the slender logs tore at the gelding's legs as it broke through into the open pasture. The howling of the cowboys only increased the terror of the crazed horse.

"He'll kill yuh out there!" shouted Red. In the same breath, forgetful of the danger, seeing only a masterful rider subduing an outlaw: "Come on, yuh four-flusher. Rake him! Scratch him!"

Through the poles, Maken and Cochita watched in breathless silence. Larimore was riding easily, his body a part of the heaving, twisting animal. Suddenly the girl's hand flew to her breast. The cowboy's leg had straightened out. The smooth boot heel, sans spurs, was playing up and down the outlaw's neck.

"Sleepin' Injuns!" whispered Mowbry hoarsely as he sighted the cowman and girl. "Look at that hombre ride. He's scratchin' Blue!" He noted the hostile glint in Vasquale's eyes. "Spaniard! Why don't yuh holler?" Reaching down quickly, he seized the man's arm. "Yell an' wave yore paw, yuh kiote!" he commanded. "That's the boy who's takin' two hundred bucks away from yuh on a hoss yuh can't set!"

Vasquale's face went red, then ashen. He dragged his arm loose with a force that almost unseated Mowbry.

"Don't start nothin'," warned the puncher, taken aback by the prodigious strength the fellow displayed. "Yuh an' me ain't any friendlier than a coupla rattlers nohow."

"I am at least thees gentlemans in the presence of the señorita."

The scathing rebuke stung the color from Red's freckled cheeks. He started to dismount, the hot blood of anger drumming in his ears. A scream from the girl straightened him about in the saddle. A whistling gasp escaped his set lips. Blue, completely out of control, was heading for a barbed-wire fence.

"Oh, daddy!" shrieked Cochita. "He'll be cut to pieces!"

"Haze him! Haze him!" shouted Maken. "Look out for the barbed wire!"

Mowbry's horse hurled chunks of 'dobe in their faces as the rowels sank home and the animal cleared the splintered gate. Inch by inch the puncher crept up on the crazed gelding. Maneuvering carefully, Red edged his mount between the outlaw and the glistening fence, crowding it away from the treacherous strands. The stirrups locked. Both horses went down in a cloud of dust. The girl reeled against her father, covering her eyes with her hands.

A moment of quivering silence, then a mighty shout. The punchers tossed their hats into the air, dancing and yelling wildly. The gelding was on its feet, staring about in a daze, trembling like a new-born colt. Larimore, wiping the dirt from his mouth and eyes, was in the saddle.

Mowbry arose shakily and helped his limping horse to a footing.

"Isn't he wonderful?" cried Cochita, forgetting her antipathy in the excitement of the moment. She clutched Vasquale's arm as the Texan dismounted and the thoroughly subdued Blue nosed his shoulders, then, dropping his head, followed his master like an old work horse. She caught her breath sharply at the glance the Spaniard shot, not at her, but at old Pedro who inadvertently had kicked up a puff of dust.

"Man, what a horse!" grinned Jack to Red. "Lookee!" Calmly he remounted, stroking the animal's lather-smeared neck. With pleading voice he coaxed the gelding back through the splintered gate and into the corral, where he swung down.

For the first time he caught sight of Maken and the girl. Vasquale, advancing, handed over a roll of bills. Larimore accepted the money without comment and turned to the cowman.

"I'll give you two hundred dollars for him. Are you on?"

Maken was silent, apparently wrapped in thought.

"No," he answered presently, "but the K-Spear'll make you a present of him if you'll take Bevens' bed roll." He climbed over the poles. "Boys, there are none of you have any love for that Double-Spear-Box gang. I'm gettin' too stove up to sit a bronc like I used to and my gun-arm's beginning to take a smart of linament. You've seen what Jack can do. He's going to run this outfit an' we're going to stop those rustlers. I'm tacking a five dollar a month raise on every mother's son of you as fighting pay. Oil up your Colts. We aren't hunting trouble but we aren't riding out of our way to dodge it, either. We're going into the Sangre brakes on the first round-up in five years. Are you with me?"

A chorus of shouts split the air.

"But those Lazy-T cows?" questioned Larimore, embarrassed and self-conscious under the steady gaze of the girl. "You know I'm a Boss Peters' man and —"

"Yep." Maken laid a fatherly hand on the youth's shoulder. "And those Lazy-T fellows have the same opinion of you I have." The cowboy looked puzzled, attempting to fathom the meaning of the words of the rancher who was crumpling a message in his hand.

"Mowbry!" Maken turned to Red who stood by slapping the dust from his chaps with his hat. "I want a man with a fast string heading for Los Pinos, Texas, before sundown. I can't tell Boss Peters what I want in a telegram, and I reckon if a K-Spear man burns up the trail with orders to ride day and night he'll get there almost as quick as I could get a letter to him."

Watching Vasquale, Jack noticed the same slight start at mention of Peters' name that had struck him as strange at Riley's cabin. Wondering, he listened to Maken.

"I want him to tell Peters to start those dogies of his north," the rancher continued. "I'll turn over that Old Woman creek range. Wise him up to bring a half dozen men who know that six-guns are for something besides to stick down under the bar when they get on a spree. Have our man pilot 'em through."

Motioning to one of the men, Red moved off to execute the command. Maken turned back to Larimore.

"Are you on?"

Unconsciously Jack caught the girl's eye. The first trace of friendship she had shown now sparkled in the blue eyes. Somewhere within him the look seemed to strike a chord of harmony. His nerves twanged tunefully.

"You danged know it!" he replied huskily, extending his hand.

He made no effort to conceal his surprise when Vasquale stepped forward to offer congratulations.

"Eet ees to be than'ful at las' Señor Maken fin' those primero wheech weel protec' 'es 'orse from spurs an' keel thees Double-Spear-Box rus'lers, si?"

Nettled at the sarcasm, Larimore flushed, but the winning, friendly smile of Ramon completely disarmed him.

He met Cochita's shy gaze as she too advanced to offer felicitations, but the nervous blood of embarrassment left him almost speechless before her. He scuffed the ground awkwardly with the toe of his boot, inwardly cursing himself for his timidity. She chanced to look at Vasquale and a flicker of fear replaced the sparkle in her eyes.

CHAPTER
SEVEN

The next few weeks were busy ones for the new foreman of the K-Spear. Overseeing the breaking of the "wild bunch", familiarizing himself with Maken's lines and range, and keeping a sharp lookout for rustlers demanded his whole attention and left little time for retrospection or further investigation into the mystery surrounding the death of Buck Riley.

The eerie "tokee" seemed to have vanished completely, and the dread it had instilled in the minds of the settlers dimmed as the days sped by. Through Maken's influence the coroner's jury inquiring into Riley's murder had laid the crime "to person or persons unknown", and had made no recommendations on which to base warrants for arrests.

While on his occasional visits to the ranch Dawson never questioned him, yet Jack knew by the officer's coldness and the care with which he followed every move that his suspicion had not been allayed. His doggedness in sticking to the trail of the mystery bade fair to bring forth a solution eventually.

Although the girl had thawed to some extent in her attitude toward the foreman, still, after her show of friendliness at the corrals the morning he had ridden

Blue, she had shrouded herself with an icy reserve which arose as a formidable barrier between them. He had attempted to talk with her, had tried to convince her that he was in no way connected with the murder, but she always seemed impatient to bring the conversation to an end. Especially was this true when Vasquale was near, at which times she all but ignored Jack, and while courteous, would never pause longer than to pass some inconsequential remark.

"I think that breed's got her buffaloed," Red commented one day as they watched the pair on the porch. "Funny ol' Ed'll stand fer it."

Larimore remained silent. Inasmuch as Vasquale had shown him nothing but friendliness, he hesitated to commit himself, choosing rather to overlook the unpleasantness that had marked their first meetings. Yet try as he would he could not overcome the suspicion Ramon had aroused at Riley's cabin which constantly annoyed him when they were thrown in contact.

He went about his work with a determination to merit the trust the cowman had imposed in him. That he was succeeding even better than he had hoped was shown by the fact that Maken not only turned over the entire management of the K-Spear, but went so far as to take him into his confidence on matters of almost a personal nature. They never discussed Vasquale, who came and went with old Pedro as freely as a member of the family, yet Larimore knew by the uneasy glances the cowman cast in the fellow's direction that before long something was certain to be said.

With almost a touch of homesickness he waited for Peters' arrival. Good luck should see the herd at the K-Spear in a little over a month. The courier had been gone but a couple of weeks when he began counting the days until the Lazy-T men would trail in, little dreaming of the events that were to pile up before they met again.

As Maken had ordered, preparations went forward for a round-up in the Sangre brakes, known to be infested with rustlers. Chafing under the routine of the ranch, the punchers were eagerly awaiting the ride which portended excitement. From his own observations and conversation with neighboring ranchers, Larimore was convinced that stock was disappearing in startling numbers. He found himself anxious to get into the work of cleaning out the thieves. This desire was increased one afternoon by his discovery of a steer that had been shot and skinned.

Maken's loud-voiced condemnation and threats when he was informed of the incident brought repeated warnings from Jack. But the cowman disregarded the advice, pursuing a policy of open hostility which could not fail to make him a marked man among the rustlers.

The foreman showed no surprise when the owner called him to the house one day and tossed over a note that had come out with the mail:

Ed Maken. Yuh shore think yuh played hell but yuh'll get yorn. Theres enuf of us up here to kill yuh an we're goin' to get yuh er lose 12 men. We want one hair apiece outa that ole chin a yorn.

We hear yore plannin' a round-up in here. Yuh've give us the worsta it all the way through so don't stick yore head in these brakes or we'll blow it off. We are 12 men waitin' to get yuh. Bewar.

Revenge Gang.

"Hell," growled Maken, proudly stroking his bristling beard. "Want a hair apiece out of my chin, do you? Well, they're waiting to be taken." Twining his spurs in the rounds of his tilted chair, he watched Larimore as the puncher bent over the scrawl. "According to this you'd think those Sangre rustlers had the whole outfit buffaloed. How do you s'pose they heard about the round-up?"

"I don't know any particular hombre I'd accuse of squealing," replied Jack thoughtfully. "There wasn't a soul on the place heard it mentioned outside our own men and Vasquale. I been telling you to lay off this loud talk."

"These birds aren't so tough they can scare all the cowmen off the range," snapped Maken. "I've been expecting something like this ever since Bevens was killed. We've cracked back at 'em occasional-like without getting anywhere and the thing's got to come to a showdown sooner or later. I'm calling their bluff right now. I'd like to have Peters and his gang with me, but I'm not waiting any longer. I'm moving into those brakes even sooner than I figured for a round-up. I'll teach 'em to hanker after my chin whiskers. 'Spect to make things right legal I better give public notice, huh?"

"Reckon so. Frame up something for the paper that you're going to ride the draws for strays, neglecting to mention, a course, you're loaded for bear."

"Well now, let's see." From a drawer in the table the cowman fished the stub of a pencil and some paper. "It's July fifteenth today. Better give thirty days' notice. How's this?"

Notice to the public. On August 15 the K-Spear, Franklin and Brewster outfits will hold a round-up in the Sangre brakes to gather up all critters wearing our brands and any stray stuff which will be turned over to stock inspectors.

Ed Maken,
Owner, K-Spear.

"Like to put something in there about those whiskers, but I don't reckon the public'd be interested," he remarked as he concluded the laborious task and leaning back in his chair, surveyed the scrawl proudly. "We'll try this anyhow. Cochita usually does all the writing, but we don't even dare tell her what we're going to do or she'd raise hell. Want to be sure she doesn't even see a paper when this comes out. You whip up those punchers, topping off that string for a fresh *cave*. I'll lope into Cibola, get this notice published, and tell the sheriff what we're aiming to do, so as to kind of calm things down if there's too much stink raised."

The men met Cochita and Vasquale at the door as they started outside.

"What are you two scheming?" she demanded, eying her father closely.

"Oh, nothing," he answered, avoiding her gaze and winking at Larimore for silence.

"You are too! Jack Larimore, I can tell by your face that you two have planned something."

"You're right, Cochita," put in her father before Jack could reply. "Larimore's going to hurry them cowhands up forking those broncs, an' I'm going to drive into Cibola right away."

"I'm going with you," she announced decisively. Before he could stop her she had dashed into the house, leaving Ramon standing alone.

"Whew!" exclaimed Maken, ignoring him and continuing on to the corrals with Larimore. "Don't ever let her find out or we'll never move a man off the place."

"Kind of wish you'd taken those bays," remarked Jack later as he helped the cowman hook a pair of snorting, wild-eyed ponies to a buckboard. "These cayuses aren't to be trusted."

"They'll be all right," replied Maken, edging in cautiously to fasten a tug strap. "I'll run 'em most of the way and tire 'em out."

The foreman opened the gate and stood watching them as the cowman swung the racing horses toward Cibola. He turned back to face Vasquale who had ridden up, apparently having decided to quit the ranch, which held no attraction with the girl absent.

"Señor Maken ees goin' to town suddenly," he observed. "Perhaps eet has sometheeng to do weeth thees round-up?"

Larimore glanced at him quickly, wondering where the fellow could have obtained his information, or why, if it was but a conjecture, it was so nearly correct.

"It's none of my business what he's going for," he replied tartly, wheeling and starting toward the barn. "Reckon if he'd wanted you to know what he was doing he'd have told you."

Vasquale colored and sat watching Jack as he strode away. A smile overspread his face. Setting spurs to his horse, he headed north.

Maken attempted to maintain silence during the ride to town, but the girl insisted on knowing what was worrying him.

"Nothing," he answered evasively. "Just thinking!"

"About what?"

"Rustlers. We're losin' too many cows. Larimore found another steer skinned yonder in those brakes t'other day. Can't go on any longer."

"What are you planning?" she demanded anxiously. "Has this trip to town anything to do with —"

"Yep." The word slipped out. Having bared his hand unintentionally he determined to brave her anger. "I'm plumb sick of it. It's going to stop, that's all."

"What are you going to do?"

"Round up our stuff in those brakes."

"Daddy!" she gasped. "Please don't! It will mean all kinds of trouble and more enemies."

"Don't care," he returned stubbornly. "I listened to your ma for years and I'm not going to listen to you. My mind's set. I'm going in, rustlers or no rustlers."

72

Silence again fell between them after his outburst. She realized that it was useless to attempt further dissuasion when his jaws were set as grimly as they now were.

Reaching Cibola he left her with friends and hunted up Dawson at the jail.

"Yore playin' with fire, Ed," the sheriff assured him, running his fingers thoughtfully through his gray hair and shifting a quid of tobacco behind discolored teeth. "Yore invitin' gunplay by movin' yore punchers into the Sangre brakes."

"Something's got to be done," flashed Maken. "Those rustlers are costing hundreds of good critters every year. We didn't holler when it came to blotching brands on a few head, but they're going too damn far when they shoot the stuff to get the calves, and skin steers and leave their carcasses for the kiotes. There's been all sorts of reports claiming the gangs are going to stop the round-ups from working in there. They'll have a hard time of it. While the K-Spear and Franklin and Brewster boys aren't hunting a scrap, they aren't running for cover either. We're looking for the dogies that belong to us.

"I'm 'lowin' to work that country the fifteenth of August. I'm going in peaceable-like, but I'm not forgetting there's twelve hombres in there waiting to get a whisker apiece out of my chin." He tossed the note of warning from the Revenge Gang onto the table before the sheriff. "If the outlaws want to fight, when we know we're right, I say fight, that's all."

"It's that threat 'bout them whiskers that's rilin' yuh more'n the rus'lin', I reckon, Ed," smiled Dawson as he concluded reading the scrawl. Then soberly: "I'll admit I didn't know they was gettin' bold enough to warn yuh through the mail. Somethin' shore has got to be done, but gallopin' in there with a gang a punchers all hostile-like ain't goin' to get yuh nowheres. They ain't men to be monkeyed with 'ceptin' yore shootin' to kill. They're slick hombres. I'd a had 'em long ago if I coulda got the goods on 'em an' found out who's leadin' 'em."

"Blow the cussed heads off some of 'em," growled Maken. "That'll bring 'em to time quicker than anythin'."

"Blowin' the heads off'n some of 'em ain't goin' to stop rustlin'. If all of 'em turned up missin' yuh might be able to get somewheres. Hell's due to pop on this range soon enough without forcin' no showdown. I got plenty on my han's right now tryin' to figger out the 'tokee' killin's. It'd drive a man loco. Nothin' to work on. Jes' mill aroun' in the dark. Sit tight till we get them hombres dead to rights, then I'm willin' to overlook a lotta things."

"Maybe you're right, John," conceded Maken, "but we been at you for five years now waiting for you to get 'em with the goods. We'd like as not wait five more if they hadn't made a crack about my whiskers. Reckon we'll get a line on those 'tokee' murders when we get us some rustlers. I'm dead set on going in there now. I'm serving notice on you that the K-Spear punchers'll start riding at daylight the morning of August fifteenth, and all the rustlers this side of hell aren't going to stop us."

"I allus played square with yuh, Ed." Dawson's tone was half-pleading.

"We've come awful near a split a right smart o' times, but underneath it we'd both give each other our shirts. I ain't hankerin' to rile them outlaws yet. We're all certain there's a gang swingin' long ropes, but suspectin' ain't goin' to send 'em up. Let's catch one of 'em, find out who's leadin' 'em, an' then work down. There's a pile o' nesters that ain't brandin' illegal."

"Can't be done," protested the cowman. "We've been trying to nab those hombres with the goods for months. As for their leader, if we ever did get one of these evaporating rustlers cornered, they're not the squealin' kind. He's plumb under cover, an' got the whole crew tongue-tied with fear. I won't wait any longer. We're going in!"

"Awright." Dawson's teeth clicked. "But I'm warnin' yuh to be damn shore who yuh shoot. I'm keepin' tally on yuh an' holdin' yuh responsible fer any killin's."

"Nice way to talk to a friend," snapped Maken savagely, rising and stamping to the door. "I'm loping in just the same. There's going to be gunplay if anybody tries to stop me from rounding up K-Spear stuff, too. I'm right proud of these whiskers, and rustlers don't come hard enough to throw a scare into me after forty years on this range. As for you, if you want to sit there and do nothing, just hop to it, old rabbit hunter." He slammed outside, leaving the officer staring after him.

CHAPTER
EIGHT

Cibola was one of those numberless cowtowns which seemed to have been dumped haphazardly on the most uninviting spot of the alkali-clotted plains. Unsheltered from the winter storms that whipped in from the Sangre de Cristos, unshaded against the blinding sun which in the summertime turned the range into an inferno of swirling dust and glaring wastes, its weather-beaten, unpainted buildings gave the impression of lifeless monsters huddled within warped, withered shells for protection against the merciless elements.

Its sole claim to existence lay in the cattle-loading racks bunched beyond the tiny, red station at which trains stopped only on signal. Before the advent of the mail-order house catalog it had served as a trading point for the big cow outfits and homesteaders alike, but the coming of the railroad had changed all this. Now, save for an occasional supply wagon from one of the larger ranches, and the semi-annual shipping celebration of the bow-legged, dust-streaked punchers, it had settled down into little more than a village of the dead, living on poignant memories of yesteryear.

Cibola was typical of the frontier towns that once flourished throughout the west. The passing of the range days had left the citizens too deeply engulfed in the maelstrom of apathy to move, too content to attempt to do other than eke out a meager existence.

There was no pretense at beauty; civic pride was unknown. If the supply of the "makin's" and staple groceries was adequate for the wants of the unexacting cowmen, and the store of liquor sufficient to soak the parched throats at shipping time, then Cibola had fulfilled its duty as a town.

Five saloons, three general stores which handled everything from beans to saddle-trees, a court-house and a jail, hotel, a livery barn, and the deserted, heat-warped railroad station made the village; these and a citizenry of some hundred souls augmented by a floating population of raucous-voiced punchers.

Making his way down the rickety boardwalk toward the "Last Chance" saloon, Ed Maken paid no attention to the hummocks of dirty sand fringing the one street, nor to the knots of citizens idling before the places of business discussing the mysterious murders which had been the sole topic of conversation for weeks. The blazing sun was no hotter than his own boiling thoughts. Dawson's unruffled exterior had rubbed him wrong. Added to his contempt for the sheriff now came his point-blank refusal to be a party to a showdown with the rustlers. The unsatisfactory conference had fired Maken to a fury which threatened momentarily to blow off like an overfilled steam chamber.

Leaving his item concerning the round-up at the "Cibola Weekly News" office, he passed on to the Last Chance. Here he unexpectedly came upon Brewster and Franklin — fire-eaters of the same stripe as himself — tying their ponies to the hitching rail in front of the saloon.

An hour later, over three fingers of rye at the bar, he gave vent to his pent-up feelings, exploding with the suddenness of a gunshot.

"The K-Spear's stood all the loss it's going to as a result of these rustlers," he announced decisively. "I estimate a thousand head have disappeared in the last two years. You fellows have lost as many."

He made no attempt to conceal the bitterness in his voice, hurling his remarks at anyone within earshot. He glared at Franklin and Brewster, then swept the small crowd of hangers-on who had stopped their games to listen.

"The whole country's living on stolen beef." Fired by the liquor he rushed on, seemingly resolved to unload himself of the thing that had been weighing on his mind for months. "Carloads of critters with run brands are being shipped from the Cibola loading racks right along. Between sheep tramping out our forage and rainbeaters and cow thieves, we're facing a showdown that we aren't going to weather if we don't get busy *pronto!*"

Franklin and Brewster shifted nervously, glancing at the men about them, many of them homesteaders whom Maken had included in his arraignment of rustlers. The strain was beginning to make itself felt on the group. It was lessened somewhat by the entrance of two breed cowboys who plainly showed evidence of hard riding by the dust on their faces and the reeking odor of saddle leather clinging to them. Sauntering over to a table near the door, they ordered a brace of drinks with signs. Franklin nudged Maken. Now seemed a good time to check the cowman's outburst and conclude in private the conversation in which they were both deeply interested.

Maken, however, appeared determined to force any hostile declaration in the house. In spite of the uneasy glances of his companions, he continued his discourse, meanwhile watching the two strangers who sat sipping their liquor and toying with a deck of cards.

"I didn't mind losing a few head. Even rustlers must live. I realize that swinging a long rope hasn't always been frowned on —" He winked significantly. Nervous grins appeared on the faces of his companions, who themselves had known what it was to toss a lariat about the neck of a racing maverick, "— but when it comes to killing she stuff and rustling veal it's time to call a halt."

The two breeds had started a game of "Seven Up". The unlighted cigarettes dangling from their lower lips and the studied expression with which they examined their cards were ample evidence that they were hanging onto every word uttered by the cowman. Noting this, Franklin took hold of Maken's arm and piloted him across the room. Even then the thoroughly aroused baron was not to be denied his loud-voiced denunciation of lawlessness.

"Stock laws aren't worth a damn," he growled as they seated themselves at a table directly opposite the breed punchers, who now, to all appearances, were deeply engrossed in their game. "We've brought detectives onto the range and posted big rewards. We've tried the courts. Arrests have been made, yet rustler after rustler has been turned loose for lack of evidence. Those gangs have held round-ups in violation of the law."

Franklin and Brewster, sensing some definite plan behind the words, now were paying the strictest attention, oblivious to the crowd which had collected about them, shutting from view the two breed riders.

"We got out an injunction to stop 'em last fall." Maken's big voice penetrated to every corner of the room. "What happened? The United States Marshal and his deputies who tried to serve the order stampeded after one of 'em had been plugged. We've tried every lawful means to protect our herds. Now what are we going to do about it?"

A breathless silence followed the question. The outburst suddenly had brought the showdown in rangeland. Maken's words had fallen with the deadliness of a prophecy of disaster. The hatred which for years had been smoldering sprang into flame. The listeners shifted uneasily, realizing that within the hands of the three cattle barons lay the very life of the range. A word from them could send dozens of armed men onto the plains with orders to kill.

Brewster drummed nervously on the table. Franklin alternately toyed with his liquor glass and attempted to

80

watch the two breeds, who had risen from their table and sauntered over to the bar.

Maken glared at the pair framed in the mirror that ran the length of the back bar. When he spoke he seemed to be hurling his scathing remarks directly at them.

"I just got a warning. Me, Ed Maken, who's been on this range for forty years, warned to stay out of those Sangre brakes!" He tossed the note he had received at the K-Spear face upward on the table. "Now what do you think of that?" He waited, rubbing his beard savagely.

"Well, I'm damned!" burst from Franklin.

"Gone too far!" commented Brewster tersely. " 'Pears that the time has come to make ever-buddy show their true colors. We're with yuh, Ed. Whaddaya suggest?"

"I already took the liberty of putting a notice in the paper that our three outfits were riding the fifteenth of August. But I'm going to start moving even before that. Dawson can't or won't do anything. It's not only rustling we've got to stop. It's those mysterious 'tokee' murders too. Reckon they're hand in hand. If you'll notice, all the killings have been men who were just a step behind the cow thieves, and like as not knowing something that wouldn't't've helped these rustlers' cases any in court." His voice dropped to a hoarse whisper which was yet plainly audible over the entire room. "Beat the law to it!"

"What's your plan?" Brewster's weazened little face was deadly serious.

"Fight fire with fire!" Maken's words set the crowd to shifting nervously. "I've got a bunch of gunmen coming up the trail from the Rio Grande. I turned my north pasture over free gratis so's to have 'em handy. They probably won't be in by the time we want to start, but they'll be here by the fifteenth. We'll swing into those breaks anyhow with every hand we can muster, and pick the Texans up later. We won't start anything 'less we get the goods, but if we do —" He jerked his head significantly.

Still maintaining their attitude of disinterest, the two breeds paid for their drinks and sauntered outside as a gang of punchers entered.

"Yore on." Franklin arose and extended his hand. "Our wagons'll meet yuh on Ol' Woman crik the mornin' o' the fifteenth of August." Then in an undertone: "Or any time yuh say." The last was lost to the listeners, who mentally set down August the fifteenth as the date when cowland would spring to arms.

"I've got a new foreman out at the ranch that's a wampus cat," Maken proudly smiled as the three made their way toward the door. "He'll be all set and snorting to fight, so don't forget. Get your wagons stocked. I'm liable to holler for 'em any day. I'm depending on you."

With assurance of cooperation from the two he swung into the street, just as the breed cowpunchers spurred out of town.

Calling for Cochita and throwing a few supplies into the buckboard consumed some time. It was not until almost dusk that Maken cracked the whip across the backs of the bit-fighting broncs and headed homeward. He drove in silence, turning over in his mind the plans for the coming round-up which was certain to precipitate a range war. Cochita, too, had nothing to say, apparently being satisfied to think and gaze dreamily at the rising moon, which was piercing the twilight gloom with shafts of silver.

Semi-darkness crept upon them. The prairie world was wrapped in slumber. A peaceful hush lay over the adobe flats. No sound broke the silence, save the chirp of the cricket, the distant cry of a night bird, or the drumming of insects.

With considerable difficulty Maken held the team in the road, now shimmering like a ribbon in the wan light.

"Wish I'd taken a gentler pair of broncs," he grunted, as he sawed on the animals' mouths. "I'm plumb worn out fighting these mullet heads."

There was a note of weariness in his voice which was new. She placed an arm about him tenderly and patted him on the cheek.

"Daddy," she murmured, "you need a rest. You're tired out. Let's get away for a while."

"Soon as I get a little work cleaned up I planned for the fifteenth of August, you and me'll skin out for a while and let Jack run the shebang," he answered.

They had left the open prairie behind and had swung into a stretch of country choked with thickets of greasewood which skirted the road like grotesque ogres in the moonlight.

"Whoa! What's the matter?" Maken dragged the horses to their haunches as the buckboard sidled dangerously in a streak of sandy road and a tug strap came unhooked.

"That's a nice note," he snarled, handing the reins to the girl and crawling over the wheel. "Hope the darn thing isn't torn out. Keep a tight hold on 'em," he cautioned.

Soothing the prancing horses and patting them on the rumps, he moved in to fasten the leather.

Suddenly, from directly behind him, a finger of flame stabbed the gloom. The bullet splattered against the side of the buckboard.

Throwing himself clear of the team, Maken dropped in his tracks.

"Turn 'em loose, gal!" he shouted. "Don't stop this side of the ranch. I'll be all right."

Springing to his feet, he dodged into the greasewood clump.

She brought the whip down across the backs of the snorting horses. The light wagon creaked as it lurched forward. Clinging desperately to the reins, she struggled with all her strength to keep the racing animals in the road as they tore toward the K-Spear.

During the cowman's absence in Cibola, Larimore had gone about his duties mechanically, unable to shake off a feeling of depression. Nor was that uneasiness, aroused by the note of warning Maken had received, placated by Vasquale's question concerning the roundup. Goaded to action by his restlessness, he finally called Red aside and laid the subject before him.

"I just can't help but feel there's something wrong," he said. "The old man went out of here madder'n a wet hen to have a pow-wow with Dawson. There's liable to be trouble. If he doesn't have it with the sheriff he will with that Double-Spear-Box gang if he meets with any of 'em. Reckon we'd better mosey along in and see nothing happens — to — Cochita — anyhow!"

"Thought that was the way the wind was blowin'," laughed Red. Then, soberly: "But the boss'd be plumb riled if we pulled out fer town, 'specially if he got it into his head we was comin' to pertect him. He'll be in afore long on a high lope. Don't worry 'bout ol' Ed."

"I'm not so sure," returned Jack thoughtfully, recalling the note of warning yet hesitating to violate Maken's confidence and tell Mowbry of it. "Reckon if you'll stay here and keep your eye on things, I'll drill into town with a couple of hands and meet him, under pretext of riding that south pasture."

"Jake with me," announced Red, "but God help yuh if he ever gets it into his head yore ridin' guard over him."

Without answering Jack strode to the barns. Ten minutes later, accompanied by two punchers, he pounded through the lane gate and started along the trail for town.

Their mounts had eaten up several miles of the twenty, when suddenly a shot blasted the stillness.

"Guess my hunch wasn't so far off at that," observed Larimore, jerking Blue to his haunches. The three waited for a moment, listening. When the shot was not repeated they threw the spurs into their mounts and raced toward Cibola.

Blue quickly outdistanced his running mates. In three miles Jack was riding alone, his companions lost in the haze of the moonlit night. Ahead he could hear the rumble of wheels. Pulling up, he waited beside the road. A careening buckboard took shape. He noted quickly that it had but one occupant. Setting his jaws grimly, he jerked loose the lariat at his saddle bow and, wheeling Blue, cantered back along the trail in the direction in which the team was racing.

Unable to recognize the dimly outlined horseman, Cochita sawed frantically to swing the broncs about in the road. With sinking heart she realized that they were completely out of control. She stifled the scream that came to her lips. Bracing herself as best she could in the swaying, bouncing vehicle, she watched from the corner of her eye the rider who now had set spurs to his horse and was galloping beside her.

Suddenly his face was revealed in the moonlight. With almost a thrill she recognized Larimore.

His rope cut the air and encircled the near horse's neck. The animals slackened their pace under the restraining leash. Before they had been dragged to a complete stop, Blue, head down, emitted a bawl of rage and pitched back along the road. Busied with keeping his seat, Larimore tossed the loose end of the lariat to the girl.

"Choke 'em down if I can't get this here mullet-head quiet!" he shouted as he flashed past.

86

With all her strength she pulled the slip knot tighter about the throat of the animal. A few minutes, broken only by the rasping breathing of the team and the thumpity-thumpity of Blue as his hoofs clipped the ground, and Larimore rode back alongside. Dismounting, he stroked his mount's arched neck.

"He's not to be blamed, Cochita," he said, apologizing for the actions of the pony. "He's never been broken to do snubbing or roping. Where's Ed?"

She told him of the ambush, her arms meanwhile working to and fro as the team fought the bits. He glanced down the road to where the two K-Spear hands were galloping toward them.

"The chico brush, back a couple of miles," he said thoughtfully. "Sure Ed wasn't hit?"

"No," she replied. "The bullet struck the buckboard, and daddy ducked so quickly they didn't have a chance to shoot again. He dropped right there in the brush."

Larimore halted the punchers as they rode up, and repeated her story of the attack. He turned back to her in perplexity. "What are you going to do?" he asked.

"I'll drive on to the ranch," she answered. "I can handle these horses now." The words were scarcely out of her mouth when the broncs, straining on the reins, clamped the bits between their teeth and bolted.

"Ride to the chico brush and scout around," shouted Larimore to his men. "Don't get far away. If you start doing any following, leave me a trail. I'll bring some of the boys from the ranch."

The cowboys galloped toward Cibola as Jack started in pursuit of the run-away team.

Overtaking the buckboard, he loped beside it for a time. Freeing his feet from the stirrups, he swung cross-ways in the saddle and leaped into the seat at the side of the girl. He thought he detected just a sigh of relief as he took the reins from her cramped fingers, but a hasty glance failed to detect anything that denoted fear in her pretty, firm-set face.

CHAPTER
NINE

It was not until they were within a mile of the K-Spear that Jack was able to bring the maddened horses under control. Blue was waiting at the lane when they dashed up. Undoing the gate while Cochita steadied the panting animals, they raced on to the corrals.

"Who do you want to stay on the ranch with you?" asked Larimore under his breath as Red, in answer to his shout, came on a dog trot from the bunk house. "I'm taking every man I can scare up to look for your pa."

"I don't need anyone," she smiled bravely. "Help daddy."

"Where are all the hands?" inquired Jack, as Mowbry came up. "I'm needing 'em bad."

"Let most of 'em go over to the Willer Crik dance. There's four down to the barn. What's wrong?"

"Round 'em up and run in some fresh horses, Ed's missing."

"Missin'?" queried Red blankly. "How come?"

"Ambushed at the chico brush," explained Jack as he helped the girl over the wheel and set about unhitching the team, now docile with weariness. "Somebody took a shot at him. The broncs bolted with Miss Cochita. Sent the two fellows with me ahead to look around. Whip up those punchers. We got to be traveling."

Mowbry sped for the barn. Before Jack had dragged the harness from the reeking broncs he was back with the four punchers and fresh mounts. They had little trouble in corraling Blue, who, in spite of his display of temper when the rope had whistled by his ear, now seemed penitent and was nosing about with an inquisitive hang-dog air.

Dragging the saddle from the animal, Jack tossed it on to a long-legged bay. Cochita extended her hand as he swung up.

"Thank you, Mr. Larimore," she said half timidly. "And please — please — find daddy."

"You know it, miss," he pledged. "We'll find him or dust this country with powder, and don't you forget it. But I'd like to leave somebody here with —"

The thud of hoofs on the road to the gate interrupted him. The group waited expectantly, straining for a glimpse of the newcomer. Vasquale galloped up. A wave of unreasonable anger surged through Jack. He spurred forward, his hand involuntarily dropping to his gun. The man's sudden appearance from nowhere set the hot blood hammering in his temples.

The girl's soft voice brought him to himself.

"I'll be all right now, Mr. Larimore. Ramon will stay with me."

"Always, señorita," smiled the fellow gallantly. "Eet ees the greates' pleasure I 'ave. Ees something wrong?"

"Hell!" snorted Jack disgustedly under his breath. "Where do you suppose that fellow came from?"

With a word to Red, inaudible to the others, he jerked his horse about savagely and, followed by the four men, pounded into the night.

Cochita flashed Mowbry a questioning look as he dismounted and started slowly back toward the barn.

"Aren't you going?" she demanded.

"No, ma'am."

"Why?"

"Larimore told me to stay here."

"What for?"

"Didn't say."

"You go with those boys just as fast as you can. They need you to help find daddy!" A note of scorn crept into her voice. "I can't imagine Red Mowbry here on the ranch when there's any action in sight."

"Neither can I," he admitted ruefully. "I'm sorry, Cochita, but orders is orders. Jack says stay. I stay."

"You'll do nothing of the kind!" she blazed. "I'm telling you to go. I'll show him that my orders take precedence over his on this ranch. Are you going to obey him or me?"

"Sorry," he repeated stubbornly, "but I'm staying here."

"Oh!" She stamped her foot angrily. "Oh! Just wait until I see Jack Larimore! I'll — I'll —"

Mowbry passed from earshot into the barn, leaving her speechless with rage. Downhearted at being denied a part in the search that promised real thrills after the inactivity at the ranch, he moped about until she and

Vasquale, followed by the shuffling Pedro, made their way to the house. Pondering over the story of the ambush, he unsaddled his horse, closed the door of the barn and went to the bunk house, keeping his eye on the glowing end of Ramon's cigarette on the porch.

Arriving at the chico brush, Larimore and his four men were challenged by the two punchers, who reported that they had seen or heard nothing.

"Nothing to do but lay low till morning," remarked Jack, seating himself and twisting a cigarette.

The others followed suit, and, holding to their bridle reins, sprawled about waiting for dawn. Chafing under the delay, Larimore presently rose and, taking advantage of the moonlight, scouted around. Picking up a trail, he followed it some distance.

"Three horses," he mused, as he traced an imaginary course across the plains toward Old Woman Creek. "To track 'em's going to take time. They can't go south because they'd hit Cibola. They're heading straight for the Sangre Brakes. We'd better lope along and be in those draws 'fore daylight."

Returning to the camp, he told the cowboys of his discovery. They agreed that there was but one route the kidnappers could take, and, mounting, they rode north.

CHAPTER
TEN

A throbbing pain in his head brought Ed Maken back to consciousness. He was trussed face downward across a hard-gaited pony. Each stiff-legged step of the animal drove the breath from his aching body.

He gazed about dully in the moonlight, his burning eyes, when he raised his cramped neck, on a level with the blurred, indistinct skyline. He chewed viciously on the gag that locked his jaws, making it impossible for him to swallow. He attempted to wriggle his hands, but they were bound tightly behind him.

Craning his neck to look over the swaying rump of the horse across which he was bundled, he glimpsed two riders moving along at a leisurely pace. Even in the wan light the figures struck him as familiar.

Suddenly he recognized them as the two breeds who had idled about the Last Chance during his scathing denunciation of rustling. The Revenge Gang flashed into his mind! The pair had been spies; had remained only long enough to learn his plans, then had sneaked away to ambush him on his homeward journey.

With that thought came a fervent hope for Cochita's safety. He remembered telling her to run for it. The crazed team tearing through the night stood out with terrifying vividness.

The sensation that shook his big frame as he squirmed in his fetters across the lumbering pony was not fear; rather a consuming anger that brought livid flames to the pupils of his eyes and steeled his muscles beneath the thongs.

His captors set a course straight toward the Sangre Brakes, while he, stoically nursing his discomfiture, passed the endless hours reviewing the events that had tumbled upon him in such a jumble of uncertainty. The drive from Cibola; the dropping of the tug strap at the ambush with a precision that was little short of uncanny; and the shot in the darkness, stalked through his muddled mind. Yet the incident of the unhooked tug undoubtedly had been the means of saving his life. Silhouetted in the moonlight, he would have made an excellent target, while in the shadows of the team he had escaped the bullet that had spattered harmlessly against the buckboard. He had leaped into the brush for cover only to be felled by a blow on the head from behind.

His own predicament grew insignificant as he again thought of Cochita. A silent prayer for her safety sprang to his lips. Her peril, he realized, was not so great at the hands of the assailants, if by chance there had been more than the two, as from the broncs he himself had had difficulty in controlling. He cursed himself for not having taken Larimore's advice and driven a gentler team.

The farther they traveled toward the brakes, the angrier he became, until as they paused above the bluffs of Old Woman Creek he was in a towering rage.

The lowering moon had scudded behind a cloud, leaving the brakes gloomy and foreboding. Ignoring his inarticulate gurgles, after assuring themselves that the thongs with which he was bound were secure, his captors took the slippery, dangerous trail into the valley.

Turning sharply at the foot, they rode into a dense grove of pine and halted.

Dismounting, they dragged Maken from his horse and deposited him on his feet, where he swayed, sickened and dizzy from the jolting ride.

Stooping, one of the pair cut the rope from his tightly bound legs, then, shoving a six-gun into his ribs, ordered him forward. He stumbled ahead in the Stygian darkness, the rage, that left his great body quivering, increasing as they advanced.

They halted presently before a shack. Throwing open the door, his captors pushed Maken within and lighted a smutty-globed lantern. Again making certain the bonds on his wrists were secure, they jerked the gag from his mouth.

"What the hell?" he demanded as the crisp air cut his lungs. "Do you know who I am?" He took a step forward threateningly, but a .45 held him at his distance.

"No sabe," shrugged the man with the gun, while the other set about undoing some tarpaulin beds stacked in the corner. Maken watched him closely, struck with the number of rolls. "Hangout for this Revenge Gang," he thought. "They sure have their guts, too, moving right into my pasture and building a cabin to steal me ragged!"

He surveyed the interior of the unfurnished shack, seeking some way of escape, but the man with the gun was between him and the door and one window. Realizing that resistance was useless, he lay down on the roll toward which his captors pointed.

In spite of his exhaustion he fought against sleep. While he did not believe that the gang would dare follow out their threat and kill him, still he did not doubt that the two breeds were tools of the rustlers, and had kidnapped him as a part of a scheme to thwart the round-up in the brakes.

As he lay thinking, he squirmed uncomfortably, attempting to move his aching body off of something hard protruding from the floor.

If Cochita had reached the K-Spear, he mused, Larimore already was on the trail, yet the darkness, along with the uncertainty as to the course to follow, precluded any chance of rescue before late morning. The constant thought that the girl had not been able to master the broncs and was lying unconscious somewhere on the prairie added to his uneasiness and brought the cold sweat to his brow.

Pulling his scattered thoughts together with an effort, he centered on the task of trying to figure a way out of his predicament. The bed roll to which he had been allotted consisted of a soogin and canvas tarpaulin below and a dirty blanket above. The thing beneath him was becoming unbearable.

Unable to twist himself to a comfortable position, he worked his tethered arms to the spot. His heart missed a beat! The breeds had thrown the roll directly over a big spike protruding at least half an inch from the floor, which now was gouging him unmercifully in the hip. The head had been sharpened by a glancing blow from a hammer.

By the uneven breathing of his captors he knew they were not asleep. Moving cautiously, lest he alarm them, he succeeded in wearing away the canvas and soogin with his finger-nails until the point of the spike was bare.

Gritting his teeth with pain, he maneuvered the rope about his wrists over the nail and began sawing steadily. Feigning a measured, raucous snore, he labored away, fearful lest the breeds hear the almost soundless scraping even above the noise he was making. One by one the strands parted!

With a surge of exultation he felt the last braid give. Working the cord from his numbed and bleeding wrists, he ceased his snoring and lay listening. Still not satisfied that the two were asleep, he stretched his long legs. One of the men sprang to his feet, gun in hand.

"Water!" gasped Maken hoarsely.

Peering at him through the flickering lantern light, and apparently satisfied that there was not trickery behind the request, the fellow put his .45 on the table and stepped to the opposite corner of the room.

In a single leap Maken was from the bed roll. Before the breed could collect his thoughts, or his companion could win his feet, the cowman seized the six-gun and had them covered.

"Now stick 'em up!" His voice trembled with the pent-up fury he had nursed since the ambush. "First I want to know who you are, and who you're working for!"

The two stared blankly.

"No sabe," they shrugged.

"Who's behind this kidnapping? Who's the Revenge Gang?"

"No sabe."

"Make talk fast, you polecats!" roared Maken. "I've got no time to listen to your no sabes. Who's your boss?"

The breeds slunk back in terror, yet his threats of vengeance unless they furnished the information he sought were futile. They were hopelessly tongue-tied.

Undecided whether their lack of knowledge of English was pretense or ignorance, he realized that he was but wasting precious moments in attempting to make them talk. Through the window he could see the first streaks of dawn tinging the horizon. Deciding suddenly to make them prisoners and turn them over to Dawson, he ordered them to advance. Backing to the door, he opened it behind him and kicked it wide with his foot.

Taking advantage of the gloom within the room, one of the breeds stealthily closed a hand over the .45 that lay beside his bed roll. Firing under the crook in his arm, he sent the cowman reeling through the door.

As Maken dropped to his knees, the other leaped forward and seized the six-gun which fell from the cowman's nerveless fingers.

He swung it up. A shrill cry issued from his lips. His arms flayed wildly. He took a few uncertain steps, plunged through the door and was swallowed up in the thicket of pine.

Only stunned by the bullet which had creased his side, Maken lurched to his feet, clutched the .45 the other had dropped, and wheeled.

"Hold your fire!" came a gruff command from behind a tree. "Move back there. How many of those hombres are in the cabin?"

"One!" barked the cowman. "But I've got nothing to do with 'em! I'm Ed Maken of the K-Spear. Reckon you're the Revenge Gang. Come on out in the open, yuh kiotes, and shoot it out!"

"Get under cover, Ed. We're sure glad we found you so easy!" came the voice. "We just followed this trail in the dark by guess and, by God, stumbled onto this shack!"

Unable to place the voice, and wary against surprise, the cowman ducked behind a tree. Then he recognized Larimore.

"Kind of expecting you, boy, but didn't figure it 'ud be so soon," he said, joining the foreman in a clump of jackpine which commanded a view of the shack. "You saw Cochita. Is she all right?"

"Sure. That's how we knew you'd been ambushed! But we didn't figure on the kidnapping. She's at the ranch. Not a scratch or anything. Come loping in behind those cayuses that ran most of the way from the chico brush."

"Thank God!" There was a note of relief in the cowman's tone. "I wasn't so much afraid of the shooting as I was that team. But if she pulled through let's give that fellow in the shack hell. If we're right quiet he'll poke his nose out of there like a badger."

The east was shot with the flame of sunrise as the door of the cabin again swung open and the breed looked out.

A fusillade of shots drove him hastily within. Quiet again settled over the brakes. The sun climbed into the cloudless sky. Maken, Larimore and the six K-Spear punchers lay motionless, biding their time until the fellow should make another attempt to venture forth.

"Reckon we might as well drift along to the ranch and let the poor devil go," suggested Larimore, after the cowman, sprawled at his side, had reviewed the details of the kidnapping and his escape from the cabin. "He's harmless and can't raise much hell by his lonesome. The one the boys plugged when you come out I don't reckon was hurt much, or we'd 've heard something else from him."

"Let him go nothing!" growled Maken. "He tried to pot-shot me, and I'm going to get him if it takes the rest of my days! Not on your life I'm not going to the ranch and let him alone! If he doesn't show pronto, I'll smoke him out."

Seeing that he could not dissuade the cowman from bringing the breed to account, Larimore settled down again. Toward noon a buckboard and horseman appeared on the trail which led into the Cibola road.

"Stop that pair," warned Maken in an undertone as he watched the two. "That's 'Soapy' Crag and his nephew. They've got a finger in this rustling, but we have never been able to get anything on 'em. Now's a good time to call their hands."

Abandoning all thought of concealing themselves from the breed within the cabin, the men sprang to their feet and gathered along the trail.

"Get down, Crag," ordered Maken as the two came abreast. "We want to chew the fat with you."

The rider twisted nervously in his saddle. His eyes roved over the stern-faced cattlemen, who lowered their six-guns as he started to dismount. Half-way to the ground, he jabbed his horse with the spur and, laying low on the animal's side, bolted.

"Run for it!" he shouted as he streaked past the youth in the buckboard.

The driver's lash cracked across the backs of his team as he threw himself flat on the bottom of the light wagon and tore down the road in a hail of lead.

"Climb on your nags and stop 'em!" roared Maken. "If they get away they'll have every cow thief in these parts rarin' to shoot before dark."

Larimore and the punchers piled onto their horses which were tied in a thicket nearby and started in pursuit of the pair. The cowman waited impatiently, alternately watching the road and the cabin.

The foreman and the men returned dragging a buckboard at the end of a lariat.

"Well?" Maken's tone was bitterly accusing.

"They just naturally outrun us," volunteered Jack sheepishly, as he swung down. "If I'd had Blue they couldn't 've done it. Fellow in the wagon cut the traces and rode one of the team. They're sure traveling."

"You are a fine bunch," snapped the cowman. "You —"

"Easy, Ed," warned Larimore quietly. "We're not here to run horse races. We've been up all night trying to help you. Our nags are tuckered out. Anytime you don't like the way we're doing you can —"

"There, there boy," apologized Maken quickly. "I didn't mean anything. But that Crag'll stir up the whole country. The K-Spear is none too popular with these rustlers nohow." He paused, glancing from the buckboard to the shack. "I've got a scheme. Let's load the wagon with brush. Here you," he snapped to the punchers, "knot your throw ropes together."

Quickly the vehicle was heaped high with brush.

"Now hook it on the tongue. One of you ride past that cabin hell bent for election. Drag the buckboard right up to the door." He lighted a match as the man straightened out the slack in the spliced rope and took a half hitch around his saddle-horn. "The rest of us'll do the shooting if there's any needed."

The tinder-dry brush flared up. The breed opened fire. The rider stuck spurs to his horse and raced into the face of the bullets. He halted only when the blazing wagon crashed against the door.

"Guess that'll smoke the rat out," observed Maken hatefully.

"Reckon it will," was Larimore's reply, "but I'm telling you right now I've got no hankering for burning a man to death. I'll shoot when they get a break, but if that breed goes down it won't be from my gun."

He stood with his hand pressed against the butt of his .45 as though pushing it further into its holster. The cowman stared.

"Maybe you're right, boy," he conceded, "but if you'd fought with these devils as long as I have and been shot at and kidnapped and warned they were going to get you; and if you'd been cautioned not to ride your own property, like as not you'd feel the same as I do. Keep your gun stashed. I'll 'tend to this hombre. We'll need you later on when Crag gets the country riled up."

The fire spread quickly to the eaves and crept to the roof. Within a few minutes the entire shack was a mass of flames.

"He's got to come out or get burned to a crisp," remarked Maken.

As he spoke the window pane crashed and the breed sprawled headlong into the open. Leaping to his feet, he raced for a coulée. The cowman's six-gun swung up, wavered, then dropped.

"Aw, hell!" he snorted. "Guess I'm not built right to shoot him down either, Jack. You win. Let's hit the trail for home."

Larimore extended his hand.

"Didn't think you were the back-shooting kind, Ed," he said soberly. "You and me are going to hit it off fine."

The sincerity of the tone brought a lump to the cowman's throat. Jack turned back to the blaze which had reduced the dry cabin to ruins and was eating its way through the grass toward the trees.

"Here, you fellows," he ordered. "Drag off your saddles and get your blankets. We'd better check it while we're able."

Uncinching his own saddle he seized his blanket and leaped forward, beating at the creeping flames. After a half-hour of choking work they succeeded in stamping out the fire.

"Catch me one of those breeds' nags," said Maken as the men came up. "They left 'em yonder in the brush. Guess if we let 'em off with their lives they hadn't ought to kick if we borrow a pony."

He entered the thicket into which the breeds had disappeared. Two of the three horses were missing.

"Those fellows weren't as scared as we figured they were, not by a damn sight, seeing as how they stopped long enough to get their horses! Reckon they'd had me riding shanks ponies if they hadn't been in such a hell of a sweat. That reminds me," he swung into the saddle, "Franklin and Brewster is rarin' to go. I called the round-up for August fifteenth but in the face of this we'll fudge a couple of weeks and ride quick as we can load up the chuck wagon."

"You can't begin any too quick to suit me." Larimore ducked the low branches of a pine. "I'd sure like to get a crack at some of those birds in the open."

The words were scarcely out of his mouth when, clearing the timber, they sighted six riders coming from the adjoining arroyo.

104

"Looks like you're going to get a chance," observed Maken. He scrutinized the approaching horsemen. "Don't know a one of 'em. But you can just lay your last nickel it's some of that Revenge Gang as wants a whisker apiece out of my chin. They're not itching to get 'em any more'n I am to have 'em try, either. Those hombres got wind somehow or other I was going to town, planted those breeds to kidnap me and now they're heading to that shack to get me. Hell's going to pop pronto, fellows. Get your gun-arm slinging loose."

"Howdy," greeted a stocky-built fellow with an evil face as the six came up. "Lookin' for strays?"

"Yep." Maken's voice was casual. He threw one leg carelessly over the saddlehorn and reached for his makin's. "Milling 'round a bit to see if we can't find some beef stuff. Seen any K-Spear or Franklin or Brewster critters?"

"No, we ain't seen none a yore dogies, Maken," replied the man. The cowman started at the sound of his name on the lips of the stranger. "They don't prowl 'roun' these breaks much. Only occasional we sight a cow packin' yore bran'. Reckon yuh didn't shave them whiskers afore yuh come in, did yuh?"

Maken winced. The man's question immediately marked the six as part of the Revenge Gang. He glanced at Larimore. His calm poise gave the baron assurance.

"I'm wearing them long on purpose," he answered evenly. "Got wind there was some rustlers hankering to shoot 'em out and I 'lowed to save the time of shaving."

"We warned yuh not to come nosin' in these brakes, didn't we?" Anger unsteadied the stocky man's voice.

"Yep. Leastwise some rattlesnakes calling themselves the Revenge Gang, not having guts enough to use their real monickers, did. That doesn't cut any ice with me. I'm hunting dogies, not trouble. I don't mind telling you though we aren't losing any sleep over shooting down a rustler now and then."

"We didn't give yuh credit fer a hell of a lot a sense after the way yuh shot off yore mouth in town yestidday." Maken started. The remark showed that the breeds had reported immediately his escape from the cabin and the six had come for no other purpose than to carry out their threat. "If yuh'd a minded yore own bus'ness yuh'd probably lived a hull lot longer than Cline and Bevens and Riley did. They got nosey jes like yuh. Now we're warnin' yuh fer the las' time to be outta these brakes inside a hour an' not to show up in 'em again."

Maken's punchers closed in at the mention of Bevens. By the man's own admission the Revenge Gang had been connected with the mysterious "tokee" killings. It proved Maken's contention that the three had been slain because they knew too much.

Larimore also was weighing the rider's words.

"If I don't go?"

The cowman bit off the words, determined to bring a showdown and if possible capture the men, who under a third degree might be made to shed some light on the triple slayings.

"We're packin' shootin' irons!"

"Guess all the shooting you'll do won't stampede anybody. Hombres like you fire from ambush like your breeds did at the chico brush last night."

The taunt brought color to the fellow's face.

"Is that so?" he sneered. "I'll show yuh — yuh —"

His six-gun leaped from its holster and spat flame. Maken fired wild.

With a movement as quick as that of a striking snake, Larimore's .45 belched. The stocky man reeled in his saddle, clutched at his side, then grabbed for the horn as his horse plunged, wheeled, and bolted from sight in the arroyo. Jack, his smoking Colt sweeping the crew, sat calmly dragging on his cigarette.

A second of breathless silence. The loss of their leader temporarily demoralized the gang. Then with an oath another reached for his gun. His companions, waiting nervously for the break, blazed away.

With blood-curdling yells, the K-Spear punchers cut loose. Crazed by the fusillade of shots, the ponies bellowed and pitched. Bullets hailed through the cloud of dust kicked up by the dancing hoofs. Lead clipped at saddle-leather, but the swaying, jerking riders were almost impossible targets.

A scream of agony arose above the curses and shouts. One of the outlaws' horses fell, beating its head on the ground. The rider was thrown clear. Dazedly he scrambled to his feet and dived into the arroyo.

The battle ceased as suddenly as it had begun. Rowelling through the blanket of suffocating dirt, Maken leaped to the ground and peered into the ravine. The six men had disappeared. At their feet stretched the motionless form of one of the rustlers' horses.

"Reckon we better lope down that draw?"

"Be plumb foolish," advised Larimore. "Those fellows got their guts full of lead up here in the open, but stashed down there in those coulees they'd pick us off without a show. Our play right now is to head for the K-Spear while we're all whole."

"You're right," admitted Maken.

He turned back to his men, two of whom were nursing flesh wounds. A trickle of blood splattered on his shirt. He blinked and fingered an open gash in his chin gingerly.

"Hell," he growled savagely. "Those buzzards sure were shooting for my chin. And they got some of those whiskers." A broad grin spread over his grimy face. "But they didn't get all of 'em. I'm right sorry we haven't got a little game to snake in to show the fellows at the ranch we really had a scrap with these hombres, but I reckon some of them'll be sore in spots tomorrow where they were sliced up with lead." He swung into the saddle. "Let's be moving along and get patched up, boys."

"Ed," said Larimore, as they jogged back to the K-Spear, "this range is going to be burning up from now on. We started the ball rolling toward bringing a showdown, but something seems to tell me some of the fellows are going to take the big tally before it's over."

"Yep." The cowman's voice was strained. "Reckon I'm one of the lads that's marked. But before I kick off there's a lot of doings I'm going to be wise about. Right now the one thing that interests me is who is the leader of this gang, and what those 'tokee' killings have got to do with the rustling?"

CHAPTER
ELEVEN

Toward dusk the eight galloped up to the corrals of the K-Spear. They were met by the other punchers, who, having ridden in for food and fresh mounts after hours of fruitless search, again were preparing to take the trail. Cochita was one of the waiting group. With a little cry of joy she threw herself into her father's arms.

"Pretty nigh scared to death, gal?" he asked tenderly.

Her face went ashen at sight of the wound on his chin.

"Oh, daddy!" she cried. "You're hurt! What's happened? Where on earth have you been?"

"Nothing but a scratch," he assured her. "Little warm water and a wash'll fix it up fine. We've been scouting around those north brakes a bit. Sure you're all right?"

"Yes," she replied. "Ramon and Pedro were with me. And Red —" Her eyes snapped at sight of Jack climbing down wearily. "You see, Mr. Larimore took it upon himself to disobey my orders and make Red stay. I wanted every man on the ranch to help you out, but Mr. Larimore was so capable he didn't need anyone but himself." The scorn in her voice set Jack twisting uneasily.

"Aw hell, Ed," he blurted out, swinging back into the saddle, "I did the best I could. I left Red here because the rest of the fellows were down at the Willow Creek dance when we pulled out."

"You knew Ramon was here," she accused.

"That's why I left Red," he retorted angrily. Then to Maken. "If I'm foreman of this ranch, I'm going to be foreman. If I'm not, I'll start riding now. I'm not caring either way."

"There, there! Don't get on your high horse," interposed the cowman, his eyes twinkling. "You did plumb right in leaving Red."

"But, daddy!" she gasped incredulously. "Ramon —"

"Jack just told you that's why he left Mowbry," he returned brutally.

"But —"

"That'll do now. He was plumb within his rights. By the way, Cochita," Maken attempted to forestall the storm brewing in her eyes, "how did you come out with those broncs after we were ambushed?"

"Why —" she floundered hopelessly, ashamed of her outburst as she recalled the risk the foreman had taken to save her from the runaway team. "Mr. Larimore," she gulped bravely, "I'm sorry for what I said just now. I want to thank you for your help."

"What help?" put in her father.

"Didn't he tell you, daddy?" she asked in surprise. "He stopped those broncs yesterday. They bolted after the ambush. Mr. Larimore met me and stopped the team just as I was beginning to lose my nerve. Then he drove me on to the ranch."

"What were you doing there?" queried Maken.

"Playing a hunch," grinned Jack. "Nobody was hurt because I went, were they?"

"You're there and over, boy," admitted the cowman warmly. "If I'd listened to you I wouldn't have taken those broncs. But it came out right as it is, 'cepting of course you disobeyed Cochita here in making Red stay on the ranch." His smile faded as Vasquale quit his seat on the porch and sauntered toward the group. His pleasant tone became flint-like, "And I want to thank you for being thoughtful enough not to let my little gal stay alone on the ranch."

Before the indignant Cochita could speak he turned, and taking her by the arm strode to the house, leaving Ramon staring after him.

Larimore was surrounded by the punchers, who plied him with questions. Still smarting under the girl's remarks he gave them the story as briefly as possible, then making his way toward the kitchen routed out the growling cook to prepare supper.

Apparently having nothing to do while Cochita bathed Maken's wound and the two discussed the affair, Vasquale sauntered in where the cowboys were eating.

"Eet ees the fine work, meester Larimore," he began with a friendly grin. "I would exten' thees thanks in the name of the señorita."

Jack was in no mood for conversation with the fellow. His very presence irritated him.

"Save your thanks," he snapped discourteously. "You're liable to need all your breath before long."

Ramon colored but was silent under the veiled threat. Wheeling abruptly, Larimore stamped from the room, made his way to the bunk house, pulled off his boots, and threw himself on the bed. Later, when he fell into a fitful sleep, the angry face of Cochita as he had seen her at the corrals tormented him.

Daylight found him superintending the preparations for the round-up. Breakfast scarcely had been finished when Dawson galloped up. Leaving his horse at the corral, he strode past the punchers with a surly grunt and making his way to the door demanded an immediate audience with Maken.

Larimore went at his work, casting furtive glances in the direction of the house. The cowman appeared presently and motioned him within. The sheriff eyed him sharply as he entered, but did not speak.

"Jack," Maken broke the embarrassing silence. "Half the rustlers and nesters in the county are up in arms. Crag and that kid pulled into town yesterday and raised particular hell. He's even got out a complaint against me —"

"What for?" interrupted the foreman.

"Holding him up on the road and stealing his buckboard. Anything just to get me where I can't do anything."

"Why don't you do some complaining against being ambushed, and kidnapped, and shot?"

"What's that?" demanded Dawson, suspiciously.

"It's a long yarn, sheriff," put in Maken, "but we might as well get the low-down on it here."

Quickly he unfolded the story from the time he had left the sheriff in Cibola until they had returned to the K-Spear.

"Know any of 'em?" asked the officer, referring to the rustlers who had been routed in the gun battle, as Maken concluded his tale.

"Nary a one. Yet they knew my name. The whole country's lousy with breed-looking guys. Reckon we crippled one of 'em right bad and punctured a couple more!"

"Yore plumb certain yuh didn't kill none of 'em?" blazed Dawson.

"Not certain of anything," returned Maken hotly. "If I didn't croak some of 'em it wasn't my fault, because I sure as hell was trying! They isn't anybody shooting whiskers off my chin and getting away with it."

"Just a minute," interrupted Jack, scenting the usual trouble between the two. "If you ever get to the bottom of this thing you're going to have to cut out the rag chewing. Ed had plenty of cause to kill both those hombres up at that cabin, but didn't." He ignored Dawson's hostile glance. "Let's begin at the beginning. First there was those 'tokee' murders. We don't know any more about 'em now than when they happened. Then Ed gets that warning. He takes it right in to you and gets ambushed and kidnapped on the way home. They drag him up yonder to that cabin. If me and the boys hadn't been Johnny-on-the-spot they'd have turned him over to that gang we had the gun fight with."

"Ain't gettin' us nowhere to re-hash all that," snapped the sheriff testily.

"Maybe not, but let's do it anyhow," grinned Jack. "You're hunting clews for so many things you like as not'll forget 'em and arrest me for 'em all."

Dawson's tilted chair came down with a bang.

"Don't get —" he exploded, his face purple with rage. But Larimore continued calmly:

"This here Crag came snooping around when we didn't know what we were up against. We asked him plumb peaceable to get down and talk things over and he ran like he was guiltier'n hell. He might have been one of that Revenge Gang coming after Ed for all we knew. Sure we snaked his buckboard out of the road. We'd have dragged him into jail if we'd caught him. Then, when we're moving back to the ranch, those six strangers open fire . . . The rustlers have started things, but we're going to finish 'em!"

He eyed the officer steadily. "I know you don't like me, Dawson. You've always had a hunch I did that Riley killing. Forget that damn foolishness for awhile and play like you were a regular fellow, instead of a sheriff suspecting everybody. On the square," he asked earnestly, "are we guilty of robbery, or ought we to have laid down like a whipped dog and let 'em run us off our own place?"

"Yuh might be right," admitted Dawson reluctantly. "We'll ferget this warrant Soapy swore out fer the time bein'. What's puzzlin' me though is who's behind all this?"

114

"You're not the only one that's bogged down there." Maken fingered his gun butt thoughtfully. "They don't seem to have any leader, but you can bet your last cent somebody with brains is backing 'em. He's sure keeping well hid, too. Those breeds that ambushed me couldn't or wouldn't, say anything but 'no sabe.' Reckon that's a stall, but I didn't get anything out of 'em."

"I'll sneak up to that burned cabin an' get my bearin's." Dawson rose and turned to the cowman, completely ignoring Larimore. "If there happens to be any of 'em slip into Cibola after a doctor, or there's any inquests, I 'low I'll need yuh. Meanwhile I wisht yuh'd stick close to the ranch an' not start nothin'. Lemme get a break on the thing afore we opens up. There's goin' to be enough hell poppin' pronto to keep ever'-buddy on the jump. An' I'm tellin' yuh, Maken, watch out! Every rus'ler in the county is gunnin' fer yuh."

They watched him as he rode from the corrals.

"You're about as strong with him as I am," grinned Maken turning back to Jack, "but we've got plenty to do without fretting over being sheriff's buddy. We're running on the edge of this thing, and getting the drop on the gang that pulled those killings. Dawson won't do any more'n he's always done. It's up to you and me. It's a dead mortal cinch we haven't heard the last of that scrap yesterday, and we want to be loaded for bear when things break. We —"

He stopped, gazing at a cloud of dust whirling down the trail from the brakes.

"He's sure in a hell of a hurry," he remarked as a rider jerked his mount to its haunches at the gate.

"Wonder who he is? . . . Reckon it's about five hundred mile down to Los Pinos." He took up the thread of his conversation, meanwhile watching the horseman as he mounted and raced for the corrals. "With steady trailing Boss and his gang ought to be here in a few days. I'd kind of like to hold things back till he comes, because aside from you and Red and a couple of the hands I haven't a man worth a damn in a pinch. Do you 'low Boss'll be with us?"

"That's Peters' failing," replied Larimore quickly. "He's been scrapping ever since I met up with him. He'll plumb admire to join in where there's liable to be fast shooting."

"That's good," observed the cowman. "Whatever we do now we've got to keep from Cochita. She's dead set against range wars, and I don't believe she's right sure there're rustlers around, even after all that's happened." He peered at the horseman, whom they now recognized as a line rider. "Let's see what's the trouble."

The man swung down at the corrals to be surrounded quickly by a knot of punchers. Red left the group and trotted toward the house.

"Something's wrong," growled Maken as they hurried out to meet him.

"They're movin' a herd of our dogies outta the north pasture!" shouted Mowbry, sighting them.

"Who?" demanded the cowman.

"Don't know," put in the rider. "Couldn't see no-buddy drivin' 'em, but I could tell by the way the critters was bunched they was bein' trailed."

116

"There you are, boy." Maken turned to Larimore. "They're eggin' us on to a showdown right now. Will they get it?"

"You damn know it!"

"All right then. Remember, I'm behind you with everything I've got."

Attracted by the loud voices, Cochita came from the house and stood at her father's side.

"Daddy," she pleaded, "don't send the men out with orders to fight. There's enough trouble around here without any more, please —"

"And let these hombres break me, shoot me down, and single-foot along my carcass? Sorry, gal, but we're going to show those wallopers a thing or two right now. Boys!" — he turned back to the men — "Don't forget poor old Bevens."

One of the men led up Blue. Larimore mounted and sat looking down at the girl. Her eyes were wistful. He found himself pitying her. Her tense body was evidence of the mental anguish she was enduring. Yet in spite of it all, she smiled up at him bravely.

Suddenly the smile faded and a haunted look crept into her eyes. He shifted in the saddle. In his usual manner of appearing from nowhere, Vasquale had ridden up quietly, followed by Pedro.

"Where are they headed, señor?" he asked with an elaborate display of unconcern.

"Gunning for rustlers," snarled Maken. "We're going to clean this range if it takes everything I've got. Get the leader of the gang, boys, if you can, and we'll swing him from the first tree we find." His eyes bored into

117

Vasquale's. "You've been around that Double-Spear-Box outfit quite considerable. Don't you know who owns it; who is this hombre they say hangs out in Mexico?"

The fellow shrugged his shoulders.

"I am not the one to ask who ees their primero."

"Whoever it is you can lay your last dollar he's the guy behind this rustling and these killings," snapped Maken. "They're bound to be connected. And let me tell you fellows" — this to the impatient punchers — "if you ever get an inkling as to where we can find this fellow, let me know. We'll get him if we have to go clean to Mexico! . . . I'm offering my check for one thousand dollars to any hombre that snakes him in dead or alive. If he's a corpse I'll go to the mat with everything I've got to get you cleared in court!"

The cowman was working himself into a towering rage.

"They killed Bevens and stole my stock. They've shot me and warned me off my own property. Yet there isn't nary a man sighted 'em rustling. They must have wings, for it's a dead cinch they drive those cows somehow. Next thing they'll be after you!" He wheeled on the girl. "Brewster and Franklin are with us, and so help me God, I'm going to clean 'em out if I lay in jail the rest of my life! Up and at 'em, fellows, and if you can't capture the hombres driving that herd, snake 'em in in hunks!"

With a shout the men struck spurs to their mounts. Larimore turned in his saddle as they reached the lane. Cochita had not moved. She stood transfixed, her eyes like those of a terror-stricken fawn. He experienced a wild desire to ride back; to take her in his arms and comfort her; but setting his teeth grimly he roweled the snorting Blue through the gate and swung north at a gallop.

"There, there! Don't take on so," consoled Maken tenderly after the punchers had disappeared.

"But daddy," she choked, "why must we start a range war? I — I — there must be some other way to handle things. The boys will —"

The tears that had hovered on her lashes since the ordeal at the ambush, burst forth. Throwing an arm about her, Maken moved toward the house.

With a quick nod to Pedro, who was stretched on the ground beside his horse, Vasquale brought the old peon to his feet. Heeding a few whispered words in gibberish that would have puzzled either a Spaniard or Mexican, the creature slunk to the corrals, and, dodging from sight, reappeared behind the barn at his shuffling trot.

"Where's he going?" demanded Maken, turning suddenly.

"To trail those vaqueros, 'e says," smiled Ramon. " 'E ees take liking to thees Larimore an' would geeve 'eem those protection."

The girl stopped crying suddenly and stood dabbing at her eyes.

"I'll be all right now, daddy," she smiled. "Don't mind my foolish tears."

A puzzled look crossed her father's face, to be replaced by just the trace of a grin.

"Oh!" he muttered as they entered the house. "The wind's beginning to come up in another direction, huh?"

"I don't know what you mean," she flashed, blushing prettily. "If you are referring to Jack Larimore, I hate him. I hate him!"

She stamped her foot angrily, as though defying her father to come to Jack's defense.

"I didn't mention Jack, did I?" he answered blandly. "Fact is, I was just surmising."

"Well, don't surmise," she advised, making no attempt to question him and avoiding Vasquale's eyes.

CHAPTER
TWELVE

The blazing sun was bathing the adobe flats with shimmering waves of heat as the K-Spear punchers, headed by Larimore, pulled up on the ragged bluffs above Old Woman Creek.

Below them were the charred ruins of the cabin Maken had fired, a blackened heap, rimmed with half-burned tufts of grass, lying like a splotch of ink in the emerald setting of pine. Although Jack had told him the night before of the kidnapping and battle, and had elaborated on the story as they loped out from the ranch, it was Mowbry's first glimpse of the deserted place.

"I'm damned!" he exclaimed, throwing a leg over the horn of his saddle. "They shore got their nerve to move right into Ed's pasture."

Larimore twisted a cigarette and gazed across the arroyo-gashed plains.

"Now where'd you see those critters?" he demanded of the line rider.

"A mite further along," replied the cowboy. "They'd like as not —"

He stopped suddenly and pointed toward the south. A serpentine string of cattle was writhing down a dry ravine a couple of miles distant.

The party advanced cautiously, then, detouring, halted at a spot from which they had an open view of the blind draw and the herd a few hundred yards ahead.

"Can you see anybody driving 'em?" asked Larimore as he watched the tier of swaying rumps.

"That's what I been tryin' to locate," returned Red. "Them's K-Spear dogies awright, 'cause I know that brindle steer. But who in hell's trailin' 'em?"

"It was around in here we had that set-to with the Revenge Gang," said Jack thoughtfully, "so I reckon it's them or some of their breed helpers." He settled his gun more comfortably at his thigh. "Be sure your .45's working because they're bad hombres. Ride circle on that herd and cut 'em back. I'll mosey along behind here and take a whirl with anybody that tries to sneak this way."

"Better let a coupla us fellers stick with yuh," suggested Mowbry. "They might be 'lowin' to get even with Ed by knockin' us off from ambush."

"I'll take care of myself," replied Larimore shortly.

"Yuh got guts to spare, ol' hoss." Red's voice was filled with admiration. "I'm fer yuh till hell freezes plumb over an' through."

"Thanks," returned the foreman dryly, "but let's save the tradelasts till we find out whether we're all coming out of this mess. Lope on and head those critters off."

The cowboys spurred forward, leaving Jack alone. He sat quietly until they had become dots, bobbing like corks on water in the prairie haze, then advanced slowly.

Alert, tense, his lips parched with dust, he followed the rim of the draw, occasionally patting the neck of his mount as it picked its way daintily through the cactus beds.

He jerked up as he topped a rise above the broad ravine down which the cattle were ambling. Having ridden circle on the herd the punchers suddenly galloped down the fissure-gashed side of the arroyo and into the floor-like bottom, which afforded no shelter from an attack.

"I thought you had better sense than that, Mowbry," he muttered aloud as he threw himself from his horse and bellied his way to the edge of the draw.

From his perch he watched in amazement as the boys dismounted and seating themselves cross-legged on the ground, dragged forth their cigarettes. Climbing back into the saddle, he urged Blue over the steep side wall toward the group.

"Have you gone plumb loco, Red? Where's the rustlers?" he demanded as he raced up.

Mowbry grinned and pointed to a clump of greasewood. Calmly nibbling at the tufts of grass, stood a fleabitten burro.

"That's them," he observed dryly.

"This is no time to get funny," snapped Jack. "Where are the hombres trailing the herd? We'd better get to cover or they'll pick us off like flies out here in the open."

"That burro was drivin' 'em, I'm tellin' yuh," repeated Red stubbornly.

"Wouldn't that stump you now?" snorted Larimore, scratching his head in perplexity. The sleepy donkey, carrying a bedraggled pack, stared at him from baggy, half-closed eyes and edged away as he spurred closer. "I've trailed a lot of rustlers in my time and some of 'em were human jackasses, but this is the first real one I ever caught stealing cows." He pulled up, gazing at the animal which again dropped its head and went to grazing, watching him, however, from the corner of an uneasy eye. "What do you think of it, Red? Isn't there something in that pack?"

"Sticks out like it. Le's see, can we rope the little devil an' search it."

Guarding against frightening the animal, he uncoiled his lariat.

"She's a puzzler," he admitted. "Them cows has been trailed a long way since the line rider first sighted 'em. That burro's drivin' 'em shore as hell. It's strange he's headin' straight fer them north brakes where we know the rus'lers hang out."

"He isn't any stray on account of that pack," Jack reasoned aloud. "He belongs to somebody around here. Who'd have a burro?"

"Yuh got me guessin'. This here's a cow country, not a hang-out fer mountain canaries. Looks like the nifty riggin' ol' Pedro'd have if he was single-footin' 'roun' a-courtin'," grinned Red.

"Uh, huh," mused Larimore thoughtfully. "Now I'll holler right sharp-like and get him to raise his head. You pop that riata over him. Are you ready?"

124

Red nodded. The two rode nearer. The animal sidled further away, fearful to allow them within roping distance yet loath to stop eating long enough to move far.

"Yip-pe-ye-e-e!" bellowed Larimore suddenly. "Yip-ee-e-e—"

The yell died in his throat. The burro came to life, a bundle of knotted muscles and flying hoofs. Red threw his lariat. It fell a full length short. From somewhere came the weird:

"*Tokee! Tokee! Tokee!*"

"Owe-e-e!" wailed Mowbry nervously, jerking up, then breaking into the strains of "Nearer, My God, to Thee".

Jack's gun was from its holster. Head up, tail straight behind, the burro galloped madly toward the brakes.

The punchers leaped forward, .45's drawn. They scanned the ground carefully. The spot where the burro had been grazing was deserted.

"Where'd that holler come from?" demanded Larimore gazing about in perplexity.

"Sounded like it was here close somewheres," replied Mowbry. "Couldn't a been more'n a few feet." He glanced above him at the rim of the arroyo. Not a blade of grass stirred.

"Ride this coulée for a ways," shouted the foreman. "Red, you and some of the fellows skin up there on top and look into the neighboring draws. It's a goat hair cinch the ground didn't make that noise, nor did the jackass."

The men spurred forward to do his bidding, while he remained motionless, watching the fleeing donkey as it dropped from sight in another draw.

The punchers rode back presently and reported having seen nothing suspicious.

"Of all the damn fool things I ever heard of!" muttered Jack. "Somebody gets croaked and a singing lizard hollers 'tokee.' We ride up on a flea-bit burro trailing a bunch of stolen dogies and something hollers 'tokee'! The jackass shows pronto he's no jackass." Then aloud: "But what in hell's the connection with the killings, and where's the singing lizard?"

He met the bewildered stares of the cowboys.

"Singin' lizards?" demanded Mowbry sharply. "Yuh ain't referrin' to that little tune I was hummin' quietlike while I was thinkin'?"

"No," laughed Larimore, "I was remarking about that 'tokee'!"

"We got whangadoodles an' side-hill umps," observed Red sagely, "but singin' lizards, nary a one have I seen. What kinda birds are they?"

"They aren't birds," smiled Jack. "They're reptiles. They sit around in the trees in the tropics and naturally scare the life out of everybody that comes near 'em. You just heard one. That was their 'tokee,' or a damn fine imitation." He turned in his saddle. "It's one of two things. That burro's either got a singing lizard in that pack of his to warn him of danger, or somebody hollered like one right close about here in these coulées, seeing us about to rope him."

126

"Sleepin' injuns!" breathed Mowbry reverently. "Rus'lers! Ambushes! Jackasses! Singin' lizards! Don't reckon us fellers drink enough."

"Let's ride those draws again sharp," cut in Larimore. "There's sure some reason for all these things. But I'm playing a hunch that burro's toting singing lizards in that pack. You recollect, Red, we both remarked it was full of something?"

"Who'd load a burro with singin' lizards?" snorted Mowbry disgustedly.

"Who'd expect a burro to be rustling?" countered Larimore, spurring forward.

Riding a mile circle, the trained eyes of the punchers let no greasewood or clump of chico brush escape. Their hunt was fruitless. With long faces they returned to the spot where the burro had stood.

"Let's hold a pow-wow on this thing," suggested Larimore, dismounting and rolling a cigarette. "The tokee's been hollered after those killings, so it's a cinch this burro's mixed up in the business somewhere. Those rustlers admitted knowing about why Bevens and Riley and Cline were croaked, but I don't think they did it. Here's what I reckon they meant — the gang was responsible for 'em, but to my way of thinking there wasn't a breed in the outfit that had sense enough to pull anything as slick as that. They'd have shot somebody betwixt the shoulder-blades, but there wasn't any shooting done."

"That burro's trained to rus'le, that's a cinch," announced Mowbry.

"I believe you're right, Red," exclaimed Larimore. "That accounts for none of the fellows ever sighting the cow thieves. This jackass has been doing all the cutting out in the herds, those hombres knowing damn well nobody'd ever think anything of a burro meandering around. We've stumbled onto something and I'm following it down before I quit." He mopped the sweat from his dust-powdered face. "I'm going to try and trail that critter. If he's trained to rustle I'll find out who for. You boys drive this herd closer to the ranch. If I don't show up in a day or two, start somebody after me. I'm riding due north from here after that jackass."

Loath to leave him, the men mounted, and with sharp barks started the staring leaders back toward the K-Spear.

Jack watched them until they were lost in a bend of the arroyo, then turned the reluctant Blue in the opposite direction.

CHAPTER
THIRTEEN

Meanwhile at the ranch, Maken, ignoring Cochita's efforts to quiet him, paced about restlessly, his annoyance at Ramon's presence plainly visible.

"Vasquale," he said, halting suddenly, "you must know something about that Double-Spear-Box outfit. Who are they? They don't hire anybody but breeds over there."

"I am uninformed, Meester Maken," the fellow shrugged. "I ride over there sometimes 'cause Pedro 'c ees lonesome an' would talk weeth the Mexicans. As for me, I understan' leetle of what they say. I spik the pure Castilian, not these jingo. They tell Pedro the primero ees Menendez in Mexico Ceety."

"That's what they tell everybody. It isn't the boss I'm after right now, though I sure would like to tie up with him. It's the rattler here on the K-Spear that's playing spy and peddling tales to that gang." His savage tone startled the girl.

"Daddy," she reprimanded tartly, "you don't suspect Ramon, do you?"

"Nope!" The hasty denial itself was little short of an accusation. "But the day we went to town he was the only one beside Larimore that had a hunch that it was some sort of hurry-up call. Every time we scheme something the rustlers know about it. I'm getting plumb sick and tired of having to talk in a whisper to keep my own shadow from taking a shot at me. If I ever get my hands on the squealer you can bet your life I'll bust him in two. I'm not charging you with anything," he hurled at Vasquale, "but after you wind up your pow-wow with Cochita tonight, I'd just as leave you and that grinning bob-cat Pedro'd stay off the place!"

Ramon flushed.

"Eef that ees the weesh of the señor," he said bowing courteously, "then eet shall be so. I 'ave already accept the invitation of the señorita for supper, an' trust that eet weel be all right for me to remain. After that I go, not to return."

Maken twisted uncomfortably under the angry gaze of the girl.

"Maybe I was a mite hasty," he admitted reluctantly. "I'm plumb upset and boiling inside. I don't care a damn whether you stay or go, but if it wasn't for Cochita I'd run you right now just on general principles."

The tone whipped the color from Vasquale's face. Unconsciously his hand fell to his gun, but the girl, springing between them, checked his draw. Maken backed off, his blazing eyes revealing his eagerness for a fight, but before those of Cochita he stood embarrassed.

"Aren't you ashamed of yourself, to make a guest in our home feel like a spy?" she chided. "At least you could be a gentleman! Come, Ramon." She took the fellow's arm. "You'll have to overlook daddy's outburst. He's been under a terrible strain lately and seems to have picked you as the object on which to vent his spite."

"Damn!" blurted out Maken as he watched her lead Vasquale onto the porch, where they were soon chatting chummily.

CHAPTER
FOURTEEN

While this little play was being enacted at the ranch Larimore was scouting the brakes of Old Woman Creek for trace of the burro which seemed to have been swallowed up completely in the wild country.

"Lord," he mused as he halted toward dusk, and sat sweeping the broken skyline for a glimpse of the fleeing animal, whose trail he long since had lost in the bewildering ravines, "I didn't know those little devils could travel that way. Reckon I better be heading for home. Hunting jackasses isn't much in my line no-how." He swung the eager Blue about. "A burro trained to rustle! Now wouldn't that stump you? Wish I could've got into his pack. Something tells me there's a heap of connection between these killings and that donkey."

A few miles from the K-Spear he jerked up, listening. The pounding of hoofs sounded on the road leading from the ranch.

"Must be a scared colt," he muttered, peering across the flats, murky in the twilight glow. "Doesn't make noise enough for a big horse."

He waited, tense in the saddle, Blue ambling along fighting the bit. A riderless animal flashed into sight.

Almost upon him, it veered sharply in the trail and sped past.

His hand fell to his gun. A shot blazed into the night. The hoofbeats quickened. Reining about, he raced after the animal. It dropped into an arroyo and was lost. The thud of hoofs grew fainter — ceased.

"Well, I'm damned!" Completely mystified, he again turned back to the ranch. "It was that burro, sure as I'm alive, and its pack was missing!"

"If that wouldn't give a fellow the chills," he lamented as he pulled up at the corrals and dismounted. "Leave that jackass running north after hearing that 'tokee' holler, hunt around for him all afternoon, itching to get into his pack, then meet him hot-footing it from the opposite direction a few hours later without any pack. I'm sure showing all the symptoms of loco."

Having cared for his pony, he went to the house where a light still twinkled, resolved to tell Maken of the strange discovery before rolling in. At the door he met Mowbry tip-toeing onto the porch.

"It's the boss," whispered the puncher hoarsely, "he's croaked!"

"What?" Larimore stared at him in dismay.

"Cochita says it was right after dark afore the moon came up. He died jes like the rest of 'em. That 'tokee' hollered. It's another one of them mystery —"

Not waiting for Red to finish, Jack brushed past him into the house. An atmosphere of gloom pervaded the place. He found himself fighting against the strange sensation he had felt at Riley's — of unseen eyes following every move.

"Eet ees for me to see you crying peetiful, *bonita*," came the voice of Vasquale from the living room. "We shall make the padre comfortable, then I shall close my rancho."

Conscious of eavesdropping, Larimore turned the knob noisily and stepped within. Cochita, her face buried in her hands, was sobbing bitterly.

"Miss Cochita —" he stammered, at a loss what to say.

She glanced up, startled. Vasquale wheeled, then stared coolly.

"Oh, Mr. Larimore," she choked. "It's too terrible!"

"It sure is," he sympathized. "I just rode up a few minutes ago. Red told me. Would you mind my taking a look?"

She pointed to an adjoining room. Thankful to escape the pain in her eyes, he left the two.

A hasty examination of the body revealed that the cowman had been killed in the same manner as the others. The throat was discolored as though by a thong, the bruise over the heart was identical with the mark he had found on Riley.

"Will you go over the details of just what happened when — you — when — we — can be — alone?" he asked, rejoining the silent couple.

Unconsciously he centered his gaze on Vasquale. While he had realized since his first appearance on the range that fate seemed determined to make them enemies, he was scarcely prepared for the hatred that

134

lurked in the man's eyes. He jerked his head toward the door. Ramon only smiled blandly and ignored the invitation to retire.

"I'd like to talk with Miss Cochita." Larimore strove to keep the rage he felt from his voice. "Would you mind leaving us alone?"

The girl glanced up quickly. Jack sensed that she was on the point of asking Vasquale to retire, yet in her eyes as they met those of Vasquale the haunted look he had seen at the corrals replaced the grief. "What — what — is there to say that Ramon cannot — hear?" she faltered.

Larimore stared in amazement, puzzling over the change. A tenseness that charged the air settled over the room.

"Nothing, I expect," he floundered, nonplused by her attitude which suddenly had become unfriendly. "I just wanted to get the story from you as it really happened, that's all."

"Well, Ramon won't interfere with that." Her voice was as colorless as her cheeks. "There is little to tell. Ramon stayed for supper and we sat on the porch for a long time talking. Daddy and Ramon had —" She stopped short biting her lip. "Daddy went into the house," she rushed on, as though attempting to cover up the thing she had been about to reveal. "Suddenly that 'tokee' screamed right at the corner. We rushed inside and found Daddy — dead!"

Hysterical sobs choked her. Mystified by her unfinished sentence, which stood out even above the details of the murder, Larimore stepped forward, fighting down a desire to comfort her. Ramon eyed him venomously.

The foreman started to speak, but was interrupted by the sound of voices at the door. Vasquale answered his look of inquiry.

"Thees weel be the sheriff," he said easily. "I shall 'ave thees talk weeth Meester Dawson, *bonita*." He sauntered across the room. "An' Señor Larimore," he threw over his shoulder, "the poseetion padre Maken gave — of course, we no longer need yuh."

"Oh, that's your game is it?" snapped Jack. "I begin to get your drift, you breed."

"Mister Larimore!" flashed Cochita. "It occurs to me that this is no time to start one of those hasty arguments of yours. Ramon has been kind enough to sacrifice his own ranch in order to devote his time to my interests. Knowing this range far better than you it is only natural that he assume the position of foreman. Your connection with the K-Spear need last no longer than right now."

"Fired!" exclaimed Larimore. "Well, that's hunkydory with me. How about that pasture your pa turned over to the Lazy-T? Peters'll be drifting in here any day now with a bunch of tired dogies."

" 'As Meester Larimore these lease in writing?" queried Vasquale, his hand on the knob.

"You sure got the cards stacked, haven't you, you snake?" snarled Jack. "What's your next play going to be — off the bottom of the deck?"

"To turn yuh over to the law," was the smooth reply. "I deed not like the look of theengs up to Riley's. Yuh

136

'ave been gone all day — an' Señor Maken —" He stopped significantly and threw open the door. "*Entrar en sheriff.* Once again 'ave we found yore 'ombre."

"Oh, it's yuh, is it?" grated Dawson in surprise, as he stepped within followed by the silent K-Spear punchers. "Reckon I made a mistake in lettin' yuh go up to Riley's. An' pore ol' Ed's been made to suffer for tryin' to be white —"

"Finish that sentence and I'll plug you, even if you are a sheriff." Larimore's voice was deadly. "Ed Maken never had a better friend than I've been since he helped me up yonder that night. I'm guilty of nothing, and you aren't the right caliber to accuse me."

His tone, as he took command of the situation, was almost purring. The compelling personality that had held the crowd motionless the night of his first appearance on the range again sent the punchers crowding back against the wall.

"I could have plugged you up at Riley's but I hadn't a mind to. I'm giving you fair warning now — you've charged me with the last thing. I didn't kill Ed Maken nor Riley and I'm plumb sick of having you and this breed laying things on me. Unless you back down pronto you're going to have me shooting. Every man's got a limit and I've reached mine. If you've a mind to talk this thing over peaceable-like you'll find me plumb eager to help you — but the next time you accuse me of killing old Ed Maken, you want to do it while you're reaching for your gun!"

He paused sweeping the row of faces before him, sifting those that were friendly from those that were hostile. With satisfaction he noted that there were but two of the latter — Vasquale and Dawson. Yet the entire group was immovable under his livid rage. The hot blood was pounding through his veins, throbbing with sickening regularity against his brain. He struggled valiantly against a wild desire to draw and shoot his way out. He glanced at the girl. Her expression was unfathomable.

"You're a woman," he said between clenched teeth. "You know things about men we don't even know about ourselves. You've seen your dad and me together. Do I look like a man that would kill him?"

He found himself hoping that she would come to his aid, that with a word she would defend him against the accusations she must know were false. She started to reply, but as before Vasquale interrupted.

"I would rather you would not question Meesus — Mees Cochita."

"I wasn't talking to you, you breed!" flared Larimore. "When I've got anything to say to you it'll be said just like I always said it — at the end of a six-gun. In the first place you've got your crust even to be placing yourself on an equal with pure-bred stuff. You're no Spaniard. I spotted you the minute I laid eyes on you. You're a Navajo breed and I dare you to deny it! Come on, you polecat, you're so ready with your gun! I'm calling you the worst thing a man can be called in front of a lady — a dirty, low-down Navajo breed — a treacherous, knife-packing skunk that's been educated by the government.

"Don't try to fool me. You might've slipped it over these white folks up here, but I know your pedigree better'n you know it yourself."

Vasquale went ashen with rage. His hand hovered near his gun, but the steely eyes of the puncher held it there. Jack again spoke to the girl who was staring at him in amazement, scarcely able to realize the charge he was hurling into the man's face, and which was not denied.

"Answer me, Cochita. Do I look like a man who'd kill a fellow in cold blood?" he demanded brutally.

As before Vasquale started to reply.

"I'm warning you to shut up," snarled Larimore. "I'm waiting, Cochita." A note which was almost a caress crept into his voice. "Don't be afraid of him any longer. He's not going to hurt you, even if he has got the fear of God in old Pedro. He daren't touch you because he knows I'll get him if it takes the rest of my life. Come on — give me your answer."

His tone brought the old color into the girl's eyes. She met his gaze frankly.

"No," her voice was clear and determined. "I do not think you killed —"

She choked on the word.

Cochita's words fell like a bombshell on the group.

"What?" gasped Dawson incredulously. "Do yuh mean to sit there with yore paw dead an' tell us yuh don't believe this feller done the killin'?"

"That's exactly what I mean, John Dawson," she replied with a show of spirit. "I don't think Mr. Larimore killed my — my — father, and nothing you can say or do will ever make me think so!" Her gaze met Jack's. He stood rigid, his face bloodless, but his eyes betrayed his thanks for her defense. "But your absence this afternoon," she faltered. "Why did you send the men back alone — then — come — in after — after — this — horrible —"

His hopes, which had soared as she rushed to his aid, now plunged with sickening speed. She had defended him only to admit there was a doubt in her mind.

"God!" he muttered hoarsely. "The whole deal's stacked against me." He tore his gaze from her and stared evenly at Dawson. "Here I am. What are you going to do?"

"Arrest yuh fer the murder of Riley an' — an' — !"

"That's enough," cut in Larimore hotly. "I tell you I was trailing a burro all afternoon. I wasn't near the K-Spear. The boys'll back me up. I couldn't possibly have beat 'em here."

"Trailin' a burro?" scoffed the sheriff. "That's a new job. What kinda burro?"

"There's only two kinds," flashed Jack. "Your kind and the ones they use for packs. This was a pack animal. Ask the boys — they'll tell you."

"Is that right, fellers?"

Dawson turned to the punchers who stood casting sidelong glances at the girl and twirling their hats uncomfortably.

"Plumb right, sheriff," volunteered Red. "He was trailing a burro, just like he says he was."

The officer stared at him blankly.

"Whaddaya mean, trailin' a burro?"

140

"Jes what I said," barked Mowbry. "We found out what's doin' the rus'lin. It's a pack burro."

"Are yuh fellers all drunk or crazy?" snorted Dawson.

"Don't get heavy," warned Red. "We ain't drunk an' we know what we're talkin' 'bout as of'en as yuh do. There was a burro hazin' them K-Spear steers toward the north fence. We come on back to the ranch with the cattle, an' Larimore trailed the donkey. Where'd he go, Jack?"

"Lost him in the brakes. Then I come on in. You know when I got here. I —"

He started to tell of having met the animal leaving the K-Spear but checked himself. As long as the sheriff did not believe his story, he reasoned, he would gain nothing by revealing another clew which probably would be scoffed at even more than the first.

"Meester Maken made Señor Larimore thees primero," said Vasquale presently, when the silence had begun to be oppressive. "I shall now take charge of thees K-Spear. Therefore we shall not need the Señor Larimore."

"Jake with me," snapped Jack, "but Ed turned over that north pasture to me for them Lazy-T dogies."

"Of course," shrugged Vasquale indifferently, "the arrangement ees now off, onless yuh 'ave thees lease."

"Lease, hell!" flared Larimore. "You know I haven't got a lease. You heard the boss make the dicker though, and so did all the fellows. Didn't you, boys?"

"Yuh damn know it!" replied Mowbry. "An' we're behind yuh in anythin' yuh do 'bout it."

"Then I take eet yuh do not care to be employ at these K-Spear longer?" Vasquale's voice was metallic but not unpleasant.

"Whaddaya drivin' at, yuh blear-eyed outlaw?" demanded Mowbry.

"That'll do, Red," interrupted the girl. "Mr. Vasquale is going to take charge of the ranch. He has a perfect right to make what arrangements he sees fit, provided they are for the best."

"That bein' the case, Miss Cochita," answered the cowboy penitently, "we'll hang 'round to see yuh get a square deal, but I reckon yuh better take my time. I got too much regard fer myself to work for a —"

"We ain't got no time to stan' here an' chaw the rag," snarled Dawson. "Larimore, I'm going to arrest yuh!"

"Go ahead if you're feeling lucky," smiled the Texan. "I've told you I'm not guilty now, and I wasn't the other time. I don't calculate to be run in for something I don't know anything about."

His gun was from its holster. He started backing for the door.

"Take him!" ordered Vasquale, making no move to draw. "He killed —"

"You're a liar, you breed!" Jack's voice was deadly cold. "I never croaked anybody, and it's not for hombres of your caliber and color to say so. Another crack like that and this here sheriff *will* have a case against me."

The punchers remained stationary, completely ignoring Ramon's command, the expressions on their

142

faces revealing sympathy for Larimore. Not so the girl. She sprang to her feet.

"I'm in charge of this ranch!" she blazed. "You're accused of a double murder. I'm not so positive from your actions in the last few minutes that you are not guilty. I was willing to give you the benefit of a doubt, but you seem to resent —" She met his hurt gaze. What she had intended saying died on her lips. "At least," she finished brokenly, "if you are innocent you will have no objection to submitting to arrest and proving your innocence."

"And let Boss Peters drill in here with a thousand head of dogies that're all tuckered out, and find I lied to him and didn't have a range? I'm sorry, Miss Cochita, but as long as this breed allows I've got no job or pasture I reckon I'll travel."

"No yore not! Yore comin' with me!" Dawson's hand fell fearlessly to his six-gun.

"If he goes yore goin' to have to take the hull gang!" challenged Red. "We're with yuh, Jack, if yuh feel like stirrin' up some hell!"

Larimore found the knob behind his back with his free hand.

"I'm right sorry, sheriff," he grinned with an exasperation that set Dawson fuming with rage, "but you're arresting the wrong man again, and I'm a kind of mule myself. Adios!"

He stepped through the door and disappeared into the night.

"Stop him!" screamed Vasquale, going for his .45.

"Why don't yuh?" taunted Mowbry, blocking the way. "Yore plumb welcome. Ain't none a the resta us got any hankerin' to trot in fronta one of them slugs that hombre's able to put through a ace of spades from his hip. Go ahead! If he don't drop yuh, I will!"

While Red had made no move toward drawing, Dawson sprang between them prepared for gunplay. Something in Mowbry's steady eyes told him that the puncher was ready to fight, at the drop of a hat, for the fugitive. That the other K-Spear hands were behind him to a man was plain to be seen.

Vasquale too, was eager for action. He cast sidelong glances at Cochita, as though but waiting a signal from her to open up. In spite of his failure to intercept the flight of Larimore there was neither fear nor terror in his eyes.

Seconds ticked by. From the corrals came the creak of saddle-leather. A horse pounded into the night.

The girl's hand flew to her breast as she strained forward listening. A sigh escaped her tight-set teeth.

Mowbry stepped away from the door.

"Now get him, yuh bad men," he grinned. "He's straddled Blue, an' there ain't a bronc-forkin' vaquero in all Colorado that'll ever catch sight of him agin!" He peered into the semi-darkness. "Ride yuh Texan, ride!"

"I'm deputizin' ever'one a yuh!" shouted Dawson, stirred to action by the sound of hoofs. "Yuh'll go after that hombre or I'll arrest yuh fer aidin' an escape."

"Shore, we'll ride," chuckled Red. "We ain't got no job at the K-Spear. We might as well be deputy sheriffs. But yuh wanna remember," — his voice grew hard —

144

"when it comes to any us fellers runnin' Jack Larimore down, ever' pony on the place is hamstrung and spavined. Can we catch up with that hoss-killin' Texan on Blue, boys?"

"Not a ghost of a show!" came the answer of one of the smiling men, who were now enjoying Dawson's dilemma immensely. "He's straddlin' the outgoin'est bronc in the state an' ridin' like hell, but we're a all-fired willin' posse."

They trooped from the house as though eager to be away from the tenseness surcharging the place. Mowbry lingered. Ignoring Vasquale, he stepped to the side of the girl, who again had buried her face in her hands.

"The K-Spear han's want yuh to know they're fer yuh stronger'n hoss-radish, Miss Cochita," he said quietly. "Do we stick, or does this here hombre get a new crew?"

"Thanks, Red," she choked. "I want you boys to stay. I know you will understand Mr. Vasquale better when our nerves relax a little. He is simply trying to unravel the mystery. But everyone is so upset we seem to suspect each other. Isn't that right, Ramon?"

"I was perhaps the leetle 'asty," granted the man graciously. "Eet ees as the señorita says. We are all nervous an' anxious to start the fray pronto. Eet geeve me pleasure to exten' my 'and in these good frien'ship. Si?"

"Keep yore dirty paw," blurted out Red. "We ain't friends an' we never will be. Yore the boss the way the cards lay now, an' we're the gang. But don't start

145

nothin'. We got some rights. Don't yuh fergit it! I ain't overlookin' that I heard ol' Ed order yuh off'n the place this afternoon."

"Red!" put in the girl. "Don't you repeat that. It has nothing whatever to do with it."

" 'Ave a care, señor," snarled Vasquale. "You are walking on what you call thees thin ice."

"Go get yore gun, if yuh feel lucky!" challenged the puncher hotly. Then to Cochita: "Mebbyso the chawin' match this hombre had with yore paw didn't mean nothin', but I know enough 'bout courts to see right off that it wouldn't sound good to a jury."

"How foolish," she exclaimed angrily. "Ramon was with me constantly. He was sitting on the porch beside me when that 'tokee' screamed. Why, Red, have you lost your mind?"

"I ain't so shore I ain't got a touch o' loco," he admitted, shamed by her explanation, "but anyhow, ol' Ed promised that north pasture to Larimore fer them Lazy-T dogies. Does he get it or not?"

"Yes." She answered before Vasquale could reply. "Father did say he could have it, and we'll stand by our word."

"Then I'll keep mum about the rag-chewin'," bargained the puncher, "an' the boys'll stick. But you remember —" his steady gaze bored into Vasquale's blazing eyes, — "we're protectin' Larimore at ever' bend in the road!"

"That at your own reesk," said Ramon smoothly. " 'Ees guilty —"

146

"Yuh don't know nothin' 'bout it. We seen some things this afternoon that points in a different direction. An' even if I don't squeal, yuh wanna remember I heard ol' Ed order yuh to get to ridin' an' not come back!"

Turning on his heel, he strode from the house leaving Vasquale staring after him and the girl flushed, yet with almost a trace of happiness discernible in her tear-stained eyes.

She looked up startled as old Pedro glided into the room.

"Pedro!" snapped Vasquale. "Get back down to the barn where you belong. I would talk weeth the señorita. Keep yore eyes on these hombre, an' eef anythin' ees start let me know *instante*."

The peon nodded but made no move to obey. Instead he stood motionless, casting furtive glances at the girl, then back to his master, as though attempting to read the thoughts of the two.

"Vamoos!"

Ramon spat the word and advanced threateningly. Pedro skinned his lips across toothless gums like a snarling wolf and remained stationary. He slunk back, presently, and dropped to his haunches in the corner, his eyes never leaving Cochita.

"What is it, Pedro?" she asked kindly. "Where have you been all afternoon?"

A look which the girl could not fathom passed between the peon and Vasquale. Pedro smiled at her question and shrugged his shoulders.

" 'E ees wanna be by yuh to geeve yuh theese protection," volunteered Vasquale quickly. "Can 'e stay een the 'ouse?"

"Why certainly," she granted, puzzled.

A few words of gibberish with the creature and Ramon turned back to her.

" 'E come over 'ere to see eef we all right. 'E does not yet know about — padre Maken. There ees no need to tell 'eem. Eet weel only make 'eem franteek — 'ard to control."

Unable to imagine the meek, half-witted dog of a man out of control, she remained silent . . . wondering.

CHAPTER
FIFTEEN

Larimore soon put considerable distance between him and the ranch. He pulled up presently, listening to hoof-beats thundering in the opposite direction.

"Good old Red," he muttered, heading south. "He's leading Dawson to the brake knowing darn well I'll start for the Rio Grande."

Blue hit an easy gallop which steadily ate up the miles. Sunrise found Jack near the New Mexico line. Stopping at a ranch he rubbed down and fed his pony. Having breakfasted while a shifty-eyed breed attempted to draw him into conversation, he re-saddled and loped on.

Half-dead for lack of sleep, he pushed ahead, determined to meet Peters as far from the K-Spear as possible and thus shorten the drive if Boss decided to swing back to the Lazy-T.

During the long, sultry hours in the saddle, he reviewed the events which had forced him to assume the role of fugitive and had branded him with the stamp of Cain. He cursed Dawson violently to Blue, who flapped his ears understandingly, yet at the same time he thrilled to the thought of the friendship Red and the K-Spear men had extended him. The picture of Vasquale in his mind brought a cold smile to his lips.

"That breed knows more'n they give him credit for," was his muttered comment. "He's a smart hombre and there's nothing yellow about him either even if he does swallow some stuff I wouldn't take once in a while." His teeth clicked savagely.

"You can't blame Cochita much. He's a good-looking devil, and treats her like she was the whole cheese. Reckon it's those fetching little ways of his, that bowing and palavering soft-like that makes a hit with the women folks."

His anger subsided with the recollection of the grief-stricken girl. In spite of the doubt she had expressed as to his innocence and which now brought a leaden sensation to his heart, in the face of the damning evidence continually arising against him, he could not condemn her, but pitied her instead.

"That Vasquale's sure got her buffaloed," he admitted to himself ruefully, "and like as not'll marry her. Well, I've got no show nohow. Nothing but a common forty-dollar cowhand. She's too good for me in the first place, but —" he brought his open hand down on the horse's neck with a resounding whack that sent the animal plunging forward and nearly unseated him — "she's too good for a breed, too, and she's not going to hook up with him if I can help it."

Despite his resolution, he knew his chances for preventing the match were slight. Jamming his hat further down over his brow to shut out the glaring alkali flats, he roweled the leg-weary Blue ahead.

Stopping only long enough to feed his mount, allow it to roll and stretch and throw a feed under his own belt, it was after dark on the third day when he sighted a camp fire.

He scrutinized the punchers sprawled on bed rolls around the blaze, behind which he could distinguish the outline of a large herd of cattle on bed ground. Recognizing them as Lazy-T men, he spurred forward, jerked his pony to its haunches at the chip blaze and swung down.

"Boy, howdy!" they shouted, surrounding him.

"Mighty glad to see yuh."

Jack pumped the extended hands cordially, feeling easier among friends.

Boss Peters, a hulking man with a weather-beaten face that was brutish until it broke into a broad smile which seemed to change the man completely and invite confidence instead of arousing fear, greeted him with genuine pleasure. His soft brown eyes and low, even voice were exactly the opposite of what one would expect.

He took the puncher's hand in a grip of steel.

"Jack, old horse, didn't figure on seeing you. Where in hell did you come from?"

"Tell you later," replied Larimore, taking his arm and leading him out of earshot of the men. "There's other things more important right now."

Boss' face was expressionless as Jack unfolded the story.

"And this Vasquale," he concluded, "just naturally up and moves in war-bag and clean shirt and 'lows to run the K-Spear and the gal's backing him up in it. The little thing's scared to death. If I could've just had a talk with her when that hombre wasn't around —"

"So poor old Ed's done for?" observed the big Texan mournfully, interrupting the mention of the girl which bade fair to become endless after the telling of the main events of the story. "Vasquale?" he repeated thoughtfully. "Seems like I heard that name somewhere but for the life of me I can't place it."

"Good looking fellow 'bout my build and meaner'n hell," supplied Larimore. "And he's sure got that gal plumb loco."

Unconsciously he started to finish what he had started, but checked himself.

"I'm in a fine mess. Don't dare go back up there with that nosey sheriff always bobbing up and hanging every killing in the country on me. What do you think?"

"Got any line on those murders?"

"Not exactly, but I reckon if I could keep a jump ahead of that Dawson without running into new bog holes I could get at the bottom of 'em with what little I do know."

"How do you figure the burro?"

"I'm sure it's trained to steal cows and makes a damn fine blind for the hombres that're working brands because none of 'em trailing the stolen stuff have to show. It's eating into the K-Spear outfit to a fare-you-well and driving those dogies somewhere. We made a mistake by not letting it go on with the herd and following it up.

"Old Ed 'lowed to me that Double-Spear-Box gang was stealing stock, but he said he never could get anything on 'em and never sighted any of 'em pulling any jobs. That jackass explains why. Another thing I noticed. That burro didn't quit the flats till he heard that 'tokee' thing holler. It's a cinch the killings and rustlings are connected. That donkey's carrying something in its packs. I sighted him coming from the ranch the night Maken was killed. Those packs were missing when I'd seen him with 'em not three hours before."

"You say the gal at the K-Spear 'lows we can't have that range unless this Vasquale says so?" Peters dismissed the line of conversation summarily. "You're plumb sure the punchers up yonder are with us?"

"She let the breed tell me we couldn't have the pasture without a lease in writing," returned Larimore, "but I reckon seeing as how all the boys heard the deal she'll kick through in a pinch and keep faith with her pa. Those fellows are with us to a man. Old Ed made me foreman and Red Mowbry's my segundo. He'll wade through hell and high water for us and he's plumb against Vasquale. I'm not so sure though you want the pasture even if they'll let you have it because there's a range war cut loose that's going to be a wampus cat."

"Don't worry," commented Peters grimly, the lines in his homely face deepening. "I've got Ed's letter telling me I could have the pasture. Reckon along with it and the puncher riding clean down to Texas to give us the come-along, and your word and those hands playing with us we can cover anything this Vasquale's holding."

"But again there's the Double-Spear-Box," protested Larimore. "Maken always 'lowed that outfit was the real bog hole. Nobody seems to know who runs that gang. Ed suspected somebody. Sometimes I thought maybe it was Vasquale."

"What gave you that hunch?" demanded Peters.

"Nothing I ever saw, only it's kind of queer how that fellow was always Johnny-on-the-spot to get his ear full of everything."

Boss fell silent, digging into the soft ground with the rowel of his long-shanked spur. He looked up presently.

"I haven't got a speck of business gambling with these critters, but don't reckon I'll ever have a lick of sense. The range war doesn't scare me any. The Double-Spear-Box outfit'll be meat for our boys if we tangle up. We'll trail this herd on just like we hadn't seen you. You come along with us. I was brought up making breeds back water. If you've picked this Vasquale wrong and he does happen to be pure Spanish instead of Navajo breed like you're playing him, we'll play hell making him hunt cover. I'm betting my hand on your say-so. If he's Indian with a strain of white we'll sure have a heap of fun."

"But the gal?" Larimore bit his tongue as the question slipped out.

Peters eyed him sharply.

"If she wants to tie up with a forty-dollar cowhand we'll have you stashed handy for the bridegroom."

Jack flushed under the thrust but remained silent. Boss was grinning broadly as they rejoined the Lazy-T punchers who were eagerly awaiting an account of Larimore's trip and unexpected appearance.

154

CHAPTER
SIXTEEN

Noses to the ground, lagging feet scuffing up choking clouds of dust, the Lazy-T herd trailed past the K-Spear a week later just at sunup. The thousand rumps, jammed hip to hip, heaved with the undulations of a restless, reddish sea. A horn-torn flank, a hoarse bellow of pain, told of disputed position. Here and there a head would bob up from the reeking mass as a steer plowed a lane through the barrier of sweat-streaked backs, a wild-eyed, snorting antagonist pounding on its heels.

From the sides of the swaying drive would come the protesting grunt of a sleepy pony as the punchers, aroused from one-eyed naps in the saddle, drove home the rowels, striving with barks to steady the circle lunging to safety from the scene of combat. The leaders would stop, fore feet planted, bawling defiantly. Tails would straighten out like signals to the fray. Along the whole line would echo the bawl in a thousand different tones, increasing in volume until it was deafening. Slickers would come from saddles; six-guns from holsters. The punchers were up in their stirrups, ready to halt the stampede. Then noses again would sink wearily to the ground, and the herd move on, forgetful of its flash of life.

The early morning breeze sifting across the prairies, stirred the withered flowers on the little mound overlooking the ranch house where Ed Maken had taken up his eternal rest. The wail of a coyote floating from the brakes seemed a wild requiem over the new-turned sod. The gleaming tombstone that Cochita had ordered post-haste from Cibola stood like a sentinel in the early morn, catching up the rays of the rising sun and flashing them across the flats. It was a beacon light to travelers who once had known the hospitality of the uncouth, raw-boned man who had sacrificed his life to the mystery of the plains.

Piloted by Larimore after the K-Spear courier had swung into the ranch with sharp injunction not to breathe a word of Jack's return except to Red Mowbry, the herd trailed on. The scent of water in the north pasture spurred the heavy, mud-caked legs to action. With low bawls of anticipation, their pace quickened to a shambling trot, their alkali-powdered flanks heaving as they plunged forward and splashed ankle-deep in the springs of Old Woman Creek.

"Thank God that's over!" sighed Boss, sweeping the expanse of plain and box canyons toward the south with blood-shot eyes. "Reckon things'll begin to move now we're here."

He turned to Jack who sat on his horse watching a wisp of smoke on the skyline above the K-Spear. But the expression on the puncher's face held Peters silent, and arming himself with a cup and tin plate he joined the cowboys circling wearily about the mess wagon.

It was late afternoon before the Lazy-T herd had been established in the north pasture, guards detailed and fences inspected. In spite of their weariness, the cowboys went about their tasks cheerfully. Work finished, Larimore threw himself on a bed roll watching the trail for Dawson.

"Reckon I'll gallop on down and make my howdys to Miss Cochita, and give this Vasquale the once-over," remarked Peters riding up.

Propping a broken piece of mirror against the wheel of the mess wagon, he started a precarious toilet.

"What's the matter with you?" he demanded, lathering his week-old beard and rubbing the soap in vigorously with his fingers. "Tongue-tied or eaten a skunk?"

Jack only regarded him in silence. Abandoning the attempt to draw him into conversation, Boss Peters wiped his razor between his fingers, donned a clean, but sadly wrinkled shirt, straightened the gaudy kerchief at his throat and slapping the alkali from his chaps, swung into the saddle.

CHAPTER
SEVENTEEN

Following the burial of her father, Cochita seemed to sink into a state of utter despair. Vasquale had assumed complete charge of the K-Spear. Old Pedro had become a part of the place, much to the disgust of Red, who went about his work with a cautious eye always cocked on the house. The men sullenly attended to the things they knew needed to be done, treating the new primero with a contempt that brooded no good and threatened momentarily to flame into open revolt. But the breed was the soul of friendliness. He conferred constantly with the girl and seemed delighted to carry out her every wish.

The preparations for the round-up that Maken had planned were halted. Brewster and Franklin, who had attended the funeral, insisted that Cochita follow her father's plans, but she had refused obstinately, declaring the K-Spear would not be a party to further acts of warfare against the rustlers. While her attitude was difficult to understand, the pleas of the barons availed nothing. They had left the sad-eyed girl finally, convinced that the overwhelming tragedy had broken her spirit, a thing they had seen many times before among the women of the range.

158

She seemed to accept Vasquale's offer of help as a matter of course and had turned over the entire management of the ranch, not so much, as Red observed, " 'Cause he was a cowman or 'cause she was stuck on him, but 'cause she jes didn't give a pertic'l'r damn whether things run right or into the ground."

She stayed in the house much of the time and a blanket of gloom settled over the place. It was into this foreboding atmosphere that Boss Peters galloped. Tying his pony at the corrals, he strode to the house.

Ramon, dragging on a cigarette on the porch, looked up to meet the gaze of the Texan. He paled, but recovered his composure instantly.

"Buen day, Don Alejandro," grinned Boss.

"Señor Alejandro? The Americano 'ave make thees mistake."

A hunted look flitted across the fellow's face.

" 'E ses per'aps refer to some other 'ombre?"

"Where's Ed Maken?" Peters had determined to approach the men at the K-Spear in apparently complete ignorance of the events that had transpired and thus allay any suspicion that might arise.

"I am thees primero," parried Vasquale. "Eet ees weeth me the señor would talk."

"No, the señor wouldn't make palaver with you. Ed Maken's paying the wage checks."

The bent figure of old Pedro shuffled around the corner of the house. Boss stepped onto the porch and leaning over the rail peered into the beady eyes of the creature.

"*Hallo*, Pedro!" he shouted suddenly.

The peon stopped as though he had been shot. His withered hand flew to his heart. His wrinkled leather-colored face turned a sickly yellow.

"Madre di Dios!" he cried. "Señor Peters!"

"See, Alejandro," the Texan wheeled on Vasquale who had leaped to his feet. "Old Pedro hasn't forgotten. It's been ten years but Boss Peters doesn't forget either. Now where's Ed Maken?"

He kept up his show of ignorance.

" 'Ave yuh not 'eard?"

"Heard what?"

"The Señor Maken," the fellow crossed himself devoutly, " 'e ees dead!"

"Dead?" repeated Boss blankly. "How? When? Where?"

"Eet ees the greates' mystery. Thees creature wheech do those keelin' strike een the night. Then there ees no more Bevens, Sheriff Cline, Riley an' Padre Maken."

"Mystery, hell!" snorted Peters. "Wish I'd never butted up against anything more mysterious than this. Who's running the shebang since old Ed kicked off?"

"Señorita Cochita. She ees to be Señora Vasquale."

"The hell she is," snapped the Texan. "What are you going to do with the *pequena muchacha* down at Calientes?"

"Bastante!" grated Vasquale, his hand sliding stealthily toward his six-gun. "Señorita Cochita shall leesen to none of yore lies."

"Whoa!" warned Peters. "I'm not lying. I know your pedigree better'n I know these Lazy-T steers I'm holding up yonder in the north pasture. I've been trying

160

to locate you for quite a spell. 'Spect you're still posing as a Spaniard with a flock of estates in old Mexico, you Navajo. You're not going to pull any more phoney —"

"Ramon!" came the voice of Cochita from within. "Oh, Ramon!"

"The señor ees not goin' to accuse —" began Vasquale under his breath.

"I'd accuse you of anything, knowing you like I do," snarled Peters. "If you don't want that gal to hear you'd better dry up. She'll know a-plenty about you soon enough. Play your cards and play 'em straight. Don't try any bluffing nor deck-stacking on me."

Livid anger flashed across Vasquale's face, yet when he answered the girl his voice was purring.

"Si, bonita. Come 'ere. We 'ave Meester Peters of the Lazy-T. 'E no doubt has come about that north pasture. Shall we let 'eem 'ave eet?"

"You know damn well you'll let me have it," blazed Peters in an undertone. "Tell her to come on out, there's one white man here."

"Si, you can 'ave eet," growled Vasquale sullenly. "Eet was the weesh of Meester Maken. She weel join us, but I trust —"

"Don't trust me any more'n I trust you, you breed! I'm liable to do anything when I'm dealin' with you. I'm not squealing though, unless you try to marry her, and if you do —"

Fire glinted in the man's eyes. "But she already ees the Señora Vasquale."

"Ramon," chided the girl, hearing the remark as she came from the house and extended her hand to Peters whom she recognized instantly from the descriptions of the Texan woven into her father's tales of the old trail days. "We are not married. In fact —"

Conscious of a strained understanding between the two, Boss cut in.

"I'm sure sorry your pa's dead."

"Thank you for your sympathy," she choked. "I — we — it's been so hard since."

She halted, meeting his gaze frankly through the blinding flood of tears. He wondered at the fear that flamed in her eyes whenever she met Vasquale's stare. Pity for her welled up in his heart, a pity that caused him to hurl a glance at the breed that sent him back a step, fingering his gun-butt nervously.

"It's about that north pasture."

Again Peters changed the subject to relieve the tenseness.

"The man your pa sent down to the Lazy-T gave a letter which is a sort of long-time lease."

"Daddy meant for you to have that pasture, although I believe one of the stipulations was that your men were to help him clean up the rustlers."

She made a poor attempt to smile.

"You shall have it as he intended, but I shall forbid any trouble with other outfits, and especially the Double-Spear-Box, whose men, daddy was convinced, were stealing cattle. They are our neighbors and I do not care to become embroiled in any range feuds."

"You're plumb right, Miss Cochita," agreed Peters. "We didn't come up here all hostile-like. But of course we'll protect our own critters."

"That's to be expected," wiping away her tears. "You're convenient to the north water holes and I'm sure you will be comfortable. Mr. Vasquale will be delighted to aid you in any way. Won't you, Ramon?"

Her fingers dropped lightly to the man's arm, but Peters, watching the pair closely, thought he could detect a slight tremble.

"Trying to make me think everything's hunky-dory when she's plumb scared to death," flashed through his mind.

"Si, señor," smiled Vasquale, reaching for her hand which she withdrew quickly. "Yuh shall want for nothing."

Peters shifted his weight and stared at the breed. The girl's next question puzzled him.

"Have you heard from Mr. Larimore?" There was a note of fear in her voice. "He seemed like such a nice young chap. It's too bad —"

"Thought he was up here and was just going to ask you where he was hanging out," interrupted Boss.

"Haven't you heard? He was suspected of killing — of killing daddy?"

"That being the case I don't wonder he's not sticking around."

Vasquale recoiled under the glare Peters cast at him.

"Far as him being arrested, if he got any kind of a break with your sheriff, they don't make 'em tough enough to sit in the saddle on the trail of that walloper."

He wondered at the flush that crept into the pale cheeks of the girl.

"As for pitying him, save it. He's the squarest-shooting youngster that ever threw a leg over a horse. He didn't do this killing no more'n I did. If he ever murders it'll be plumb betwixt the eyes and the other hombre'll be reaching for his gun. I've not been here long enough to get the lay of things and Jack being suspected kind of knocks the wind out of me. But I'll nose around and when I get ready to spring an ace-full on the jackpot you can bet it'll be the best hand out."

"Will you help me run down my father's assassins?" she asked in a strained voice.

"You know it, Miss Cochita," he pledged, extending his hand. "And that's only half of it. We will round 'em up and see that you get a square deal too."

"The Meester Peters 'e 'ave mebby what you call thees suspeesion?" inquired Vasquale blandly.

"Yep." Boss bit off the word. "I've got such a damn good suspicion I'm willing to bet my hand pat right now against any that's out and I've only been in the country a few hours and don't know a soul excepting you folks."

Sensing something back of the veiled challenge lurking in the Texan's tone, the girl stared at the two. Vasquale's face was expressionless.

"That ees good," he remarked quietly. "We shall work together an' bring thees killer to time, si?"

"You know it," commented Boss as he stepped from the porch and with a pleasant smile to Cochita, started for his horse. "If you need any help, Miss, or want anything just call on the Lazy-T boys."

She looked at him strangely, then without speaking entered the house. Peters wheeled back to Vasquale.

"As for you, I've got nothing on you yet to start you traveling, but you'd better get your warbag packed. I did it once and I'll do it again. And just remember, I'm plumb set against any wedding bells. Do you understand?"

A leer twisted the breed's face.

"The señor 'e ees ver' funny," he sneered. "Eet geeves me those good laugh."

He sauntered after Cochita, leaving the Texan staring blankly.

"That hombre's sure of his ground," mused Boss as he mounted and started for camp in the twilight dusk. "But I reckon my knowing his pedigree'll kind of start the ball rolling."

CHAPTER
EIGHTEEN

After Peters' departure, the Lazy-T punchers threw themselves on their bed rolls in an attempt to catch up on the sleep they had lost during the long hours on the trail. Tired but cautious, Larimore kept one eye on the south, expecting momentarily to see Dawson put in an appearance. Nor was his vigil amiss, for the sun had scarcely sunk on the horizon when Mowbry galloped into camp.

"Is Jack here?" he demanded of the wild-eyed punchers, suddenly aroused from their naps.

Larimore himself answered.

"Climb down, Red," he invited cordially. "Why the rush?"

"There's plenty a reason to rush, onless yuh got a hankerin' to spend time in the Cibola hoosegow," said Mowbry seriously. "Dawson'll be here pronto. He's played a hunch yuh was in camp soon as he got wind the Lazy-T herd had come in. The ol' boy's been faunchin' ever since I led him on that wild turkey hunt up in the brakes the night yuh vamoosed."

"Which way's he coming from?"

While Jack had no fear of meeting Dawson in gunplay, in the face of the suspicion in which he was held, he had hoped to avert a showdown until he had had time to try and unravel the mystery of Maken's murder.

"South. Rid past the K-Spear 'while back an' 'lowed out loud to — to" — he stopped grinning foolishly. "Oh, one uh the fellers, he was headin' this way. He's a smart ol' badger even if it does take him a long time to figger what he's goin' to do next. He's lookin' fer yuh an' they ain't nothin' outside a stampede ever been known to stop him. The feller that piloted the critters tells me on the side yore with the gang so I beat Dawson here by takin' a short cut through the pasture."

"I might as well stay and have it out now," said Jack soberly. "It's coming sooner or later anyhow. Don't look to me like that sheriff'll ever get a line on who really did the killings so I reckon I'm goin' to be the goat."

"Naw yuh don't! I ain't doubtin' yuh could keep from bein' hung or sent up in a court if yuh was brought to trial, but before yuh let ol' Dawson get his mud hooks on yuh yuh'd better rus'le some proof yuh didn't do them killin's. Right now all yuh could say is that yuh was trailin' a burro an' that'd get about as far with a jedge in a cow country as it did with the sheriff. Never thought how funny it sounded till after yuh left, then me an' the fellers had a good laugh over it."

"Do you think I killed Maken?" demanded Larimore.

"I know damn well yuh didn't. I happen to know yuh was really trailin' a jackass but yuh couldn't convince nobuddy else of it."

"Got anything up your sleeve?"

"Yep. There's a cave in them bluffs yonder that ain't been used that I know of since the big rus'ler war years ago. Why not snake some soogins an' grub in there an' jes ride range on yourself an' the country in gin'r'l till yuh gumshoes out some clews?"

"You're on. Where does she lay?"

"In them brakes yuh rode that day after that jackass. Shake a laig. Dawson won't let no grass grow under his feet on the way up. I'm tellin' yuh."

"But Blue isn't broken to pack," remarked Larimore. He little dreamt of the full import of his next move and the part it was to play in the final solution of the range mystery. Nor did it enter his head that Red Mowbry his friend, was to be the unconscious cause of dragging him deeper into the mire of suspicion.

"Never had nothin' on but a saddle, not even a slicker," he apologized for the gelding. "He's liable to raise particular hell."

"Load my hoss," suggested Red. "He's the best snubbin' an' pack animal in these parts."

Without waiting for a reply, the K-Spear puncher dragged his saddle from his own mount.

"Get Blue up, *pronto*," he ordered. "We'll swap hosses now, then we won't hafta worry 'bout it later. Yore goin' to need a plumb gentle hoss ridin' that ledge trail into the cave."

Their sympathy entirely with Larimore, who had told them his story along the trail, the punchers cut the snorting Blue into the rope corral. While Jack busied himself taunting the grumbling cook as he rummaged in the chuck wagon for supplies, Mowbry tossed his saddle onto the gelding and packed Jack's bedding on his own horse. Ten minutes later the two headed north, at a gallop.

They scarcely had dropped into the shelter of an arroyo and the punchers resumed their interrupted nap, when Dawson rode in.

Posing as a traveling puncher he made several inquiries concerning the herd and requested a bed roll to spend the night. The Lazy-T bunch was more than affable and plied him with questions of the Cibola country, meanwhile chuckling under their breath at the thought of Larimore's escape.

Supper had just been announced when Peters galloped up and arming himself with a plate and cup, sat down beside the stranger. The men held their breaths as he glanced about the row of faces but said nothing.

"There ain't a feller by the name Larimore aroun', is there?" asked Dawson between loud sips of hot coffee. "He 'lowed he was from the Lazy-T."

"Larimore?" repeated Boss in surprise, while the punchers stifled grins. "He's foreman down to the K-Spear."

"Yuh jes come from there," countered Dawson. "Yuh didn't see him didja?"

"No." Peters bit his lip for his idiocy.

"Reckon if one a yore ol' men'd been down there yuh'd a looked him up, wouldn't yuh?"

The sheriff followed up his advantage.

"I went to see Miss Cochita on business," parried Boss. "Fact is I was so cut up about poor old Ed I

169

didn't think of Larimore. Are you sure he's not at the K-Spear any more?"

"He's left the country slicker'n a whistle," admitted the officer. "There ain't no use in me tryin' to cover up who I am. I'm sheriff a this county an' I gotta hunch Larimore's 'roun' clost. If yuh see anythin' of him, will yuh let me know or are yuh playin' in with him?"

"What do you want Jack for?" asked Boss.

"Killin' ol' Ed Maken! The coroner's jury didn't gimme no chanct to nab him, or I'd had a charge agin him in Buck Riley's death too."

"Murder!" Boss fairly gasped the word. "I should say we aren't playing in with any suspected murderers. We're for the law every time when it's right. But if you're connecting Larimore with these killings you'd better go to following some new clews. He never killed anybody, let alone fellows he scarcely knew."

"What makes yuh think he scarcely knowed 'em?" Dawson fired the question pointblank.

"How could he? He didn't leave the Rio Grande till a few weeks back and he'd never been north before."

Boss' reply was as quick as the sheriff's query.

"He's not the killing kind nohow!"

"Mebbyso," admitted Dawson, reaching for another helping of food, "but he's got that to prove."

"I'll tell you some things I just run onto if you'll let up on Larimore," bargained Peters later as the sheriff settled himself on a bed roll much to the chagrin of the punchers who glanced about nervously, fearful that Jack would come riding back.

170

"Yore jes like ol' Ed Maken," returned the officer testily. "I turned Larimore over to him an' he gimme the slip. What does ever'buddy seem so plumb set on tryin' to keep that hombre from provin' he's innocent fer?"

"Oh, if that's the way you feel about it," Peters' square jaws snapped viciously, "you find him, but don't expect any help from us."

CHAPTER
NINETEEN

Having picked their way through the darkness over the treacherous, rock-strewn cañon sides, Mowbry and Jack dismounted on a narrow trail skirting the rim of a precipice overhanging Old Woman Creek. They groped around the ledge and halted at the entrance to the cave.

"Nice place for a murder," growled Larimore, attempting to peer into the gloomy maw.

"Don't get too near the edge or they'll be carting pieces a yuh an' yore hoss outta the valley fer the next six weeks," warned Red. "Yuh better lay low till yuh get a line on things. In the mornin' yuh can scout aroun'. The cow-path we jest came in on is the only one leadin' into this side, an' the other's blind, so yuh don't need to worry 'bout anybuddy ridin' in here without yore knowin' it."

While he was speaking they had moved within the cave. Scratching a match he touched it to a pile of brush near the entrance.

The glare pierced every corner of the cavern and set the shadows dancing grotesquely on the corrugated, smoke-blackened walls. A careful survey failed to reveal any signs of wild animals, which long since seemed to have abandoned the place as a retreat.

172

"Too damn lonesome for 'em," snorted Larimore. "Nobody belongs in here but some hombre that's a fugitive for something he didn't do."

"Aw, keep yore lip stiff," laughed Mowbry. "Yuh ain't got no holler comin'. Think a havin' to work fer Vasquale. I'm li'ble to be a fugitive afore long myself an' when I am I won't be innocent, either."

"Red?" Larimore's voice carried a wistful note. "Do you really think Cochita's stuck on that breed and is going to hook up with him?"

"She ain't no more stuck on him than we are, Jack. She's buffaloed, that's all. That feller's throwed a scare into her jes like he has ol' Pedro. As fer tyin' up with him, yuh jes tell the world he ain't marrying her while I'm on the K-Spear. But if he should happen to, sometime when I ain't 'roun', little Cochita'll be a widder almost afore she's a bride."

"Thanks." Jack gripped his hand. "I don't reckon I got any reason to even hope, but —"

"I know," consoled Red forlornly, "I was thataway oncet, but she couldn't see me. Reckon she's why I've stayed at the K-Spear as long as I have. Ain't nothin' holdin' me now that ol' Ed's gone, but I'm jes goin' to see the gal gets a square deal an' God help the hombre who tries to stack the deck on her."

Silence fell between them. They stamped about the cave, examining the smaller holes for predatory animals and snakes which might have slunk to cover with the lighting of the fire. Finding nothing, however, they returned to the blaze, to one side of which Mowbry pointed out a spring trickling into a subterranean pit.

They walked on to the entrance. Jack stopped, and stooping, examined several small tracks in the soft sand at his feet.

"It isn't a deer or sheep," he muttered. "Looks like the print of a colt. It's too small for a weaned critter and there are no signs of a mare."

"Shore is a colt's track." Red straightened up from his survey. "Well, I better be lopin' back, I reckon. Wanna stop at the Lazy-T camp an' meet this Peters an' see if any the boys had a pow-wow with Dawson. Then I'm going on to the ranch." He paused thoughtfully. "Better leave my hoss here with yuh. Blue —"

"He's all right," protested Larimore. "I won't have to do snakin'. Nothin' but straight saddle work."

"Yuh can't never tell," were Red's soberly prophetic words. "I'm goin' to swap with yuh fer the time bein' anyhow. Blue's li'ble to get skittish comin' 'roun' that ledge an' they wouldn't be nothin' left a either a yuh. Yuh need a gentle ol' cow hoss ridin' in an' outa this cave."

In spite of Jack's protests he started back over the narrow trail, leading the snorting Blue.

"I'll lope over tomorrow with more grub an' some oats fer yore hoss," drifted to Larimore from the darkness.

After the cowboy had gone, Jack undid the pack and spread out his blankets.

"This is a nice note," he growled as he munched a cold meal. "An innocent man hiding out for a bunch of killings he doesn't know anything about."

174

He was half inclined to return to the Lazy-T camp and risk meeting Dawson. But in view of Mowbry's kindness he dismissed the thought and set about arranging the bed and gathering what loose firewood he could find close at hand.

"Old horse," he commented sorrowfully, "you're going to have to go hungry till we get the lay of things, but if you'll play with me tonight I'll sure see you're fed fine come sun-up."

Apparently satisfied with the arrangement, Red's horse arched his neck and gingerly entered the cave where it stood staring fearfully at the dancing shadows.

The first man Mowbry spotted when he galloped into the Lazy-T camp was Dawson. The officer sat within the circle of light from a camp fire talking with Peters. Cursing himself inwardly for an idiot for bursting into the group without first making a reconnaissance, the puncher started to ride away, but the sheriff sprang to his feet and challenged him. To divert suspicion he entered boldly, swung down, and stamped into the light.

"Where yuh been, Mowbry?" inquired Dawson brusquely, studying the outline of the horse in the shadows.

"The north fence was down. I fixed her up," lied Red glibly.

"Where'd Larimore go?"

The question all but threw the puncher off his guard.

"Larimore?" he repeated blankly. "Whaddaya askin' me fer?"

"Oh, nothin'."

The officer's voice was colorless as he walked over to Red's mount beside the chuck wagon. Mowbry watched him with sinking heart, hoping that he would pass up a careful inspection of the horse.

The words of the sheriff as he returned to the fire presently, dispelled any such hope.

"Only yore ridin' his hoss. If yuh'll rec'lect he was toppin' Blue when he quit the K-Spear. I remember per-tic-lar cause yuh made the remark: 'He's on Blue an' there ain't a bronco-forkin' *vaquero* in all Colorado that'll ever catch sight of him agin!' Seein' as how yuh was right about nobuddy ever seein' him agin an' this here Blue wasn't at the ranch when I was there, I reckon yuh mighta been ridin' with him lately."

Mowbry glanced at the gelding that had caused the trouble, then back to the sheriff. For an instant he regretted having traded horses with Jack, but it was a fleeting remorse for the snubbing pony might be the means of saving the cowboy's life in the treacherous brakes.

"I shore believe yore right, Dawson," he agreed grinning sheepishly. "Where'd I get this nag? Them jinglers must a got 'em mixed."

He walked over to Blue, examining him closely as though for marks that would positively identify him.

"Yore right shore as hell."

He wheeled on the officer and Peters who was smiling broadly.

"Now where do yuh 'spose I got him?"

He scratched his head in perplexity.

Dawson himself could not suppress a chuckle at the poor exhibition of acting.

"I jes can't imagine, Red," he remarked, " 'les yuh got wind a me comin' up to search the Lazy-T camp an' took a short cut an' rode in ahead a me. Larimore mighta been here. Knowin' Blue wasn't broke to a pack yuh mighta swapped hosses 'cause yor'n was. Yuh don't suppose that coulda been it, do yuh?"

Mowbry groped for an answer. Sensing that the puncher was cornered Dawson threw off his mask of pleasantry. Expecting trouble, Peters stepped forward.

"Now sheriff," he interposed quietly, "like as not he can explain it. Don't know you, young fellow, but I gather from the officer's remarks you're one of the K-Spear men toting the monicker of Red Mowbry."

He surveyed the freckled face that seemed soot-speckled in the firelight and the fiery mop of hair straggling from beneath the Stetson.

"I just can't figure out why they should call you 'Red'." He smiled broadly. "I'm Boss Peters. Let's sit down and chew this thing over friendly-like. Here," to one of his own men who had arisen from a bed roll at the sound of the voices, "run this boy's bronc into the cave. He's going to stay all night."

Red uttered no protest as the puncher unsaddled Blue and turned him over to the wrangler.

"Now let's have it, Mowbry," said Dawson when they had seated themselves. "If yuh don't come clean I'll hafta take yuh fer aidin' Larimore's escape. I come damn nigh to doin' it back yonder at the K-Spear the night he made his getaway. Yuh'll re'leck yuh led me north when yuh knowed he'd head south. 'Spose yuh thought yuh was foolin' me, but yuh wasn't.

"There was only one way fer him to go. I wired Los Pinos the next mornin' an' they'd a got him if he'd ever showed up at the Lazy-T. He hasn't, an' he's had time. There was only one other conclusion to draw. He met Peters on the trail an' come back with him. He was in camp this afternoon an' yuh helped him sneak out. Didn't yuh?"

"If yuh was so damn shore he'd go south what did yuh foller me north fer that night?" demanded Red ignoring the sheriff's question.

" 'Cause I knowed I had him at the other end. I played a hunch he'd come back an' save me a long ride. Where'd yuh get Blue?"

"Yore so all-fired smart at figgerin' things out, Dawson," he yawned sleepily, "jes go right ahead an' figger how I got holda Blue. Where can I bog down, Peters?" he asked as though the conversation had been closed definitely. "I really orter lope on to the ranch an' work them hoss jinglers over fer gettin' my broncs mixed, but I'll put it off 'till mornin'."

He arose slowly, stretched, and sauntered to the bed roll Boss pointed out. He pulled off his boots and slipped beneath the tarp.

"Now where in the devil do yuh 'spose I got that nag?" he muttered to himself.

Peters caught Dawson's eye, and broke into a hearty laugh.

178

CHAPTER
TWENTY

The first streaks of dawn found Larimore stirring about the cave. The stillness of the night had been broken by what sounded like tiny hoofs stamping at flies. The noise had brought him to his feet a dozen times only to stare into a limitless void of twinkling stars. Unable to sleep, he had spent the long hours listening and prowling about. Leading his horse from the cavern, he paused on the trail, involuntarily drawing back from the perpendicular drop into Old Woman Creek three hundred feet below.

His eye followed the valley, crisscrossed with glistening fences. Far down its floor-like stretches huddled a group of buildings.

"That'll probably be the Double-Spear-Box," he muttered aloud.

Still beyond, wisps of smoke, like Indian signal fires, marked where the homesteaders were up and about.

"One of those other places'll be Vasquale's. Wonder which one?"

Pulling himself from his observation of the quiet scene he led the horse around the tortuous ledge road, picketed it in a grove of timber to graze, and returned to his breakfast.

Sitting just within the cave munching his food and staring into the valley, he fell to musing. He found himself half-mindful to chuck the whole affair, swing the nose of his pony from the K-Spear range and never return. Accustomed as he was to freedom, the role of fugitive palled to an unbearable degree.

Springing to his feet he started gathering up his soogins. A picture of Cochita floated before his eyes. He kicked the bed roll savagely, suddenly realizing that she was the cause of his discontent. Her coldness, her accusations, had been endured for the sake of those moments when she had rallied to his defense. He slumped down with his back propped against the side wall, idly flipping pebbles across the mouth of the cavern.

"Soon as my horse gets filled up, I'd better ride over to that cabin Ed burned, and strike out from there," he mused aloud. "It's a dead cinch it was the Revenge Gang's hangout and it's a good bet they know more'n I do about the killings. I'd recognize those hombres we had the scrap with if I could get sight of 'em. Reckon the thing to do would be to lope down to the Double-Spear-Box and kind of look the crew over. Maken suspected 'em and if they haven't got any boss who comes out in the open and makes a show I 'low maybe he wasn't far from right."

He fell to dozing in the sunshine which was swiftly taking the chill from the cave. His eyes became fixed. He nodded drowsily. With an effort he pulled himself up, but the silence and peace mastered and he fell into a quiet sleep.

180

He came to with a start. The turning of a rock on the ledge path sent him scurrying on his hands and feet like a bear into the cavern. Under cover of the sheltering gloom, he slipped his six-gun from its holster and waited.

Thump! Thump! Thump! The thud of hoofs on the trail grew louder. He crouched in the darkness, determined to fight it out with whoever or whatever put in an appearance. Dawson flashed into his mind. His jaws set grimly. While he revolted at shooting down the sheriff without a show the constant suspicion was making him desperate.

The hoofbeats ceased suddenly. While the entrance to the cave was still unobstructed by any form, he could feel that whatever it was approaching was standing just out of sight. Gripping his gun tighter, he straightened up and sidled along the wall, peering toward the light for a glimpse of his hidden visitor.

A deafening noise split the stillness and reverberated through the cave. The tracks of the small hoofs Red and he had seen the night before suddenly were explained. Advancing cautiously, he looked out. Two fuzzy ears met his gaze. Then an inquisitive face framing two baggy, sunken eyes.

"That's that 'tokee' burro sure as I'm living," he muttered nervously, relieved after the start the braying of the animal had given him. "He's been using this cave and I moved in an' took his shelter."

Edging forward, he surveyed the beast curiously. The packs that had been missing when he last had seen it racing away from the K-Spear, again were in place, held with long pieces of frayed rope.

Recalling that he had used his riata to tether his horse, he moved forward stealthily hoping to get behind the staring donkey and cut off his retreat, but as he advanced the burro spun about in the trail and disappeared.

Rounding the point with all the speed he dared, Jack darted to where his horse stood grazing. Quickly slipping the bit between its teeth, he swung up and started in pursuit.

He glimpsed the burro racing along the edge of the precipice. Giving his mount free rein, he began to gain. Coiling the throw rope which he had not even taken the time to hang at his saddle bow, he whirled it out. The burro, with uncanny intuition, anticipated the move and dodging into a grove of pine, halted, watching him inquisitively.

"I'm going to take a look in those packs if we play hide-and-seek all day," he muttered, dismounting and stalking the animal as though it were a wild beast.

He advanced almost upon his quarry. His hand shot out for a hold to enable him to swing onto its back. It wheeled suddenly and started through the timber. Racing back to his horse, he threw himself into the saddle and again took up the pursuit.

CHAPTER
TWENTY-ONE

Breakfast at the Lazy-T camp found a silent group assembled. Red Mowbry, who sullenly admitted to himself that Dawson had bested him the previous night, ate glumly, glancing neither to right or left.

Always surly until he had swilled down a cup of steaming coffee, Peters sat cross-legged on the ground, his wrinkled face giving the impression of a disgruntled bear. Knowing their foreman, the punchers carefully avoided addressing him directly.

Dawson went about his meal methodically, seemingly bent on stowing away as much as he could in the least possible time. He smiled occasionally at the sallies of the men, but further than that gave no sign he even heard or saw what was going on around him.

Red arose as the remuda thundered in. His movement roused Dawson who stood up, plainly preparing for speech. Sensing something in the air, Peters spun his plate toward the cook, climbed to his feet, and brushing off his chaps, waited. Before any of the three could utter a word, a shout brought them about.

One of the guards was galloping in, motioning the men to the cave yard.

"Rus'lers!" he cried. " 'Bout half dozen of 'em! Down in one a them blind draws brandin' cattle."

The puncher threw himself from his horse at Peters' side.

"How do you know they're rustlers?" inquired Boss mildly.

" 'Cause they're brandin' Lazy-T stuff!" bellowed the cowboy excitedly.

"Ours?" Peters showed some interest.

"I ain't trailed this herd fer weeks without knowin' ever' dogie in it. I tell yuh they've got a bunch uh our critters a-brandin' 'em."

Like a bull, slow to anger, but once fired capable of a cold, relentless fury, Boss came to life.

"Buckle on your guns, boys," he barked. "We'll lope down and see what it's about."

"Ain't no use in takin' yore .45's," interposed Dawson. "There won't be no fireworks."

"That just depends on who they are and what they're doing with Lazy-T stuff," replied Peters significantly, swinging into the saddle of a roan a wrangler had dragged up.

"I don't wanna man to shoot 'less it's plumb necessary," ordered the sheriff, joining him.

"We won't unless they start something," agreed the Texan. "But let me tell you if they do I've got the lead-slingin'-est crew that ever loped across these flats."

On a bluff overlooking the arroyo to which the guard led them, the men, headed by the sheriff and Peters, threw themselves from their saddles and bellied forward. They halted on the rim of the draw and lay

184

gazing into the valley. Below stood a bunch of cattle, licking at their brands. A smoldering chip fire was ample proof that the marks were fresh, but the men whom the puncher had declared he had seen doing the work had disappeared completely.

"Like as not sighted you before you saw 'em," growled Boss as they mounted, eased their way into the ravine and circled about the staring herd. "Those brands sure have been run."

"Howsomever, they don't look like they'd been done this mornin'," said Dawson.

"Sure they don't," agreed Peters. "It's been done with a wet blanket, that's why. What the devil?"

His question was aimed at Mowbry, who stared in amazement. The Lazy-T brand had been run into a K-Spear!

"Well, I'm damned!" ejaculated Red. "Howdaya account fer that?"

"Somebody's brandin' my cows with Miss Cochita's mark, that's all," observed Peters dryly. "Are you in cahoots with 'em?"

The tone stung the color from the cowboy's face.

"Yuh know damn well I ain't in on it, Peters," he snapped.

"Glad to hear it. I believe you personally, but I'm laying even money the K-Spear's behind it."

"Whaddaya mean?" flamed Mowbry. "Miss Cochita's the K-Spear an' there ain't a man livin' goin' to call her a rus'ler."

"Just a minute," soothed Boss. "There's no use in getting yourself all lathered up. I'm not calling Miss

Cochita nor anybody else a cow thief yet. But the fact remains they're my critters and they're sporting her brand. If you can explain it I reckon everybody'll be plumb satisfied."

Mowbry twisted uncomfortably in his saddle. In the face of the evidence before his eyes he could not help but acknowledge that Peters had just cause for suspecting the girl. He was positive though, that she knew nothing of the rustling. Knowing the boys at the K-Spear as he did, he quickly dismissed the idea that they were involved in any way. A suspicion flashed into his mind. Peters voiced it.

"Vasquale's primero down there, isn't he?" asked the Texan quietly.

Dawson, studying the herd, pricked up his ears.

"Yep." Red was eagerly attentive.

Boss wheeled on the sheriff.

"I don't know what you know about that breed, an' I don't know what you want to know."

His tone was a challenge that brought the officer rigid.

"But I chased Vasquale off the Rio Grande ten years ago for brand running."

"What?" gasped Mowbry and Dawson.

"Just what I said," repeated Boss. "His name was Alejandro then. He was the slickest brand runner in the country. He works with a wet blanket. There aren't many fellows riding any range nowadays that can handle an iron that way unless they've been shown by a past master. What are you going to do?" he demanded.

186

"Stand there and let those rustlers get clean out of the country?"

"I'm ridin' to the ranch," answered Red, "an' see can I get head or tail to this thing."

"That's Jake," returned Peters. Then to Dawson: "What are you aiming to do?"

"Lope down to the Double-Spear-Box I reckon an' get a line on them breeds."

"Say —" Boss caught himself on the verge of quoting Larimore that the owner of the Double-Spear-Box was a mystery. "Who owns that place?" he finished quickly.

"Nobuddy seems to know," replied the officer. "'Sposed to be some hombre in Mexico City. I'd plumb admire to get the low-down on him."

"Was Maken ever suspicious of that outfit stealing his critters?" asked Boss.

"Yep," Red answered. "He swore time an ag'in they was workin' his herd somethin' scandalous. He was gettin' ready to ride them brakes on a round-up when he cashed in."

"Does anybody know how they come by that brand?" Peters paced about thoughtfully.

"Nope." The sheriff's tone was eager now. "I checked the mark at the inspector's office an' it belongs to some hombre named Menendez in Mexico City."

"Wow!" yelled Boss suddenly, dropping to his knees. "Lookee!" He traced the Lazy-T brand in the dirt. "There wouldn't be any cause for Cochita to steal from me, would there?"

Dawson shook his head. Red and the punchers circled about, watching the Texan with interest.

"Supposing the Double-Spear-Box gang wanted my cows and didn't want to arouse suspicion. What do you think they'd do?"

"What's that got to do with it?" demanded the officer blankly.

"A whole heap. We're working on something right now that's going to clear up this thing, killing and all, I'm betting. Something I never saw before on any range — a brand that'll run two ways."

"What?" questioned Mowbry, mystified.

"I said it. Somebody's stealing from me and branding your brand. Why? To throw suspicion on Cochita if the thing's found out because we haven't been here long enough to lose any critters without causing a lot of trouble. Supposing that's the case."

By tracing a half diamond on the top of the Lazy-T and supplying a K in front of the horizontal bar, he demonstrated how simple it had been to run the brands on the bunch of cattle into a K-Spear.

"Damn queer you hombres haven't tumbled onto this long ago. Five jabs with a straight iron and the trick's done. Burned through a blanket to make it look old."

"Where does that get 'em?" asked Dawson. "Yuh wanna recklect yuh only been in the country a coupla days an' it ain't surprisin' we ain't thought of it seein' as how the rus'lers themselves only figgered it out in the last few hours."

Peters flashed him a look that was little short of pity.

"You're playing with a gang that's backed by a fellow with brains," he snorted. "They stole my critters for the

188

K-Spear. Cochita's going to get particular hell if I've a mind to start anything. Then when the excitement blows over, lookee!"

Connecting the two points of the K with a vertical bar and taking the perpendicular side of the letter for one end of a box, he quickly enclosed the other three sides, making a finished Double-Spear-Box.

"By God, yore plumb right!" shouted Mowbry excitedly. "They branded yore stuff with Cochita's bran' to throw yuh off'n the trail an' duck the hell they knowed yuh'd raise. It's a cinch they intended to run it later into a Double-Spear-Box. They been doin' it right along on ol' Ed.

"That's the reason they picked that mark. There isn't a man on the K-Spear rustling, I'm sure of that. It's somebody connected with the Double-Spear-Box that's done this job. I'm heading for the ranch right now to call for a showdown."

"Who yuh goin' to have a showdown with?" queried Dawson.

"Dunno," admitted Red as he swung into the saddle. "First off I'm goin' to make talk with Cochita. After that —"

The rest of his sentence was lost as he rowelled his pony into a stiff lope.

"Reckon I'll ride with him," said Boss quietly. "I'm calling somebody's hand too. Those're my steers that were stolen and I —"

"We'll all meet at the Lazy-T camp toward evenin'," suggested Dawson. "I'm goin' to drift over to the Double-Spear-Box an' see what I can learn. Yuh get a line on things down yonder an' start workin' this way. Lay off'n the gunplay, though. Are yuh with me?"

He extended his hand.

"Yep." Boss accepted the offer of friendship crisply. "I'm into your game providing you'll let somebody else do some thinking once in a while."

The sheriff flushed.

"Le's play together," was his dry comment as he jabbed his horse viciously with the spurs and headed north.

Detailing four of his men to vent the run brands and re-mark the cattle with a Lazy-T, Peters and the rest of his punchers quickly overtook Red.

"What do you think?" demanded the K-Spear cowboy as they galloped along.

"It's got me guessing," admitted Boss. "I cornered Vasquale yesterday down to the ranch but he didn't back water any. I told you I chased him and Pedro off the Rio Grande for brand running. That was ten years ago. I've been gunning for him ever since. Didn't even suspect his being here until I crossed trails with him toting the monicker of primero of old Ed's outfit. He's no good.

"A Navajo breed that's a wampus cat with the ladies. He married four or five that I know of, and has two wives down to Calientes right now that'd like to get hold of him."

"Allus had a hunch he was bad," said Red thoughtfully as the Texan concluded his tale. "He's got a shifty eye. I been accusin' him more since Larimore hit the range. Them two took a dislike right off'n the

190

start an' seems like they have trouble ever' time they meet up. But how 'bout these killin's? They must have some connection with the rus'lin'. Yuh don't suspect Vasquale uh them, do yuh?"

"Vasquale didn't do those killin's." Peter's words came measured. "He's too smart. He hasn't done any rustling either. But I'm betting he's got a gang that's doing it. That running through a wet blanket's a dead give-away. As for the killings —"

"Say," blurted out Red, "ol' Ed an' Vasquale had a rag-chawin' match the day Maken was killed. Yuh don't 'spose —"

"They did?" demanded Peters. "What was it about?"

"Don't know, but I heard Ed order that breed off the place. Do yuh 'spose —"

"Let's don't 'spose anything," growled Boss. "Let's travel."

CHAPTER
TWENTY-TWO

A stiff ride brought them to the ranch. The corrals and barnyard were deserted when they pounded down the lane and tied their mounts. The cook, a question in his sunken eyes, met them at the kitchen door as they came up.

"Where's Cochita?" demanded Red.

The sourdough wiped his hands on his apron.

"Rid out awhile back with that dago, or whatever he is," he replied gruffly. "He single-foots to the house soon as he got up an' had me call her. She come down an' they et together, then rid off. She shore was tellin' him a thing er two."

"Which way?" asked Mowbry anxiously.

"Toward the brakes." The cook waddled to his side. "'Low the dago was tryin' to get her to do somethin', 'cause I heard him keep a-sayin'" — his face twisted as he attempted to mimic Vasquale — " 'but ees eet not right for the señorita to even consider thees proposition.' "

"We'd better hit the grit," snapped Red, starting toward his horse. "Reckon we're a step behind 'em, Peters, but by breezin' right along we can make it up. They're somewheres between us an' Dawson. Whaddaya say we catch some fresh hosses an' do some tall ridin'?

Somethin' tells me the hull thing's wrong an' we're due fer a storm."

"Kind of surmised he'd be traveling," observed Boss.

"Sure isn't hard to figure the low-down now. He's using those branded cattle of mine to scare the life out of her, knowing I'll stumble on to it *pronto*. Wouldn't be surprised if they were branded right under our noses just to bring things to a head."

"Whaddaya calc'late he's aimin' to do?"

"Got no idea, but you can bet your hand pat he's got something up his sleeve that isn't goin' to help anybody but Mister Vasquale."

Red heard him through impatiently, then, without comment, started toward the barn for fresh mounts. A chuckle from the men brought him about. Stripping off his flour-sack apron, the cook had tossed it over the railing of the porch and reached for a wicked-looking butcher knife in the rack beside the door.

"Little Cochita in trouble?" he muttered, running his finger gingerly along the keen blade. "Gone somewheres with that dago? Somethin' wrong, me lads. I'll get — I'll get —"

His chubby face was flaming as he stopped abruptly and wheeled on one of the K-Spear men, who having sighted the group, had ridden in from the pasture and now stood watching the Lazy-T punchers quizzically.

"Run up a bunch a fresh hosses," ordered Red. "We're hittin' the trail *pronto*."

The man turned to obey.

"An' a rip-snortin', high-climbin' bronc fer yours truly," put in the cook. "Yuh don't need to pick the orneriest one in the hull herd but I deman's one that's got plenty a git-up-an'-git."

"Yuh can't go, cookie," said Mowbry. "Yore too fat to ride."

The red in the chef's face deepened to purple. He stepped forward threateningly.

"Too fat?" he blustered. "Yuh pig head, I ain't too fat to ride circles 'roun' any man in yore posse."

"Gwan in the house, grub sp'iler," grinned Red. "We want men in this here gang. Great, big, loose-limbed fellers who can stick without takin' 'long a supply a liniment an' bandages. Yuh couldn't go a mile afore yuh'd be so chafed yuh couldn't sit down fer a week."

The cook brandished the blade menacingly.

"An' let yuh hombres try to reckon with that dago if he turns hostile? Not on yore life. I played nurse to Cochita since she was knee-high to a prairie dog. I knowed Ed Maken an' his wife when they didn't have nothin' but one cow an' a slab of moldy bacon. If that little gal needs help, she's shore goin' to get it from ol' cookie. Yuh be damn shore an' run me up a hoss," he shouted to the wrangler, who already was riding circle on a *cave* grazing in the home pasture.

Playful and snorting, the remuda pitched into the round corrals. Quickly the Lazy-T men transferred their saddles to fresh mounts. The cook, who had followed the punchers to the yard, stood by uncertainly, his badly-bowed legs wide apart as though threatening to give way under his ponderous weight.

"Cotch me up a gentle one," he whispered aside to the wrangler. "I ain't rid fer quite a spell an' I might not be so good."

"Good?" taunted Red who overheard the request. "Yuh never was good fer nothin' only to swill down likker an' sp'ile the frijoles. Come on fellers."

"Lope right alon', yuh nasty potato!" the cook hurled at him. "That dago uses knives, yuh know, an' I reckon I'm the only hombre in these parts that'd rather stan' up agin' a blade than a six-gun any time. Jes wait," his voice arose shrilly, "yuh gun toter'll get yorn afore he gets through with yuh. I'll be comin' 'long though, so yuh can allus figger on reinforcements."

With a brief word of instruction to the wrangler to direct the K-Spear men to the Lazy-T camp as quickly as they rode in, Mowbry mounted, and followed by the posse, galloped down the lane to the outer gate.

The cook watched them sorrowfully.

"Now boy," he ordered, turning back to the jingler, "cotch me up the gentlest hoss yuh got on the place. Reckon there's a ol' saddle down yonder to the barn, ain't there?"

"Yep. One Miss Cochita usta ride when she was a kid. Ed allus kept it hangin' 'roun' kinda fer the sentiment."

The chef shook his head dubiously.

" 'Low it'd be sorta small through the seat fer me. If I'm goin' to do hard ridin' I really orter have plenty a room fer my bulk. Snake it out anyhow an' le's take a look at it."

The wrangler returned from the barn with a light buckskin saddle on his shoulder. The cook inspected it closely.

"Hell," he snorted in disgust, "I couldn't ease half myself into that thing. Are yuh right shore there ain't 'nother'n on the place I can borry fer the time bein'?"

"Nope. But I can fix yuh up a nice thick pad a blankets on a gentle hoss if yuh wanna top him bareback. It'd be the best way anyhow, then if yuh start to roll off yuh wouldn't have nothin' that could cotch yore foot an' drag yuh 'crost the flats."

The cook eyed him belligerently.

"Le's yuh an' me have this thing out oncest an' fer all," he snarled. "I usta be considered the best all-roun' puncher in these parts. I know I'm a wee bit overweight at the present, an' I ain't done a heap a ridin' o' late, but there was a time —"

"That time's gone ferever, cookie," laughed the cowboy, busy spreading several thicknesses of blanket on the back of a horse which eyed him suspiciously, its head bowed as though in shame.

"That's awright," grated the cook, "but when I starts out I allus gets there. An' yuh don't need to take all day to fixin' that hoss up, neither. I'm r'arin' to ride."

"Climb up, sire, yore steed is waitin'," announced the wrangler grandly.

"Hi, yuh!" panted the chef. "Yuh'll hafta gimme a heft."

The cowboy answered the appeal. With a mighty heave he all but threw the hapless chef over the other side of the patient, wondering animal. With a sigh the cook straightened up and gathered his reins. The horse pranced, impatient to be on its way with the strange accouterment. The chef sheathed the long knife through the belt loop on his trousers.

"If I ain't back in a day or two," he said solemnly, "tell the boys there's plenty a bread in the box an' the bacon's in the cooler. After they've et, have 'em look fer me. I'm snortin' fer blood an' like es not I'll get it."

"Yuh'll get it awright," roared the puncher, "soon as that hoss' wethers rubs the hide off yore laigs."

With a wave of adieu, the cook kicked the bewildered animal viciously in the ribs. It started out at a long swinging trot that drove the breath from the rider's bouncing body. Cookie stood it until he had dropped from sight of the corrals in an arroyo, then strove desperately to slow down his mount, meanwhile clinging frantically to the straggling mane which continually slipped from between his pudgy fingers.

"Whoa, bronc!" he shouted.

He expected every minute of the horse's wild, unbearable jerking, the unmerciful hardness of the withers as he jolted upon them, would be his last. But sighting the animals of the posse galloping three or four miles ahead, the pony only trotted the faster.

CHAPTER
TWENTY-THREE

For two hours Larimore played tag with the burro in the timber fringing the rim of the precipitous brakes. Determined to catch it and investigate the packs, he clung tenaciously to the pursuit, knowing that sooner or later he would tire the little animal to a point where it would submit to capture. He drew rein suddenly as the jackass, a few paces in the lead, slid to a halt, pricked up its long ears, then wheeling, dashed in the opposite direction.

Wondering what had caused it to change its course, he temporarily abandoned the chase and dismounted. On his guard against a trap that would give Dawson the drop, he worked his way stealthily through the trees to a spot which commanded a view of the clearing on the edge of the cañon.

From his shelter behind a big pine, he caught sight of two saddled horses grazing. Angry voices drifted to him from the bluff. His heart skipped a beat, then started pounding like a trip-hammer. Standing on the brink of the precipice was Cochita, her fists clenched tightly, arguing with Vasquale.

"I tell you I shall not!" she flared, stamping her foot. "I have given you charge of the K-Spear, but I do not propose to turn my property over to the Double-Spear-Box. Father never would have consented to such a transaction and I intend to handle the affairs of the ranch as he would have, had he lived."

"But uniting thees ranchos would make the beegest place een thees country," came the oily voice of the man. "Our 'erds would be weethout number; our ranges almos' weethout border. We could then sell an' go to ol' Mexico, thees lan' of romance an' song."

"Why your sudden interest in the Double-Spear-Box?" she demanded impatiently.

"My greatest eent'rest ees een yuh — to make yuh queen of thees rangclan'. Eet would mean so much. The Franklin an' Brewster 'erds would be nothing to what yuh would control. An' besides," he hesitated for an instant, then swept the sombrero from his head in an elaborate bow, "I 'ave the 'onor to own thees Double-Spear-Box."

"You own the Double-Spear-Box?" she repeated, stunned.

"Si, señorita."

"Oh!" The exclamation escaped her tight-set lips. "Then you lied to daddy. And to think I dismissed —"

"*Bastante!*" he snarled, advancing threateningly. "What do yuh mean, you deesmiss' —"

Larimore strained to catch her last word, but it was drowned out by the man's violent warning. Somehow he sensed that she was referring to him, and the thought set his heart to hammering against his ribs. As he watched the pair, it was easy to see that fear of the fellow dominated her every move. Her eyes were flashing, yet filled with a vague, hunted expression that brought his six-gun from its holster.

"So you own the Double-Spear-Box, do you?" he growled under his breath. "You're the *hombre* I'm looking for. You're the mysterious Menendez that's 'sposed to be in Mexico City, eh? That's enough to swing you sky high." He started up, resolved to shoot it out with the fellow regardless of what the girl could say or do, but lingered for a moment, hoping to hear more before calling Vasquale to account. The livid anger that wreathed the swarthy face was more terrible than he himself had seen at the corral the morning he had ridden Blue.

"What does the señorita mean?" The repetition of the interrogation drifting to him from the bluff, was in a different tone. Regaining control of himself, Vasquale had forced the brutality from his voice, which again was purring. "To ol' Mexico, the lan' of love an' song."

"Love — bah!" scoffed the girl. "I tell you I shall never consent to merging the K-Spear and the Double-Spear-Box, and furthermore —"

"Yuh weel," he grated. " 'Eet matters not what the padre said or thought. 'E ees no longer to be consider'. Yuh weel. I shall force —"

"You don't dare," she challenged. "You have proved to me I made a mistake in even trusting you when everyone else was against you. I hate you! I — despise you! I —"

To Larimore it seemed that she never before had been so pretty as she was now in her rage, with the color playing in and out of her cheeks. He made no attempt to stifle the secret joy he felt at the break between the girl and the breed. Human-like, he took a keen delight in hearing her forced to the admission that she had been blinded in the trust she had imposed in the fellow. But he was scarcely prepared for the trump card Vasquale played.

"*Si*, yuh weel." The tone was confident. "Even now the Señor Peters ees ridin' to thees K-Spear an' 'ees vaqueros 'ave unslung their guns."

"Why should he ride to my ranch with his men armed?" she demanded indignantly.

"Yuh made 'eem promise 'e would not start thees range war, *si?* Well, yuh 'ave start eet yoreself weeth 'eem as thees — what yuh call eet — thees goat."

"You — you —" Anger choked her. Her display of passion only brought a more hateful twist to his lips.

"Thees Lazy-T cows, 'e ees bran' the K-Spear!"

"What?" she screamed. "You have dared to steal from Mr. Peters for the K-Spear?"

Larimore heard the man's assertion in wonder, yet knowing nothing of the brand-running that Boss and Red were following up, the full significance of the disclosure was lost on him. He strained for Vasquale's reply.

"There ees always the way. Now weel yuh combine the K-Spear an' thees Double-Spear-Box, or weel the señorita go to jail tryin' to explain why thees Lazy-T cows ees brand weeth her mark?"

"You beast!"

She stepped forward as though to strike him. His hand fell to his gun. Jack straightened up, ready for action, white-hot anger searing his brain. He leaped from behind the pine; stopped in his tracks. The blood seemed to freeze in his veins. Cochita had advanced only to recoil in terror from the livid rage in the fellow's eyes and his apparent willingness to draw on a woman, then with a piercing shriek she pitched backwards over the precipice.

Larimore tore his gaze from the spot where she had disappeared. His six-gun barked. Vasquale staggered, dodged behind a tree, and raced across the clearing. Jack fired again just as the breed threw himself into the saddle, but the moving figure at long range was a difficult target and the bullet went wild.

He paused for a moment, his inclination to pursue the fleeing man, yet thought of the girl sent him on the run to the edge of the precipice. Dropping to the ground, he peered into the abyss. Lying almost a hundred feet below, head and arms down, supported only by a rotten stump sticking out from the almost perpendicular rock wall, was the crumpled body of the unconscious Cochita, suspended between blue sky and bottomless pit.

The inert figure seemed to sway in the breeze drifting across the face of the precipice and whining through the pines above. He lay watching, fascinated with terror, realizing that the insecure prop would give way at any instant and plunge her into eternity.

Forcing his legs, which suddenly had become leaden with horror, to action, he straightened up and raced to his horse. Unbuckling his lariat with awkward fingers, he sped back to the edge of the chasm. The body of the girl had shifted slightly. The stump was weakening under the strain. With the accurate eye of a cowman accustomed to measuring distance at a glance, Larimore whirled out a noose slightly larger than Cochita's body. Braiding a tuft of grass in the hondo to hold it in place, and using great care to keep from dislodging a rock that would crash down upon her and send her hurtling into space, he paid out the lariat over the precipice. His heart sank. It fell a scant half-dozen feet short!

He fought against a wild desire to climb down hand over hand, trusting to luck and strength to raise her to safety. Inexperienced as he was at climbing, hampered by his high-heeled boots, yet unable to go in his stocking feet which would be cut to ribbons on the sharp rocks, he realized that the attempt would be suicidal.

"Thank God fer Red Mowbry!" he muttered as a sudden thought sent him again dashing toward his horse. "I've got a snubbing pony that knows what to do on a rope. There's some chance at least with it. Blue'd be plumb worthless in a pinch like this."

Slackening his pace to keep from frightening the animal, he seized the bridle reins, and mounting, galloped back to the edge of the cañon. Stripping off the saddle, he wrapped the cinch several times around the bare roots of a cedar just below the rim, then buckled the latigo. With the stirrups extended it gave him perhaps three feet of advantage.

Knotting the end of the lariat through the foot-support and grasping the horn with one hand he swung himself down his full length and cautiously lowered the riata with the other. The width of the saddle bridged the gap between the end of the rope and Cochita! Rescue now depended on the strength of the pine knot supporting her weight and his ability to work the noose over her arms.

He found himself praying aloud that the stump would hold. He cursed in the same breath, as the breeze, whipping at the rope, kept it swaying along the inert figure.

Sickened at the sight, scarcely daring to hope that he could perform the delicate feat and drag her to safety, he clung to the horn. His arm grew numb with fatigue. He gritted his teeth in desperation, attempting to hang on for a few moments longer. One false move, the slightest relaxation of his fingers into which the leather was cutting, would plunge him into the bottomless pit.

To look down left him weak and trembling; to look up at the filmy clouds floating lazily across the sky nauseated him and filled him with an almost irresistible desire to let go and drop into the cañon. He swung to and fro, trying vainly to maneuver the rope over the suspended body.

A sharp report sounded through the cañon. He risked a look, then shut his eyes tightly, hanging on for grim death. His taut nerves strummed. A whistling sigh escaped his clenched teeth. The rotten stump had shifted. The decayed roots were giving way! He clutched madly for a branch of the cedar and clawed his way back to the brink of the precipice.

He sprawled full length, looking down, struggling to sift one coherent idea from his chaotic thoughts. The perspiration dripped from his forehead. He shook it from his eyes savagely. He was swiftly reaching a point where his powerlessness was driving him to employ some foolhardy expedient which in no way would help the girl and might spell his own doom.

A movement below. The blood froze in his veins. Disturbed by the knot groaning under its human load, a rattlesnake glided from a fissure in the side-wall and stretched itself on the warm ledge at the side of Cochita.

Leaping to his feet, he slipped his six-gun from its holster and sped along the rim. Reaching a boulder overhanging the chasm, he crawled out on it on all fours to a point which commanded an angling view of the rock shelf. He hugged the stone, fighting to control his jumping heart, knowing that the reptile would not strike as long as the girl remained motionless.

The odds were overwhelmingly against him. If he killed the snake there still was the possibility of the bullet glancing on the sidewall and wounding Cochita, or the impact loosening the pith-eaten stump.

Again the rotten log creaked. The snake coiled, ready to lunge.

"God!" he breathed fervently. "It's my one chance."

Drawing as fine a bead as possible on the constantly moving triangular head of the rattler, he fired, realizing that to score a bull's eye would be luck, but trusting to the force of the bullet to sweep the snake from the shelf. The thought that the shot might bring Dawson down upon him never entered his head. His own freedom was forgotten — the rescue of the girl was paramount. He waited anxiously until the dust thrown up by the pellet of lead had settled.

His aim had been true. The snake uncoiled, whipped helplessly, but the danger was not yet past. The flashing fangs missed the girl by little more than a hair as the reptile slid into space.

As if the episode had been the turning point, a sudden breeze caught up the swaying noose and slipped it over Cochita's arms.

Filled with new hope, he raced back to the saddle strapped to the cedar. Throwing caution to the winds, he grasped the horn with one hand and swung himself over the cliff. Gently he worked the lariat along her body with his free hand. It settled under her arm-pits. A quick jerk. The grass wrappings on the hondo gave way. The rope grew taut about her body.

This much of the rescue effected, he attempted to drag himself up with sheer strength. The cedar from which the saddle was suspended sagged sickeningly. He fought for a foothold, thankful that any rock now dislodged could not send the girl plunging into the chasm.

With an almost superhuman effort he pulled himself to the brink. A splintering crash brought him about. Mustering courage, he glanced down fearfully. The stump had given way. It rebounded like a ball against the face of the wall, tore loose an avalanche of small rock, threw up a cloud of dust, then smashed to splinters in the cañon.

206

The body of the girl swung clear below the ledge and dangled at the end of the rope.

"Thank God!" he muttered brokenly, wiping the beads of perspiration from his dirt-streaked forehead. "If the throw rope'll only hold!"

Powerless to raise the dead weight over the edge of the chasm, he cast about wildly for some way to drag her to safety. The lariat was too short to attach to a tree. Red's thoughtfulness in supplying him with a snubbing horse seemed to have counted for naught. He could not put the animal to use because the saddle was the link between Cochita and death.

His one course seemed to lie in riding bareback for help. He started for his pony. A deafening sound directly behind halted him. Leaping behind a tree he jerked his gun free and peered around cautiously.

His set face relaxed in a happy grin. The .45 slid back into its holster. Before him stood the burro braying loudly.

"Didn't have enough hide-an'-seek, you little devil?" he challenged. "What's the matter? Lonesome?" His eyes fell on the several pieces of frayed rope about the packs. "You're sure the fellow I'm looking for. You're just in time with that rope. Reckon if you are a rus'ler you might lend a hand at saving a lady."

The burro cocked its hairy ears quizzically, but as Jack edged forward it sidled away.

"Come on you ornery cuss and be caught," he pleaded. "Be a gent once in your life. I'm not goin' to hurt you. I just want to get my mud hooks on those ropes. I won't even look in your packs if you'll help me out."

The coaxing had no effect on the little beast, which continued to back off. Its rump came in sudden contact with a tree. It wheeled and started wandering away, apparently dissatisfied with the surroundings. A few steps and it stopped to graze as unconcerned as though it were alone in a trackless, uninhabited waste.

"I'm not much on killing other folks' stock," growled Larimore, "but as long as you won't stand for being caught, I'm plumb forced to crease you. I need that rope and I'm going to have it."

Again drawing his gun, he sighted directly between the animal's lazily-flapping ears. Using his greatest skill to keep from killing it, he fired. The burro dropped like a log.

"I'm shore glad I didn't kill you, you little devil," sympathized Jack leaping forward and standing over the twitching animal. "You seem to be about the only fellow in these parts that's not chasing me, trying to arrest me for something. But then I reckon us rustlers and murderers have to kind of play together. Hate to take anything from a pal, but I sure need that rope."

Sheathing his .45 he stooped quickly and unwinding the hemp, dragged it from around the brute's belly, and jerked it free.

In spite of his haste now that there was at least a chance to rescue the girl, curiosity drove him to open the packs. Gingerly reaching within one side, he pulled forth a heavy piece of leather, weighted at either end. Suddenly the discolored marks about the throats of the victims of the mysterious murders flashed into his mind.

"Bolo!" he muttered blankly. "Why in hell didn't I think of that before? Those hombres were choked off with a bolo. Didn't look like rope marks."

In his eagerness, he tore the pack open and started to reach within. With an oath he jerked his hand back and sprang to his feet.

A flash of orange!

His six-gun leaped from its holster. At the same instant from somewhere about him came the shrill:

"*Tokee! Tokee! Tokee!*"

He spun around, the streak of orange within the pack forgotten in the light of the eerie cry.

"That isn't any singing lizard!" he muttered, fingering the trigger of his .45 nervously. "That's a human being imitating a singing lizard sure as I'm living."

As if the weird call had pulled the burro back from oblivion, it struggled to its feet and stood blinking uncertainly.

"Hold on little fellow," commanded Jack. "We can't turn you loose yet with those packs you're carrying. Whew!"

He pushed the hat back from his forehead. With staggering suddenness the manner in which the mysterious murders had been committed came to him. The bolos! The flash of orange!

He sprang forward. The burro wheeled, shook from his grasp, and raced toward the timber from which the cry seemed to have come.

He made a frantic grab for the packs hanging by one strand but they were torn from his grasp.

"Well, I'm damned!" The gamut of emotions was registered in his violent explosion. "That's all I can say — I'm damned! I'm gunning for a human singing lizard!"

CHAPTER
TWENTY-FOUR

Jack hesitated, torn by indecision. He shuddered at the vivid recollection of the terrifying cry echoing in his ears. What he had seen in the packs was enough to convince him that to trail down the fleeing animal would lead to the solution of the murders. To ferret out the mysterious "tokee" would remove the loathsome taint of suspicion.

He twisted uneasily, conscious of unseen eyes following his every move, yet a hasty survey of the timber revealed nothing. The eerie thing — man or beast — had vanished. The only sound was the whining of the breeze through the pines and the champing of the bit in the pony's mouth as it nipped at the tufts of grass.

Minutes sped by. A picture of the unconscious girl at the end of the lariat flashed into his mind. It tore him from his introspection. With startling clearness he visioned the strands being cut, one by one, by the sharp rocks; saw Cochita lying, bruised and bleeding, on the jagged boulders in the cañon. He covered his eyes with his hands to shut out the horrible phantom, at the same time condemning himself bitterly for even considering his own plight.

He dragged his thoughts back with an effort. Praying that he had not delayed too long, he steeled himself to face the unknown terror. Gathering up the rope he had stripped from the packs, he moved boldly into the open and raced to the precipice. Turning at the rim, he swept the timber for sight of the burro. It had disappeared as completely and mysteriously as the "tokee" itself.

Anxiety quickly drove the disquieting incident from his mind. He dreaded to look into the cañon. Fear that the lariat had snapped with its precious load left him in a cold sweat.

Finally, summoning his courage, he peered over the bluff. He stifled the shout that sprang to his lips. The lifeless body of the girl still hung suspended above the chasm.

Tossing aside one length for future use, he dropped to the ground and set about splicing the rope. His six-gun was in his lap, ready for action, but nothing occurred to interrupt him. Braiding the frayed strands, he knotted them into a single piece of perhaps fifty feet, and tying one end to the trunk of a large pine beside him, let the other over the ledge.

"Sure nothing to spare," he muttered, "but I reckon I can make it do."

Running a leg through the loose stirrup, he locked his spurred feet and lowered himself, head down.

After many futile attempts, while the blood crashed against his ear drums with maddening regularity, he succeeded in wedging his body between the taut rope which held the girl and the rock wall.

Using his shoulder as a lever, he gathered every ounce of strength and slowly dragged the helpless Cochita back to the ledge from which she had swung clear when the stump gave way.

Almost blinded with dizziness, scarcely able to keep his numbed legs locked, he pulled up the slack in the lariat, and, with violently trembling fingers, knotted the two ropes.

Suddenly he felt himself giving under the strain. His body, drained of every particle of strength, was going limp. His head was splitting. The cañon became a whirling inferno.

He relaxed. A few moments' rest gave him renewed courage and strength. He struggled back to the cañon rim. Taking up the spare rope, he knotted it to the saddle horn, making it doubly secure with several half hitches.

Using great care to prevent a fatal slip, he untied the hemp from the tree, and wrapping the slack about the trunk, spliced the two pieces. The connection completed, he led the pony around the pine, unwinding the snub rope. Bracing his own feet against a rock, he held the girl as the animal snorted and reared forward; the dead weight far below swung on the horn.

"God bless old Red!" he groaned, his aching muscles standing out like whip-cord. "Giddap bronc! If you never snake another dogie as long as you live, drag that gal out!"

Ears laid back hatefully, its rump teetering as the taut rope rubbed its side, the animal lunged ahead. Once started, it pulled evenly. Jack sprang to his feet and stood full-length, face downward over the chasm, allowing the riata to run across his shoulder to hold the swaying body of Cochita away from the rocks. He clenched his teeth with pain as the blistering strands seared the palms of his bare hands.

After seemingly endless hours, the inert figure of the girl came within reach. He threw his arm about her to keep from plunging headlong into the cañon. The horse staggered under the double load, dropping almost to its knees in its struggle to obtain a footing.

A mighty effort. The weight eased. The panting pony halted. The girl lay inertly on the rim of the precipice.

With a hoarse gasp Larimore threw himself beside her, clawing frantically at his throat, through which his breath sucked raspingly. Mastering his twitching nerves, presently, he succeeded in again dragging forth his jackknife. Crawling over to her he sawed the rope which was shutting off the circulation. Gingerly he felt for broken bones. Finding none he climbed weakly to his knees and set about in an attempt to restore her to consciousness.

She lay as if dead, her breath coming faintly through bruised and swollen lips. A haunting fear that she had been injured seriously in the fall gripped him. A new strength was born of that fear. A strange emotion that set his blood pounding drove him to frantic haste in his efforts to restore her.

"Speak to me, Cochita," he pleaded earnestly. "Everything's all right. Say something. Don't just lay there like you were dead. God isn't going to let things end this way after the fight I put up. He can't!"

214

The love for the girl he had admitted timidly to himself since the first time he had seen her that night at Riley's cabin, burst on him with appalling suddenness. He patted her disarrayed hair with the tenderness of a mother. But she did not move.

"He let me fight for you like a man and I won," he breathed fervently. "You're mine! Speak to me!" Stooping he gathered her in his arms, crushing her to him. "You're mine!" he murmured. "Mine! Do you hear?"

Again he stretched her full-length and started chafing her wrists, watching her anxiously. After an infinity of time his efforts were rewarded by a slight color in her cheeks. She shuddered violently.

"Oh!" she whispered hoarsely. "I'm falling! Save me!"

"There, there," he told her tenderly. "Don't go loco now that it's all over. You're plumb safe. When you feel like moving we'll be hunting help."

Unconsciously he was brushing the dust from his clothes and attempting to smooth back his sweat-damp hair. Her eyes rested on him questioningly.

"Jack Larimore?" she gasped. "Where on earth did you come from? I thought —"

"Don't try to think for awhile," he cautioned. "Just let your mind rest. It's a plumb wonder you weren't killed."

"I'm all right now," she protested. "My pony is around here somewhere."

"Yep. I saw him when you were arguing with that breed."

She started and her cheeks, into which the color was returning, paled.

"Did you hear?" she demanded.

"We better be getting where you can rest," he answered, ignoring her query. "Guess your horse isn't very far away unless he followed Vasquale's pony off."

Seeing she was about to question him further he quickly changed the subject. "Would you mind — that is, don't you think — I'd better —" he avoided her eyes and scuffed the ground with the toe of his boot. "— Aw hell!" he blurted out. "I'm going to pack yuh."

His embarrassment brought just the trace of a smile to her lips.

"No, thank you, I can walk," she said. She attempted to arise, but sank back with a groan.

"If that's a sample of the singlefooting you're able to do, I still reckon I'd better carry you," he observed.

She lay with her eyes closed, offering no further protest as he lifted her gently in his arms and carried her to the thicket of trees from which he had first sighted her. Easing her down, he went in search of her pony which he found grazing a short distance away. Securing his own mount, he tailed the two, and gathering up the ropes, came back to her side. Raising her into the saddle, where she sat swaying dizzily, he climbed up behind. Her horse kicked as he touched its flanks, then sidled along smoothly under the double load.

Strangely content with the silent girl resting against his shoulder he deliberately took more time than necessary in guiding the nervous pony back to the cave.

216

At the ledge trail he dismounted, and lifting her down carried her around the precipice and put her gently on his bed roll within the cavern. Bringing water from the spring, he bathed her face and smoothed back her disarranged hair.

She lay quietly — so quietly in fact that he began to grow fearful that she again had slipped into unconsciousness. Leaning over, he felt of her pulse. She opened her eyes at the touch.

"I'll leave you here for a spell," he announced abruptly, arising and starting toward the entrance. "You'll be all right. I'll lope down to the Lazy-T camp and get some help to move you on to the K-Spear."

"Mr. Larimore," her voice was low. "I don't know where you came from nor how you happened to be near when — when — I needed help. You've treated me far better than I've treated you. I appreciate it with all my heart. Can you — can you — ever — forgive me?"

The penitent tone thrilled him. Cochita Maken was actually asking his forgiveness. His inclination was to be harsh; to hurt her as she had hurt him at the ranch house. A flood of scathing rebukes surged to his tongue, but he could not voice them.

"That's all right, Miss," he found himself saying awkwardly. "All of us have had a kind of skittish time lately. There's one thing I'd like to know though, if — if —"

"If you're going to ask me about — about Ramon," she interrupted, "please don't." She buried her face in her hands. "It's — it's —"

217

"You've got me all wrong," he protested quickly, yet in spite of his denial she had read his thoughts with uncanny precision. He was consumed with a desire to know what had brought on the argument that had preceded the fall. Vasquale's admission that he owned the Double-Spear Box had startled him, but the breed's reference to the Lazy-T herd was causing him the greatest concern. "I'm not aiming to pry into your business, but there was a mention of Boss Peters' critters that interests me."

"How much did you hear?" anxiously.

"Most everything that was said. But I couldn't get the drift of what you were talking about."

"I'll tell you," she said bravely. "I see things more clearly now. I realize he was just trying to get hold of the ranch. That's why he wanted you arrested. You didn't kill my father, did you?" she demanded fiercely.

"It sure grieves me to have you even suspect me." Larimore's voice was husky. "It isn't often we hands out here on the range give a tinker's damn what the other fellow thinks of us, but once in a long spell we run across somebody whose opinion, if it isn't good, just plumb worries us."

He avoided her quizzical gaze and rushed on, as though unable to stem the torrent of words that sprang to his tongue.

"In your case it's kind of hard. Of course, I didn't have any reason to expect that you'd ever pay any attention to me. I'm just a plain puncher and you're the boss's gal. But I found myself hoping, fool-like, up there at Riley's cabin, that you wouldn't be too hard on

218

me. There was a little catch right here under my shoulder blade when I first saw you. Seemed like there wasn't anything else left to see. Then I came under a cloud of doubt, and I don't reckon I'll ever be able to shake it. When I asked you back yonder at the K-Spear if I looked like a hombre that'd kill yore pa in cold blood, you said — you said —"

She struggled weakly to her feet, biting her lip with the pain racking her throbbing body. There was a strange unfathomable light in her eyes.

"Don't!" she pleaded, clutching his arm. "After the way you have treated me today I am utterly ashamed of what occurred down there that night. I wouldn't have blamed you if you'd have ridden on and let me die in the cañon."

"No," he smiled grimly. "Don't make any difference to a hombre what the other feller's done, it just isn't human nature to let him suffer real suffering. I've snaked many a critter out of bog holes when I knew good and well that the guy that owned 'em wouldn't even thank me for my trouble. Thanks aren't the only reason for trying to do good in this old world — just the idea you're helping the other fellow kind of gives you a satisfying feeling."

She started to cry again. He stared at her in amazement, trying to discover the reason for the new outburst, but gave up in despair. He wondered if he had said anything to hurt her. Failing to recall it he stood by awkwardly, fighting against a desire to seize her in his arms and comfort her.

"I never did think you were guilty," she sobbed. "Even up at Riley's that night I knew, way down in my heart, you couldn't stoop to such a thing. It was your assurance, as you backed to the door, holding all those men at bay, that angered me. I was disgusted with the K-Spear boys. I wished for a minute that I had a gun. I'd have stopped you. I couldn't understand it. Red is usually fearless, yet as I looked at him that night it just seemed as though he were frozen in his tracks. I hated you, not because I thought you were guilty, but because you seemed to have the upper hand at every turn. Then you struck Ramon.

"Oh, what a fool I've been! I guess it was the way he looked at me. It just seemed as though I had no will of my own. He did my thinking for me. I was afraid — afraid of him — terrified to cross him — fearful to tell daddy of my foolish terror. I was like old Pedro. I saw Ramon beat the old peon with a whip. He is afraid to call his soul his own. Oh, how I hate him! He left me out there to die. Why didn't I see it like this before? I would have been closer to daddy, and perhaps this thing never would have happened." The tears fell unheeded.

"Don't go to blaming yourself, Miss," he pleaded, his voice vibrant with a note strange even to himself. "You didn't know." The hot blood pounding through his veins left him trembling, made him uncertain of his words. "If we could figure things ahead, don't reckon any of us'd follow the same trail we did otherwise. But we don't know, so all we can do is bow our necks and make mistakes." His tone, which had grown hard at

220

thought of his own predicament, softened. "I'm not criticizing. I'm just — I'm just — oh hell, I don't know what I'm trying to say!"

"I know," she smiled wanly. "You're trying to say that I made a terrible mistake when I allowed myself to fall under the influence of Vasquale. You are condemning me because I condemned you."

"Reckon you've got me all wrong again," he replied simply. "I'm not condemning you. I haven't got the heart. That breed was plain to me. I've known a flock of his caliber. But I'm not criticizing you."

Their eyes met and clung for an instant. Hers fell.

"Go right ahead and bawl," he told her gently, patting her arm. "You've got it coming after all you've been through. Have your cry out here alone and I'll scout around a bit. There's a pile to be done to clean up things in this country, and I reckon if I can keep just a step ahead of that sheriff that's always accusing me of something new, I'm right on the trail of running down the mystery of these killings."

"What do you mean?" she sobbed, dropping back onto the bed roll. "Do you think you have a clue to who killed daddy?"

"I wouldn't put it just that way," he replied thoughtfully. "But with the things I've run across it shouldn't be hard to figure who did it. Your pa always 'lowed there was a gang rustling. He was aiming to make it so hot for 'em with his round-up that they'd have skipped or swung. There was nothing for 'em to do but kill him off."

221

His brutally frank assertion only increased her anguish, but she heard him bravely.

"Please go on," she begged as he hesitated.

"I'm just thinking out loud," he reminded her, reluctant to add to her grief. "Maybe I'm all wrong. If you'll recall your dad was — the killings in all the cases was the same. Wasn't any shooting. Just some marks around the neck and those little punctures over the heart. I've figured out what made 'em."

"You have?" She sat upright on the tarpaulin. "The entire mystery seems to me to hinge on the manner of the killings. What have you discovered?"

She leaned forward breathlessly, her eyes sparkling with tears. He started to reply. A thunderous noise broke the silence and reverberated through the cave.

She shrank back in terror. Reaching for his gun he sprang forward, but quickly recovering his wits, stopped, smiling broadly.

"Nothing to be afraid of," he assured her. "Just that burro brayin'. He and I take turns about chasing each other. It's my turn next. He's the little cuss at the bottom of all this devilment."

"Were you really trailing a burro like you told John Dawson the night daddy — died?" she asked incredulously, nervous in spite of his explanation.

"Sure," he retorted tartly. "I followed it all that afternoon. I wasn't near the K-Spear till I loped in after dark. Everything was over by then. You thought I was lying, didn't you?"

She bit her lip, conscious from his tone that her question had nettled him.

222

"No, but —"

"But it was kind of hard to swallow — the idea I was riding after a jackass!" he completed the sentence for her, smiling sardonically. "That's just exactly what I was doing. He's the key to the whole thing, I'm thinking."

"Why do you think that? What time have you had to run on to these clues you mention? You know," she added hastily, "you haven't told me when nor why you came back after you left the ranch that night."

Her eyes dropped under his steady gaze.

"There's nothing to tell. I joined Peters down the trail and rode in with the Lazy-T bunch. As to why, well I'm not admitting just yet."

"But how did you find this cave?" she persisted. "It used to be a rustler rendezvous. I didn't know anyone but daddy and a very few of the K-Spear boys knew of it."

"I slipped Red the word when I come back."

"Yes, I know —" she caught herself up quickly.

"Know what?" he demanded suspiciously.

"Oh, nothing," she flushed. "I was thinking of something else."

He stared at her strangely, wondering at her embarrassment. Unable to fathom it he continued:

"Mowbry loped into camp while Boss was down at the ranch palavering with you. 'Lowed Dawson was on his way up, kind of suspecting I'd trailed in, so he showed me this hole. It turned out to be this burro's hang-out. He came meandering in here this morning nosing around. Almost scared the life out of me with that bray of his. I went in after him trying to get the low-down on what he had in those packs, when I ran onto you arguing with Vasquale. I let him go and tossed a hunk of lead at that breed after you fell over the cliff. Later, when I needed a rope to splice my lariat to reach you down yonder in the cañon, the little cuss showed up. I come nigh jumping clean out of my boots when he hee-hawed. I had to crease him to make him lay quiet on the bed ground while I was taking the pack rope. He's the rustling cowhand all right."

"Rustling cowhand?" she exclaimed. "What do you mean?"

"I'm telling you," he replied stubbornly. "I know it sounds plumb loco, but I'm not lying. He was rustling K-Spear critters the day your pa —"

Her hand flew to her breast.

"I believe you, but please be more explicit. I was so dazed that night I didn't know what to think. It sounded so impossible."

"Then what did you mean out there on the bluff when you said to Vasquale: 'And to think I dismissed — '. Meaning me?"

"Please!" she pleaded, arising stiffly and moving over to his side. "Things have come so fast! I'm beginning to understand lots I couldn't see at first. I was blinded. You'll confess a story that you were trailing a burro sounded — well — at — least —"

"Fishy as hell!" he supplied soberly. "I didn't expect to be believed. I told the truth anyhow and that's more'n some other folks were doing."

"Don't!" she implored. "I'll admit that I was wrong."

224

He stared, scarcely able to believe his ears. Was this sobbing, contrite woman the fearless, impetuous Cochita who many times had made men quail before the scorn of her blazing eyes?

CHAPTER
TWENTY-FIVE

Filled with wonder at the metamorphosis, uneasy before the tears that again began tracing a course over Cochita's cheeks, Jack Larimore moved toward the entrance. Beneath an overhanging ledge at the side, the burro was slapping at the flies with its thatched tail and watching him sleepily. He stopped abruptly. The packs which a short time before he had left bound by one rope, were missing.

"Somebody's been around that jackass sure as the world since he skinned away from that cliff," he muttered to himself. "I'm betting even money they took those packs." He shuddered. "But what in the devil would they want with 'em? Cochita —" he flushed at his bravery in using her given name. "I'm dead certain this burro's the key to the whole thing — killings, rustling and singing lizards. Wish there was some way to make him talk."

"Killings, rustling and singing lizards?" she repeated, puzzled. "What are you talking about, anyway? Are you positive that all the accusations haven't made you just a little — well, overly suspicious?"

"Loco, you mean," he laughed. "Not on your life. I reckon they have worried me a heap, but I know what

I'm talking about. Don't 'low you ever did hear anything quite so crazy on this range, but it's what I mean — killings, rustling and singing lizards!"

"What are singing lizards? And what have they got to do with this burro and the — the — murders?"

"That's what I'm asking you?" he remarked sagely. "If I knew I'd have had the killer strung up long ago."

"I never heard of a singing lizard. What is it?"

"It's a reptile that hangs out in trees in the tropics."

"Is it poisonous?"

"Don't reckon so, no more'n any other lizard. 'Course some are, the Gila monster for instance." He stopped, idly watching the burro. She waited impatiently for him to continue but he remained silent.

"Jack Larimore!" she flashed with a show of spirit. "What has a reptile that sits in a tree in the tropics got to do with these — tragedies?"

"That's what I'm asking you?" he repeated aggravatingly. "Search me. A singing lizard hollers 'tokee! tokee!' when it's scared."

" 'Tokee!' " she shuddered violently. "That's the cry at the time of all the crimes. Dawson thinks it's some beast. He believes —"

"That's where he's wrong, along with the rest of 'em. That's where your pa got off on the wrong foot. They didn't stop to figure the thing out with common sense. You've loped over these brakes enough to know that, outside a lion or bear now and then, there's nothing that'll scrap a man, let alone kill 'em like these *hombres* have been croaked. That's the trouble with sheriffs. They always take the hardest trail to run down a killing.

Nine times out of ten there's no mystery at all." He came over to her and dropped cross-legged to the ground. "We've got as much brains between us as the next couple of fellows, and I reckon a whole heap more'n this Dawson. Let's figure the thing out."

He extended his hand to help her back onto the bed roll. Her fingers met his in a tight clasp. He tingled at the contact. She settled herself on the tarpaulin, but made no effort to withdraw her hand. He looked at her and smiled. He could feel the blood burning his face, pulsing in his ears.

He broke the clasp roughly, fearful of his own emotions. The trace of a smile played at the corners of her mouth, but she remained silent, eyes downcast. He attempted to speak, but had forgotten what he was going to say. He gulped awkwardly, and shaking himself as though preparing for some terrible ordeal, reached over quickly and picked up the fingers which were toying with her tiny spur rowels.

She made no resistance. The fingers lay, cool and blood-stirring, in his feverish palm. He gazed at their slender loveliness.

"Aw hell!" he sheepishly grinned. "I can't seem to think of anything to talk about."

She snatched her hand away.

"I didn't ask you to hold my hand," she pouted.

"Now don't get riled up," he pleaded. "I just haven't any polish when it comes to these things. I like to hold it sure enough. Do you?"

"No I don't!" she snapped. "Let's figure out the mystery as you suggested in the first place."

"Clean forgot where I left off now," he admitted foolishly. "You're not sore, are you?"

"You had just remarked," she reminded caustically, "that sheriffs were the dumbest things in existence."

"Aw, Cochita!" he implored. "You're not really mad, are you?"

"No!" bitingly. "Just why should I be angry, Mr. Larimore?"

"Well, now." He pushed his Stetson back from his hot brow. "I was thinking —"

"Don't think," she interrupted. "That's what you told me back there at the precipice. Jack," her impulsive mood had vanished and her voice was caressing as she laid her hand in his again at the hurt look that flashed into his eyes. "Let's collect what clues you have and go over them now."

He caught his breath sharply and avoided her gaze.

"Taking for granted that there's never been singing lizards on this range," he plunged into his course of reasoning, "and I don't reckon there has been, seeing as how they live in hot countries and nobody up here ever heard tell of 'em, that's the first thing to consider. All right, there's a killing!"

He stopped abruptly and looked down. Her hand still rested in his. He was fearful to move lest he disturb it. She watched him, perplexity in her eyes.

"The reason for any crime has to be figured out before they can get to the bottom of it." His voice trembled slightly. "I never hunted criminals, I'm just telling you what I've doped out during the time I've been sidestepping Dawson. The motive for these killings is just as plain as your nose. In every case it was men who knew too much or were pushing the rustlers too hard.

"Starting with Riley — I wasn't here when Bevens and Cline cashed in! I rode up to his cabin and found old Buck dead. On the way I heard that 'tokee' holler. Struck me as odd right off, because I've heard singing lizards before but not in the range country."

Arising he sauntered toward the entrance to the cave, where he stood flipping pebbles at the burro, which was watching him quizzically, as though listening to correct any error in his reasoning.

"Your pa had the low-down on the whole thing. If you'll recollect, he told me at the K-Spear the first night, that there was rustling. You denied it, saying you were shipping as many cows as you had been five years ago. He was plumb right that his herds ought to be increasing, but seemed like you couldn't see it, or else you were so all-fired mad at me you wouldn't."

He could not resist the thrust which brought the color into her cheeks, but the anger that flashed in her eyes was gone in an instant.

"I was mad," she admitted. "You were so confident of everything. Your assurance rubbed me the wrong way."

"Well, anyhow," he smiled, "your pa was right. There was rustling and heaps of it. Old Buck had been gum-shoeing. He got something on the cow thieves. That's why he was croaked. The motive of the crimes, then, is to cover up rustling. Doesn't that sound reasonable?"

230

"Yes," she answered in a low voice. "But the mystery? It seems to me that men who had nerve enough to rustle would have nerve enough to shoot. You recall the ambush and the kidnapping?"

"I am coming to that," he explained. "Don't think for one minute that bunch won't use their .45's. They tried to plug Ed on the Cibola road, and it wasn't any picnic when we tied up with that Revenge Gang either, I'm telling you. But unless it came to a place where those thieves were cornered there wasn't any use in 'em shooting. They had a different way. A way nobody'd suspect. They schemed out a little mystery to scare the life out of everybody and throw Dawson off the real trail.

"They sent your pa that letter trying to stampede him. He wasn't the skittish kind and they hit a snag pronto. Instead of doing what they figured he would, it riled him to the gizzard, and first thing he did was to get blood in his eye, drive into Cibola, haze Franklin and Brewster together, and decide to call a round-up to clean out those brakes. Somebody must have overheard 'em talking and got word to the leader — Ed 'lowed it was the two breeds themselves who took him for the next thing we knew you'd been ambushed, and the kidnapping pulled."

She shuddered at the recollection.

"And if it hadn't been for you," she put in quickly, "I'd have been killed in a runaway."

"I did a whole lot!" he deprecated. "Took down my throw rope and tossed it over one of those bronc's heads. That was a heap to brag about, wasn't it? You've

231

got Blue to thank for it — 'cause — 'cause he was fast, even if he did act up a bit. But that same Blue, I calculate, was the beginning of all my trouble at the K-Spear after the Riley deal."

"Why do you say that?"

"Because I might have been friends — at least on speaking terms with Vasquale — if I hadn't topped off that horse after he'd been thrown. You don't know how near we came to real shooting out there in the corrals that morning. Your pa knew though, and that's why he was leary. He'd tell you if he was here, just like any other man who really loves good horse flesh, that any *hombre* that'll cut a pony to pieces with spurs isn't to be trusted. That's what worried Ed. Vasquale hanging around you. He was just ready to pack you up and ship you east when he — when he — died."

"Oh, daddy!" she sobbed passionately, burying her face in her hands. "If I'd only known! But I didn't — I didn't! How I hate Ramon! I never loved him. I was afraid of him."

"That's all right now." He consoled her tenderly, but made no move to return to the seat beside her. "Don't take on like that. Let's get the thing figured out. Those cow thieves knew mighty well if Ed Maken ever swung into those brakes with a round-up crew that they were a goner. He got away when they kidnapped him. They had to come to the ranch to get him. They did."

He finished grimly and stood staring at the burro.

"It was that 'tokee' that got him. Ed was killed by a singing lizard, and singing lizards aren't dangerous. Now what do you think?"

"I don't know," she confessed, again brushing aside her tears.

"Reckon I do," he said slowly, as though talking to himself. "The rustlers didn't have a chance to pull the job at the K-Spear, so they got somebody else to do it. They keep him handy to fool the sheriff. Dawson and the rest of 'em are huntin' wild animals and whanga-doodles instead of men like they ought to.

"That singing lizard has hollered during every killing. It hollered up yonder that afternoon when we found this burro rustling. The donkey quit the flats pronto. It hollered down to the ranch that night, and I met this burro coming out of the ranch on the high lope after I'd been riding those brakes for it. That 'tokee' hollered up there at the cañon this afternoon when I was trying to pull you up."

"Yes?" she questioned tensely. "But the mystery?"

"Mystery?" he grinned. "Mystery hell! There's nothing mysterious about it. It hasn't got a thing to do with the murders at all, only that the killer needs those packs. It's the way somebody that doesn't want to be seen has of calling this jackass when he gets in a tight place, or when he has to get what's in those packs to murder somebody! We're looking for a *hombre* that hollers like a singing lizard and owns this burro!"

CHAPTER
TWENTY-SIX

Jack's assertion dumbfounded the girl. She watched him closely as he paced between the bed roll and the entrance to the cave.

"Supposing I am right," he asked, halting above her, "and this 'tokee' is the way the killer calls that burro, doesn't that shoot the mystery all to pieces?"

"It looks like it," she confessed, "although I can't imagine a burro being the go-between in all these — deaths. Who's is it?"

"If I even had an idea, I'd know who pulled the crimes," he answered shortly. "It's a cinch that we hit on the real thing, because every time I've tried to get into those packs somebody's hollered and the jackass has vamoosed. We can't get a line on that killer unless we catch him with the burro. We aren't going to be able to do that as long as it answers to this 'tokee'. We just have to figure out who he is by the way the victims cashed in."

"Oh, must we go into that?" she pleaded. "It seems to me that I haven't been able to think of anything else since that terrible night!"

"No," he assured her solicitously. "If you'd rather I took you back to the ranch now, I can go ahead an' figure it out alone."

"I don't want you to take me to the K-Spear!" she flashed. "I — guess — I'd rather — help — you." He stared at her in amazement. Her changing moods were as far beyond his comprehension as the mystery itself. "Don't pay any attention to me," she whispered penitently. "One minute I want to laugh and the next I want to cry. I'll be all right presently. But Jack" — she shivered with nervousness — "I'd feel a lot better if you'd — hold — my hand."

The invitation nonplussed him. He swallowed hard, but was game. Dropping beside her on the tarpaulin, he picked up the slender fingers, which nestled confidingly in his palm.

"Now let's get down to business," he remarked in an unnatural voice. "As I was saying, we've got to figure out who did the work by the way the victims were shuffled off."

"There were those marks around the neck." She shuddered and edged nearer to him.

"Bolo marks." He sidled further along the bed roll, wiping the sweat of embarrassment from his brow. "A rope was too unhandy. The bolo was tossed around the necks of those hombres and they were choked to death." He attempted to soften the brutal statement with his voice, but in spite of his effort she winced. "I know it isn't pleasant to discuss, but somebody's got to do it, and it looks like we're picked for the job."

"What's a bolo?" she inquired timidly.

"A piece of leather they use in southern countries to catch critters with. It's weighted on each end. When the

235

puncher throws it it wraps around whatever he's aiming at."

"It seems to me that that's a good clue," she chimed in. "I never saw anyone throw a bolo."

"Me either," he admitted. "So we're looking for a bolo tosser."

"But how do you know it was a bolo?" she questioned.

"'Cause I was plumb certain it wasn't a rope mark on the necks of those victims, and there wasn't any rope laying around. Whoever did 'em used a bolo, so they could take it with 'em in a hurry. I found a bolo in that burro's pack this afternoon!"

"You did?"

"Yep. Now we've figured out the mystery of the 'tokee' and how the victims were killed, let's —"

"But the discolored marks over the heart?" she questioned.

"I'm coming to that. I was in the army. I saw service in the Philippines. The savage tribes used to practice what they called fetishism. It's a mutilation of the victim as a part of a religious ceremony."

"I don't understand."

Her head dropped to his shoulder. He braced himself, glanced sideways at her, then grew rigid.

"The victims of this 'tokee' were killed with a bolo. The marks over the heart were fetishism, and were only a way to make sure that if the hombre wasn't dead he'd die pronto."

"Oh!" A gasp escaped her. "It's too terrible! I can't stand any more! Please, Jack, let's forget it for awhile."

236

"Just a minute and we will," he agreed. "First tell me who all was at the K-Spear the night when your pa — died —"

"Aside from the boys and Red, who came in with a herd of cattle, there was the cook, daddy, Ramon and myself," she replied puzzled.

"And Pedro," he reminded her.

"Why, no. He went with you."

"He did not, begging your pardon. Who said he was with us?"

"Ramon. I recall it particularly. After you boys started we went from the corrals to the house. Daddy stopped at the porch just as Pedro started across the prairie. Daddy asked Ramon where the peon was going. He said that the old fellow had taken a liking to you and that he was going along to protect you."

"Protect me nothing!" he growled. "I never laid eyes on him." His clasp tightened until her fingers tingled. "Did Pedro come back to the ranch after I made my getaway?"

"Yes. He came into the room shortly after you escaped and refused to leave when Ramon ordered him out."

"Did he hear you discussing the — death?"

"No," thoughtfully. "Ramon requested that I would not tell him for fear it would make him — a madman — was the expression he used."

"A madman?" he ejaculated. "I've got a picture of that old half-wit turning madman!"

"That's exactly the way it struck me at the time." She raised her head from his shoulder and met his eyes squarely. "I couldn't imagine the poor, twisted creature going wild with rage."

"I don't know what the game was, but I reckon Pedro was scouting around that afternoon for something. I never saw him. It's a puzzler, isn't it? Where does old Pedro hang out?"

"He has a shack down on Ramon's homestead," she answered.

"Do you feel like riding?"

"Yes, why?" in surprise. "Where are you going?"

"Let's get our horses and lope around a bit. I'd like to drill down to the Double-Spear-Box and then over to Vasquale's place. Are you game?"

"Game?" she uttered the word scornfully. "Certainly."

"Well, let's go. Don't know what we can run on to but it doesn't seem like it ought to be hard now." He sprang to his feet and helped her up. She swayed weakly against him. His nerves strummed, but he shook himself and put her aside.

"Let's travel!" he announced.

"Jack!" her voice was soft. "Will you ever forgive me?"

"For what?" he demanded.

"I — I," she faltered. "You've been so wonderful to me and I — I — well I never really believed you — were — guilty. You were just so sure of yourself. I wanted to show you —"

"But what about Vasquale?" he demanded brutally.

"I was afraid of him," she admitted frankly. "I didn't realize until today, although I tried to understand the utter helplessness I felt when he commanded. I didn't

238

want to turn the K-Spear over to him. I wanted you to stay and carry on the work for daddy, but when he dismissed you it seemed I didn't have the stamina to oppose him." She shuddered. "He wields an uncanny power over a person. I can readily understand how he forces old Pedro to do his will. It's like a bird and a snake. The bird doesn't want to die any more than a human being, but there's something in the snake's eyes that holds it helpless while doom creeps upon it. That's the way Ramon affected me. I couldn't think clearly. I knew what I wanted to do, but somehow I was powerless even to work my will when he was around. I never cared for him — honestly, Jack! It wasn't even infatuation. I've been spoiled. I wanted him around just to torment daddy — and now — I'm so sorry!"

"I'm mighty glad," he managed to gulp.

"Glad of what?" she asked quickly.

"That you never cared for that breed."

"Why? Did it make any difference to you?"

The strange light shining in her eyes spoke to him in an unknown tongue. He took a step forward. With a little sigh of contentment she slipped into his arms and buried her face against his shoulder.

Dismayed at his own courage, his heart beating wildly, he took her face between his hands and peered into her eyes. Before he could control the madness surging in his blood he planted a kiss squarely on her lips. He backed off, expecting an outburst, but she only smiled up at him sweetly.

"I guess we'd better be going now, Jack."

"I'd rather you wouldn't go," he answered, suddenly seeing the whole affair in a different light. She stared at him in surprise, but the look he gave her in return was full of determination. "There's liable to be some tall mixing with gunplay if we do run into anything, and it's no place for a gal."

"You've had enough grief since you've ridden this range," she flashed with spirit. "Now suppose you share some of it — with me." The last in a tiny voice that was little above a whisper.

"Yes, but —"

"Look here, young man," she said sternly, her eyes, however, belying her serious tone, "don't overlook the fact that I am the owner of the K-Spear and you are my foreman. I mean it when I say that I am going!"

"Then I'm not fired at all?"

Her hand found his. "I mean," she faltered, "that whatever arrangement Ramon may have made at my ranch is off. You stay as daddy intended, if you will — please?"

"Come on," he urged gently, moving toward the entrance with her at his side. "I reckon as long as you put it that way I'll just have to keep the job."

The burro backed off as they gained the ledge road outside, and he led her around the trail to their horses. Frightened, the jackass threw up its tail and sped into the timber.

Quickly lifting her into the saddle he untied the two mounts and grasped the reins of his own horse.

"Come on," he shouted, finding his stirrups. "Let's keep on that burro's trail!"

240

He stood motionless for a moment, sweeping the cañon side for a glimpse of the fleeing animal. He espied it racing madly down the trail, below which Old Woman Creek glistened in the sunshine.

"How those little devils can travel!" he exclaimed as he roweled his reluctant mount into the cowpath. "We'll do darn well if we can keep him in sight."

Throwing safety to the winds, they galloped recklessly along the steep path into the valley.

CHAPTER
TWENTY-SEVEN

Cochita and Jack had scarcely dropped from sight on the heavily wooded slope when the Lazy-T punchers, together with several K-Spear men, who had joined the posse along the way, threw themselves from their horses and followed Mowbry around the narrow ledge to the cave.

"I steered Larimore to this place yesterday to get him under cover," explained Red. "I swapped hosses with him. That's how I got holda Blue. Jack!" he called.

No answer.

"Oh, Jack!" he bellowed through cupped hands.

"He's gone!" he exclaimed. "He'd gimme a sign a' some kind if he was within callin' distance."

He looked about for the saddle horse. It, too, was missing.

"Do yuh reckon Dawson coulda come in here an' took him?"

Peters smiled grimly.

"Not unless he was asleep or crippled up so he couldn't get to his gun," was his dry comment.

"Whaddaya think we better do?" asked Red. "Search these brakes fer the gal an' that breed?"

"Supposing we lope on down to the Double-Spear-Box," suggested Boss. "There's plenty of us if they start anything. Maybe the sheriff rode in there all hostile like and needs help."

While the Texan was speaking, Mowbry was watching a cloud of dust swirling down the valley. His eyes wandered back along the trail writhing through the timber covering the cañon side. Suddenly two riders, racing recklessly down the narrow path, flashed into sight. One of them he recognized instantly as a girl.

"There's Cochita an' Vasquale!" he shouted excitedly. "Thank God, she's safe! I jes wanna get my hands on that breed. Come on," he yelled to the posse, "we'll make him hard to catch."

Followed by the punchers, he sped back to his horse, swung into the saddle and pounded down the trail.

Still another figure might have been seen dodging into an arroyo had not the riders been so intent on watching the two horsemen. It waited until they had dashed past in the direction of the Double-Spear-Box, then shifted the canvas sacks thrown across its shoulders and headed down a ravine at a peculiar shuffling trot toward a shack outlined on the horizon.

Fearful lest the girl's horse fall in the maddened race, Larimore rode sideways in the saddle, letting his own sure-footed mount pick its perilous way.

"Just try and keep that burro in sight," he shouted back to her as they reached the bottom of the cañon and galloped along a cow trail twisting beside the stream. "Like as not he'll go straight to where he belongs. It'll be pickings from then on. Wish Peters or

Red or some of the boys were here. We might have some trouble over yonder at the Double-Spear-Box and be needing help right bad."

"You're right, Jack!" She jerked her horse to its haunches, apparently realizing for the first time the seriousness of their undertaking. "The two of us can't face that whole bunch. We'd better go back to the ranch and call in the men."

"I'm not underestimating the danger in tackling those breeds, but I reckon it's just as safe riding ahead as it is to go back and meet Dawson." His lips drew in a thin line across his teeth. "I've told him a couple of times I'm not going to be taken and I'm no liar."

"It's different now," she protested, dropping a hand to his arm. "I understand. And Jack!" The ease with which she used his given name thrilled him. "The K-Spear is behind you now with every dollar and every hoof of stock to prove your innocence."

"Much obliged, little girl," he struggled with the lump that suddenly had come into his throat, "but I reckon I'll keep riding. Wish you'd go home, though. It's no place for you if the thing comes to a showdown. I can get along all right myself. At least slip up to the cave and wait there for me."

"If you go, I'm going, too," she flashed with determination. "I feel I am partly responsible for getting you into this and I propose to see it through."

He caught his breath at the picture she made as she sat tense, her eyes sparkling with excitement, her whole attitude suggestive of the courage of a young leopardess. Her golden hair, which had slipped loose, was flying in the wind. Her delicate nostrils were distended with eagerness. She reminded him of a beautiful Indian maiden. His goal faded into the haze of a day dream. They were back centuries before, riding free and unfettered — alone in a vast, primitive wild.

"God," he mused to himself, "a man'd sure be lucky to win a gal like that."

Drawn by the same irresistible impulse that had made him dare to kiss her, he reached over and took her hand.

"Partner," he whispered hoarsely.

"Plain pard, Jack," she smiled tenderly, returning his clasp. Then, dropping into the vernacular of the plains:

"We're gon' to run this thing down, pronto, ain't we?"

"You just tell a man," he grinned happily. "I could run anything down with you riding with me."

Sight of the burro as it topped a rise only to disappear into another arroyo brought him up sharply.

"We better be moseying along," he reminded her, as though dreading to break the spell of the mutual understanding which had sprung up between them.

"Let's go for the Double-Spear-Box," she replied, and giving her impatient pony the rein she started down the valley at a wild gallop.

CHAPTER
TWENTY-EIGHT

After parting with Peters and Mowbry at the Lazy-T camp, John Dawson rode north. In his peculiar, slow-thinking way, he turned the long chain of events over in his mind, but seemed powerless to arrive at any definite conclusion. The new mystery of the Texas cattle being branded with a K-Spear only added to the many puzzles already threatening to turn his grayish hair snow-white and baffled him completely. Despite the many sides of the matter that he could not reconcile, he was convinced underneath it all that Jack Larimore knew something of the crimes which he had not revealed and he was determined to drag it from him.

While he had little stomach for boldly riding into the Double-Spear-Box and demanding a showdown, when John Dawson made up his mind, nothing save a bullet between the eyes could swerve him from his purpose. He dug the rowels viciously into his horse and galloped over the bluff and down the trail into the valley of Old Woman Creek.

He jerked up a mile from the ranch and sat watching six men who had ridden into view suddenly from a ravine. Into his mind flashed the warning of the guard who had spread the alarm at the Lazy-T camp:

"There's a half a dozen punchers down there in one a them brakes brandin' cattle."

That these were the six, Dawson had little doubt. Quickly laying out a course of action in his mind, he forced his horse over a cut bank into an arroyo and riding circle on the group, came into the open directly in front of them and a short distance below the gate that closed the ribbon-like trail leading to the Double-Spear-Box buildings. The six drew rein in surprise as he loped into the path.

Dawson surveyed the crew leisurely. Swarthy-faced breeds with restless eyes and hands cager to get at the long knives that glistened in their belts.

"Tech sky!" he ordered brusquely, whipping his sixgun from its holster and getting the drop on the gang.

Without a moment's hesitation the punchers shot their hands in the air.

Riding slowly along the line, he seized their knives and guns and tossed them to the ground.

"Now, whaddaya hombres brandin'?" he demanded, catching sight of an iron tied to the saddle of one of the riders.

They regarded him sulkily but did not reply.

"Where do yuh belong?"

The sheriff failed entirely in his attempt to keep his voice friendly. The six ignored his question, looking beyond him toward the ranch house of the Double-Spear-Box. The furtive glances, the shifting, restless eyes, made him wary.

"Are yuh all tongue-tied?" Dawson's tone was nothing short of a bark, the challenge of a wolf. "Who's yore boss an' what yuh been brandin'?"

"No sabe."

One of the crew risked lowering a hand to toss aside a cigarette.

"I'll savvy yuh," snapped the officer. "I'm runnin' this here county. Lemme look at that iron an' be damned careful not to start nothin'."

Cautious against trickery, his .45 braced on the horn, he reined forward. The breed, at whom he hurled the command, untied the iron and passed it over as he rode abreast. Watching the six from the corner of his eye, Dawson examined it. There was no evidence of it having been used recently. Peters' remark back at the herd that morning recurred: "It's been done through a wet blanket so it won't look fresh." That the Texan's assertion had been correct now seemed positive.

"Whaddaya been brandin'?" repeated the officer, glaring at the man who had carried the iron and who now sat squirming nervously in his saddle. The question merely brought a shrug of the shoulders.

The stubborn silence was working Dawson into a towering rage. He was convinced that the "no sabe" was not the result of ignorance of the language, but rather the breed's way of avoiding incriminating disclosures.

Keeping the .45 trained on the crew, he fumbled at the buckle of the strap that held his lariat. Unloosening it, he dropped the rope to the ground and shifting his

248

six-gun to his left hand, whirled out the noose. The breeds watched him anxiously.

"Now, talk fast Injun," he snorted. "Who's yore primero!"

One of the men indicated the fellow who had carried the iron. The lariat whistled through the air, dropped over the rider's head as he lowered his hands to protect his face. A quick jerk! The riata grew taut about his throat.

"There's allus a way to make hombres like yuh talk," observed Dawson calmly, "an' I reckon a throw rope 'roun' your breathin' apparatus'll make my remarks clear. Now whose cows was yuh brandin'?"

After the first unsuccessful attempt to claw off the lariat, which had been stopped by Dawson's threatening gun, the fellow shrugged his shoulders with an air of disdain, but the yellow hue of his face belied his outward show of nerve. It was plain to the sheriff as he watched the breed that his command of English was limited, but the tightened rope, causing his breath to come in gasps, was quickly summoning what few words he did know.

"Lazy-T." His voice was a rasping whisper.

"What was yuh brandin' 'em?"

"K-Spear."

"Who fer?"

The fellow hesitated, glancing fearfully at his five companions, who sat watching him closely, their attitudes a challenge and a warning. He gazed back at the sheriff helplessly, but found no consolation in the stern mouth set in grim lines.

"Those primero," he muttered.

"Who's that? Talk fast Injun — this rope's gettin' powerful skittish."

The sheriff snapped out the words.

"At thees Double-Spear-Box."

"I ain't got no time to monkey. Who owns the Double-Spear-Box?"

Dawson gave the lariat a jerk.

"Señor Menendez."

"Is he the hombre that lives in Mexico City?"

The breed's eyes shifted quickly to his companions. A look of understanding passed between them which did not escape the sheriff.

"Si."

The tone was far from convincing. Again Dawson yanked the rope. The fellow's hands came down, clawing at his throat, but the bark of the sheriff's six-gun, which threw up a puff of dust and sent his horse prancing nervously, brought the trembling fingers up. The swarthy face, which had turned yellow, now faded to a sickly green.

"Yore lyin'." The officer's voice was colorless and cold. "I gotta hunch this here Menendez don't live in Mexico no more'n I do. I can tell by the way yuh say he does. Where's he hang out?"

Thoroughly cowed, the breed pointed toward the ranch house.

"There," he choked.

"There?" repeated the officer blankly, turning to the ranch, then back to the gang. "Do yuh mean to tell me this Menendez has been livin' at the Double-Spear-Box all this time?"

The gasping man nodded his head violently.

"Then get goin'," ordered Dawson curtly. "I'll drag yuh to death if yore pals make a hostile move. I'm ridin' behin' yore gang right up to that house an' yore goin' to call Mister Menendez out. Reckon it's 'bout time I was meetin' the gent an' havin' a friendly palaver."

He roweled in behind the breeds and started them slowly toward the ranch house.

CHAPTER
TWENTY-NINE

At the corrals Dawson covered and disarmed two more breeds who had slunk from the barns as the cavalcade rode up. Herding them into the group at the point of his gun, he ordered the others to dismount and precede him to the house. He drew rein in the shelter of the porch, careful to stay from range of the broken windows in the dismal, ramshackle building.

"Now le's see the color a' yore primero's hair," he grated, giving the rope a tug that brought a gasp of pain from the breed.

Yet, obviously terror-stricken at thought of the vengeance of the master of the Double-Spear-Box, he remained silent.

"Whip up there," growled Dawson. "Yip out fer the hombre that owns this dump. Tell him he's got visitors that wants to pass the time a' day. I'd plumb admire to have him come out. I've allus wanted to meet Mister Menendez, an' he orter be right tickled to see me, too."

"No sabe!"

The breed's breath came raspingly from between dry lips.

"Yuh savvy jes as good as I do," roared the sheriff. "Yuh'll talk, too."

252

In a flash he jerked the rope loose from the horn of his saddle and while the crew stared at him like hawks stalking prey, he tossed the end of it over a scantling projecting from the porch and again attached it to the horn. Touching his horse lightly with the spurs, he started forward.

"*Madre de Dios!*" choked the breed, clutching at the riata, his feet barely scraping the ground. "I weel tell. Queeck! Menendez ees no 'ombre. Vasquale 'e own thees Double-Spear Box!"

"Vasquale owns the Double-Spear-Box?" repeated the sheriff blankly, pulling back his pony a few paces and allowing the lariat to slacken. "Well, I'm damned! Trot him out. Guess he's the skunk I'm lookin' fer."

" 'ees not 'ere. 'e ees down to thees K-Spear."

"Reckon yore tellin' the truth for oncst," snorted the officer. "Did he tell yuh to brand those Lazy-T steers?"

"No sabe." The fellow shrugged his shoulders.

"What did he want yuh to slap a K-Spear on 'em fer?" persisted Dawson, paying no attention to the breed's apparent ignorance. "That's Ed Maken's bran'."

"No sabe."

"Well, we gotta have another little lesson fer yore savvin' apparatus," announced the sheriff, starting forward.

Again the fellow's toes barely touched the ground.

" 'e ees goin' to run eet when 'e marry thees Señorita Cochita," he screamed.

"That's better," observed Dawson, slackening the rope. "That's his game, is it? Pretty slick at that. Gettin' the little gal into a fine mess uh rus'lin', then hookin' up with her to pertect her. Was he the hombre that ordered yuh breeds to kidnap Ed Maken an' bring him to that shack? Are yuh the Revenge Gang?"

The fellow fingered the taut rope gingerly, then jerked his head.

"No, we not Revenge Gang. Vasquale, 'e ees say Maken goin' to keel us on round-up."

"Uh-huh. The hull thing's comin' out now. Vasquale's backin' the rus'lin' an' playin' the K-Spear fer a bluff han'." Dawson glared ferociously at the gang. "Who killed Ed Maken?"

Furtive glances passed between the men.

"Vasquale 'e say Maken die een 'ees sleep," volunteered the one with the rope about his neck.

"Yep. That's right," admitted the sheriff, "but some hombre helped him by a few years. Who done it?"

"No sabe." The breed shrugged violently.

"Mebbyso yuh don't, but I'm goin' to find out sooner or later an' I reckon the hull gang a yuh'll swing when I do. We better be about-facin' now. Straddle them nags a yor'n an' get goin'." He jerked the rope from the man's neck and coiled it. "The town a Cibola'll plumb admire to have yore bunch in jail. Start movin'."

He marched the thoroughly cowed breeds to the corrals, where they mounted and headed back toward the Lazy-T camp.

The thud of hoofs brought him rigid in the saddle, prepared for an emergency. A burro, head up, tail straight as a rudder behind, galloped through the yard, shied and kicked playfully at the corrals and kept straight on, traveling south.

"What's that burro so scairt 'bout?" he demanded of the breeds.

"Mebbyso Pedro's call."

Since his experience with the rope the one had become voluble, seemingly eager to unburden his mind of everything.

"Whaddaya mean, Pedro call?" shouted Dawson.

"Pedro, mebby 'e call thees burro."

"Whaddid he wanna call him fer?"

"That 'ees the way thees Revenge Gang rus'le. Burro 'e go out an' drive thees cows to rancho. We run bran's."

"Well, I'm damned!" exclaimed the sheriff. "No wonder I couldn't round-up no rus'lers. Larimore musta been right the night ol' Ed was killed, when he said he was trailin' a jackass. At that I ain't so shore he ain't got somethin' to do with it. Mebbyso that deal's explained, but what was the Texan Smart Aleck doin' up to Buck Riley's? Look like things is goin' to straighten out pronto."

Pulling his gaze from the jackass as it dropped from sight in its precipitous flight, he turned back to watch two riders coming down the valley. Even at the distance he recognized Cochita. But the man?

The breeds slunk around him for protection.

"Eet ees Vasquale," pleaded the spokesman fearfully. " 'e weel keel us eef 'e know we tell those secrets. We are yore prisoners. Yuh weel see 'e no keel?"

255

"What kinda hombre is this that's got the fear uh God into a gang a' eight a' yuh?" snapped the sheriff contemptuously. "Are yuh all scairt to death a' him?"

" 'E weel keel us," the whimper became a wail of terror. " 'E weel get ol' Pedro. Then 'e —" The man shuddered violently.

"He'll what?" Dawson leaned forward eagerly.

"Eet ees too terrible to theenk. 'E weel —"

It was evident that what old Pedro would do beggared the fellow's power of description. He choked on the words, terror tying his tongue.

" 'E ees do thees to one of the boys who let Maken go. Pore Juan — 'e ees suffer —"

Dawson lost the rest of the man's whimpering. He fingered his gun nervously as the riders halted at the gate and the man swung down to open it. It was Jack Larimore!

The two came on. The Texan slid his horse to a stop, eyeing the sheriff's ready .45 fearlessly.

"Yore the hombre I'm lookin' fer," snarled Dawson. "Yuh got some explainin' to do, too. Drag that six-gun a' yore'n with yore left han' an' throw it down there in the dirt."

"This is no time to stop for a chawing match," snapped Larimore. "We're right on the trail of running down the whole thing. Let's forget our little misunderstanding till we round-up that burro and then we can talk things over, if there's any use."

"Nope." Dawson was determined. "There ain't never no time like the present to get these things off'n yore chest. I'm goin' to take yuh 'long right now with the

256

resta these breeds. We can do any talkin' yuh want after yore in jail. Even if yuh ain't got nothin' to do with these murders — an' I ain't admittin' that yet — yuh shot me up to Riley's, so I got a case agin yuh."

"But we're right on the trail of these killin's, I tell you," argued Larimore. "The hombre that owns that burro's the fellow we want."

"Yep. Allus thought yuh knew somethin' 'bout 'em."

"Stop!" cut in Cochita. "I've always been your friend, John Dawson, even when daddy said you didn't have sense enough to pound sand in a prairie dog-hole."

Her flashing eyes set the officer to squirming uneasily in his saddle.

"If you don't listen to reason now I'll actually believe that he was right. Mr. Larimore knows more about this case than you do. He didn't, up until a few hours ago. I'm convinced that he's innocent. I've even gone so far as to employ him to take complete charge of the K-Spear and I'm willing to spend every cent to fight his case in court. I'll stand sponsor for him if you insist on being bull-headed, but I want you to understand we're going on now whether you like it or not. He's offering to help and can't afford to throw down his gun. Nor does he intend to.

"Jack," she turned to the cowboy, "I never in my life wanted gunplay. It was a constant source of trouble between poor daddy and me, but if John Dawson tries to disarm you I'll be a witness that you shot in selfdefense!"

The sheriff withered under the scorn, yet fire glinted in his eyes. He attempted to speak, but anger choked him.

When words finally did come he had mastered his rage.

"Well, Cochita," he said sheepishly, "it's been a kinda nervous day fer me. I was su'prised to see yuh come ridin' in with this hombre. After the way yuh talked down to the ranch I didn't know but what he was abducting yuh an' I hadta find out. Of course, feelin' like yuh do 'bout the thing there ain't nothin' —"

"It's no time for apologies, John," she reminded him sharply. "We're on the trail of that burro. Did you notice it?"

"Yep. I've found out a pile 'bout it."

"So have we, we believe," she said hastily, "but there'll be plenty of time to compare notes later. We've —"

"Never mind, Cochita," interrupted Jack. "We've no time for explaining now. Let's travel. Which way did he go, Dawson?"

"South toward Pedro's cabin yonder, an' ramblin' like a scairt rabbit."

The sheriff's attitude had changed completely. It was now bubbling with friendliness.

"Come on, then," shouted Larimore. "We'll have this thing run down in a jiffy."

"I can't go," growled the officer. "I got this hull nest a' breeds rounded up here. They're the hombres that branded them steers this mornin'."

"Good work," complimented Jack, missing the significance of the disclosure and not connecting the gang with the running of the Lazy-T brand. "How'd yuh land 'em?"

"Run 'em down. They've come clean with ever'thing. Vasquale —" he glanced at Cochita, whose face was pale, but who showed not the slightest tremor at mention of the name. "Vasquale's the mysterious Menendez an' owns the Double-Spear-Box."

"Already know that. Heard him say so this morning," was Larimore's terse reply.

"But these here are the hombres that kidnapped yore paw," persisted the sheriff, apparently set on enlightening them on at least one point.

"They are?" demanded the wide-eyed Cochita.

"Yep. They say they ain't the Revenge Gang, but I'm layin' odds they are. I got the goods on 'em."

"That's them all right," said Larimore. "I recognize 'em." He glowered at the eight who stood watching him restlessly. "I've suspected Vasquale with being mixed up with 'em for quite a spell. He got a hunch the day Ed went to town. He must've set these hombres on the trail for he pulled out right behind him. Where is he now?"

"These breeds say he's down to the K-Spear."

"He's not," announced Larimore shortly, "and that's not half of it. There's no telling where he is."

"Whaddaya mean?" asked Dawson quickly.

"Nothin'," was the cryptic reply, "only if my hunch is right I wouldn't be in his boots for anythin'."

"Holdin' a cuter?"

"We'll find out soon enough."

He attempted to dismiss the subject, but Cochita, who heard him in surprise, rode closer.

"What is it, Jack?" she asked quietly.

"Oh, nothing. But those packs are missing from that burro. I was just putting two and two together. Let's get going."

"But whaddaya figger 'bout this 'tokee'?" Dawson stopped him as he started forward.

"Singing lizards," answered Jack, plainly impatient to be on his way.

"What are they?"

"In the tropics they holler that 'tokee'!"

"This ain't the tropics," snorted Dawson. "What's that got to do with this range?"

"Nothing. There's none around here," was the aggravating reply.

"Well, what the —" exploded the sheriff, checking the oath as he glanced at the girl.

"It's just as plain as a four-ace hand, Dawson. It's got nothing to do with the killings, only indirect."

Larimore happened to glance at one of the prisoners. The fellow's face had gone pasty.

"Whaddaya know 'bout it?" he demanded.

The breed's eyes fell.

"No sabe!" he whispered hoarsely.

"They've 'no savvied' me to death," mumbled Dawson. "Yuh'll never get nothin' more'n they want to tell outa 'em. They know awright, but they ain't doin' a heap a' squealin' else they got a noose 'roun' their necks. I found out some thin's, but it was while I was hangin' one of 'em. Yuh intimate this burro's got somethin' to do with the killin's indirect? There wasn't no jackass down to the ranch the night — the night —" He hesitated out of respect for the girl's feelings. "I thought yuh was lyin' 'bout it when yuh said yuh was trailin' it up in them north brakes."

"You didn't give me time to tell you I met it coming from the K-Spear after I'd been hunting it all afternoon."

"Well, dang my pictures!" Dawson scratched his head in bewilderment, gazing along the trail to the hills where a blanket of dust hung over the path into the valley of Old Woman Creek. "Here'll be Peters an' Mowbry an' the Lazy-T bunch, I reckon," he announced. "They went on to the K-Spear 'cause Peters knew this rus'lin' was pulled this mornin'."

"What rustling are you talking about?" asked Jack.

"Didn't yuh know?" Dawson was evidently glad that at last he had found something he could explain. "These here breeds got into Peters' herd an' branded a bunch a' Lazy-T stuff with a K-Spear."

"That's what Vasquale was talking about up to the rimrock before you fell, wasn't it, Cochita?" flashed Larimore.

"Yes," reluctantly. "He said he had done it to force me to merge the two outfits."

"Well, he's plumb outa luck," broke in Dawson. "It jes happened I was Johnny-on-the-spot. Have yuh seen Vasquale?"

He glared at Jack.

"Yep."

"Yuh ain't coverin' him up, too, are yuh?"

"I should say not," blazed the puncher, "and he'll find out he's stirred up the wrong den of snakes if he's got Boss Peters and those Lazy-T hands scouting his trail."

CHAPTER
THIRTY

They sat silently watching the cloud of dust as it swirled down the valley and took shape in the forms of several riders who dashed through the gate toward them. Mowbry, his arms flapping, rode beside Peters, whose horse was eating up the miles in great, swinging strides. The determined faces of the punchers boded no good for rustlers or other breakers of the law. The K-Spear men spurred forward at sight of the girl, while Peters rode up beside Jack.

"We're plumb glad yore safe, Cochita," was Red's greeting as he dismounted and clasped her outstretched hand warmly.

"I'm fine, Red," she smiled. "But before we start explaining there's lots to be done. Jack here is in charge again and —" She paused, blushing furiously under the puncher's quizzical stare.

"We're fer yuh, ol' hoss," grinned the cowboy, shaking Larimore's hand. "Yuh know I kinda been —" Dawson moved into the circle.

"Mowbry," he said sharply, "I'm deputizin' yuh an' some a' yore men to handle these breeds. They've confessed to rus'lin' an' brandin' them Lazy-T steers this mornin'."

"Let me look at 'em close," said Peters, roweling ahead. "Did you find out if Vasquale was behind it?"

"Yep." The sheriff's tone was not overly friendly, much to the surprise of the group which watched the officer intently. "But yuh was protectin' Larimore an' tryin' to make me a goat an' I ain't calc'latin' to give yuh any too much information."

"Keep it to yourself, then," snapped Boss. "Guess all you ever did know wouldn't make a very big book. Seeing as how the cattle that were rustled were mine, I reckon I'm going to find out something about the deal, though. You're right when you say I'm protecting Larimore. I brought him back up the trail with my herd and I'm for him today, tomorrow and every other day as far as that goes. What do you think of that?"

The Texan's tone was flint-like. He edged his horse forward until he was facing Dawson in the circle. His hand hovered near the butt of his gun.

"What do you think of that?" he repeated slowly, his words dropping like icicles. "If you hadn't climbed on your high-horse and got so all-fired cocky, I might have told you a few more things I knew about this Vasquale."

"Yuh can't tell me nothin'," blurted out the sheriff. "I know all 'bout him. But yuh protected Larimore when I come to yuh askin' fer his delivery."

"You're the only one that ever thought he was guilty of anything," snapped Peters.

The two were rapidly approaching an open break. Red spurred between them, while Larimore unconsciously moved over to the girl, edging her horse among the Lazy-T men. The move did not escape Dawson, but

264

before he could voice the angry words that flared to his lips, Mowbry spoke.

"If yuh was to ask me," he smiled pleasantly, "I'd say yuh was both actin' like a pair a' day-old colts tryin' to cut capers on wobbly laigs. There ain't no use in yore gettin' riled now, when we all orter be trailin' Vasquale afore he gets clean outa the country. While we're standin' here tryin' to pick a fight among ourselves I reckon he's high-tailin' it. As fer Peters helpin' Larimore, I want yuh to know, Dawson, that he didn't. I did. An' furthermore" — he glanced at Cochita, but she avoided his eyes — "I did it under orders from the owner of the K-Spear!"

"What?" Jack's exclamation of incredulity brought a smile from the punchers. "How'd she know I was in the country?"

"I told her," replied Red promptly.

The girl was blushing prettily.

"Red," she reprimanded, "you had no right to violate my confidence."

"Mebby not, Miss Cochita," he answered penitently, "but it seems to me that it's a showdown all 'roun' an' I wanted Dawson to know that it wasn't Peters that was protectin' Jack, but that it was yuh an' me. Jack," he wheeled on the astonished Larimore, "when I brung yuh that hoss to make yore get-away from Dawson, it was under orders from Cochita. Not that I wouldn't a' done it myself, but I didn't see the sheriff an' she did. Yuh can thank her fer yore escape an' bein' free to ride till yuh got this thing figgered out."

"I thought you did a lot of hemming and hawing when your tongue slipped up yonder at the cave," Larimore accused the girl smilingly. Then to Red: "But she can thank herself for you swapping horses with me, cause if it hadn't been for that snubbing pony that worked on a rope we wouldn't have had any little gal running the ranch."

"Whaddaya mean?" demanded Mowbry.

"Vasquale backed her over that high cliff up there by the cave, threatening her with a gun, and it took me most of the morning to drag her back. Even then I couldn't have, but this little devil of a burro showed up just in time with a bunch of spare rope."

"Did he push yuh, Cochita?" cried Red.

"No," slowly, "I don't believe he did. He was angry and —"

"The dirty cur," snarled Mowbry. "That's another count agin him. He'll pay awright."

He faced Dawson.

"Are yuh goin' to sit there all day an' get rid o' yore gift uh gab, or are yuh comin' with us fellers an' help run down the hombres we're still lookin' fer?"

"Told yuh I was deputizin' yuh to take these breeds into Cibola," replied the sheriff testily. "I named yuh 'cause I was plumb certain yuh'd get there with 'em."

"I ain't anxious to lay off'n this chase," growled Red, "an' I reckon if yuh'll lemme turn 'em over to these other han's that ain't quite so int'rested it'd be healthier. I'm tellin' yuh frank, Dawson, me an' the K-Spear boys'd never get to town with 'em."

266

"Awright," snapped the officer. "If yo're threatenin' to kill, reckon I better deputize some uh Peters' men. Here, 'bout four uh yuh hombres," he beckoned the men forward, "I'm swearin' yuh in to trail these eight breeds back to the Lazy-T camp an' hold 'em till I come fer 'em. If anythin' happens I don't show up in the next few days, yuh take 'em in to Cibola. Tell the county attorney they admitted knowin' 'bout the hull deal."

Boss rode up beside the punchers.

"Don't need to tell you fellows," he said abruptly, "that you're working under Dawson's orders just like it was me. You're responsible to me and the Lazy-T for every head of 'em. Remember, they've confessed rustling our stock. I'm giving a few orders myself, though I don't reckon the sheriff'll welcome 'em. If any of these breeds make a break, you're plumb at liberty to open up. The idea is this: hold 'em at the Lazy-T camp if it's flat on their backs with a tarp pulled up over their faces. Do you understand?"

The four men nodded, and riding in behind the eight, herded them toward the outer gate. Peters swung on the sheriff.

"Now you and I have had words," he growled. "I'm willing to call quits if you're hankering that way. The Lazy-T bunch is with you to a man. But when you start on Jack Larimore you and your law and your whole damn country's got us to whip. That being off my chest, here's my paw."

Dawson met the steady gaze, hesitated for a second, then his hand went forward and clasped that of the Texan warmly.

"Which bein' done," put in Red, "reckon we'll ask Mister Larimore an' Miss Cochita to ride back to the K-Spear an' wait fer us an' we'll slip on down to Vasquale's homestead."

"Not on your life," protested Jack. "I started this here ball rolling and I'm going to follow it."

He glanced at the girl.

"That goes for me, too, Red," she said quietly. "Jack and I are not going to quit the chase now."

"But, Cochita," pleaded the cowboy, "it's no place fer yuh. There's li'ble to be shootin' an' — an ever'thin'."

"Even shooting isn't entirely new to me lately," she smiled. "I'm going, that's all there is to it. Come on, Jack, let's show this posse how to trail that 'tokee' burro!"

"'Tokee'!" shouted Dawson. "What yuh talkin' 'bout?"

"That's just the way somebody has of calling this jackass," laughed Larimore. "When we find the owner of the brute we've got the hombre that did the killings."

"Le's travel," bellowed the sheriff, jabbing his horse with the spurs and heading south toward a cabin on the skyline. "Them breeds jes told me that ol' Pedro like as not had called that burro when he went through the yard here on a high lope."

CHAPTER
THIRTY-ONE

Sunset on the prairie.

The lengthening shadows of the brush lay in serrated lines across the heat-seamed, adobe flats. A violet haze bathed the stretches in a soft, peaceful light, settling over the Sangres in a filmy blanket through which the peaks towered like tinted, fairy citadels.

Cochita and Jack galloped ahead of the party, in silence. Her hair, which she had caught up carelessly, swirled in golden strands about her face. Her eyes, sparkling with excitement, brought shy glances of admiration from the man at her side, yet in their depths lurked a wistfulness, inspired by the tragedy she had endured. Topping a rise, they drew rein, waiting for the others to come up.

"Isn't it beautiful?" she exclaimed. "But so —"

The cry of ecstasy died on her lips. She caught her breath sharply. A fleeting fear, a terror of the unknown, flashed in her eyes. She shuddered and edged her pony closer to his.

"— but so — awful. There's Pedro's cabin."

Partly concealed in a thicket of gigantic prairie sunflowers and weeds stood a dilapidated shack. Now, in the flaming sunset, its weather-curled, battered sides had taken on a blood-red hue. The slanting rays reflected from the one dirty window in crimson streamers which diffused the weed-choked yard with a stain of carnage.

The startling color increased the ominous misgivings they both felt. Reaching over he patted her hand.

"I'd rather you'd stay back here and wait, Cochita," he urged gently. "Don't know what we're going to run into."

"No, Jack, I'm going on," she answered, in spite of her forced air of bravery gazing anxiously at the cardinal scene. "Don't look so serious," she begged. "It's natural for me to want to help."

"I understand," he assured her as they jogged along, "but knowing whoever did it'll be taken care of ought to be good enough. I've got a hunch something's going to pop *pronto*. I'll have a couple of the boys stick with you. Stay here, please."

"No," she repeated firmly. "Forget I'm a girl. I'm not afraid. I'm going to fight it out just like daddy would if he were here."

Realizing that argument was useless, he changed the subject suddenly.

"Wonder where that donkey went?"

As he spoke they rounded a tottering barn. Within the rotting pole corral stood the burro, almost hidden in the swaying sunflowers, nibbling at the tufts of grass that banked the roots of the tall stalks.

"Pedro!" he exclaimed. "Maybe those breeds back yonder had cause to shiver."

"Do you really believe that burro belongs to Pedro?" she asked in a hushed voice. "If it does it means — it means Ramon —"

The arrival of the posse checked his answer.

"Reckon we're late," he remarked. "That burro's packs are still missing."

"His packs?" demanded Peters and Dawson in the same breath. "What's his packs got to do with it?"

"You'll find out they play a mighty big part in the proceedings," was the cryptic reply as Jack swung down and helped Cochita to dismount. "I'm going to have a look at that cabin."

Taking the girl by the hand, he ducked into an arroyo and started forward, their heads below the level of the sunflowers that lined the banks.

"If that's Pedro's burro I 'low he can throw a heap of light on things. Let's see if he's here."

The words were scarcely out of his mouth when a scream split the stillness, halting them with the suddenness of an enfilading fire and sending Cochita in terror against his side. The echo battered to nothing in the foothills. The only sound was a whining of the breeze through the weeds. A sinister hush like the dead calm before a storm settled over the prairie.

"Come on, Dawson!" Jack said in an undertone. "You and me'll do some scouting. Red," he turned to Mowbry, "I'm depending on you to keep Cochita back. Watch out for her."

With a squeeze of the hand which checked the angry retort that flashed to the girl's lips, Larimore whipped out his gun, sprang up the embankment and plunged into the thicket toward the cabin.

"Whaddaya reckon that screechin' was?" panted Dawson, dogging the cowboy's heels.

Jack made no reply, intently watching the shack, visible between the sunflower stalks. The sheriff shot him an admiring glance. The firmness of his step, the steadiness of his eyes, the determined set of his square jaws found the officer ashamed that he had condemned the fearless youth so harshly.

They worked their way stealthily to the side of the one-roomed cabin. Not certain that the cry had come from the hovel, yet on his guard against surprise, Larimore hugged the warped wall, edging along until he could touch the grimy window. Shifting his gun to his left hand, he reached out and wiped away the drift dirt clinging to the pane.

A low moan, ending in a gurgle, caught his ear. Moving over cautiously, he peered within, straining to pierce the gloom. As his eyes became accustomed to the dim light he could distinguish the figure of old Pedro hunched over a still form on a bed, the packs beside him.

Raising up suddenly, the peon sighted Larimore at the window. A crash! The glass shattered in scores of blinding prisms. Jack darted back, his face pricked with the stinging slivers. A spent knife fell harmlessly outside the cabin at their feet.

"Who is it?" whispered Dawson hoarsely.

"Don't move!" warned Larimore. "It's Pedro!"

They stood motionless, hugging the side of the shack, listening. Everything grew quiet within.

"We've got him cornered. He can't get away. Let's rush him!" With a vicious kick, he knocked the door sagging on its strap hinges.

"You're covered! Don't start anything!" he shouted. Followed by Dawson, he leaped within, then stopped short. "Well, I'm damned!"

A death-like silence greeted them. On the dirt floor a lizard crawled about curiously. A chameleon frolicked on the rough board table, which, with a camp stove and a bedstead of unfinished two-by-fours, was the only furnishings the hovel boasted. Aside from the reptiles which scurried to cover at their entrance the cabin was deserted!

A hasty survey of the room proved that the peon had vanished. Completely baffled, Jack turned to the bed. On a heap of filthy blankets lay the motionless figure of Vasquale.

"I saw him doing this."

He pointed to the discolored marks on Ramon's throat.

"Bolos," he said quietly.

Throwing open the shirt he revealed the purple dots above the heart.

"Nobody but a crazy man that was nuts about reptiles or religion'd think of that. Fetishism! Old Pedro's the one we're gunning for. He's the singing lizard. He was bending over Ramon when I peeked in. He saw me, threw that knife and took a sneak. But how'd he get out?"

"Yuh got me stumped," admitted Dawson blankly. "There's how!"

Beneath the table Larimore sighted a hole in the dirt floor large enough for a man to squeeze into.

"That burrow must lead outside. We'll —"

The words died on his lips. He leaped back, pushing Dawson aside. At the mouth of the passageway, blocking their advance, whirred a diamond-backed rattlesnake.

"Le's burn the place down," growled the sheriff. "That'll bring him to time if he's hidin' in that badger hole. I ain't lost no rattle-bugs."

Wheeling, he started for the door. Jack lingered a moment, but being unable to see the peon in the tunnel, followed.

"Go 'long there, yuh one way steer! Go on!"

A strange medley of sound drifting up the draw stopped them just outside. The commands were punctuated with pops like pistol shots. A weird, shrieking gibberish followed each sharp order. Breaking into a run, the two rejoined the punchers and Cochita, who stood on the rim of the ravine staring in wonder.

"What the devil?" gasped Dawson, finding his voice.

"You got me." Jack stepped to the side of the girl.

"Get 'long there, yuh —"

"Tokee! Tokee! Tokee!" arose a blood-curdling scream.

The burro in the corral threw up its tail and dashed past them down the arroyo. Unconsciously Larimore slipped his arm about Cochita. She appeared not to notice, but to Mowbry, who chanced to glance their way, the tell-tale flush tinging her face belied her apparent ease.

A strange pair hove in sight. As the first started past, broad grins broke on the faces of the possemen. Coming up the draw, a long rope whacking at his moccasined heels, the packs thrown across his shoulders, was Pedro squealing in pidgin English. Armed with a frayed picket rope and long butcher knife, and astride the jaded horse the wrangler had padded for him, the cook of the K-Spear was exhorting his captive to greater speed.

"Howdy, fellers!" shouted the chef, catching sight of the party. "I got 'em The damn —"

The burro slid to a halt at the peon's side. With an agility remarkable for the aged and withered body, he vaulted onto the animal's back. Nimbly dodging the terrific sweep of the cook's knife, the burro leaped over the rim of the ravine, and bolted from sight in another arroyo, old Pedro stretched along its lean back.

"Get our hosses, boys!" thundered Dawson. "Don't let him get away."

"I almos' had him!" shouted the chef as the possemen raced for their ponies. "I cotched him sneakin' through the weeds like a mangy coyote. That's the way, yuh know-nothin's! Get a feller like me, who really can run down bad men, an' he can't get no help from yuh grinnin' bobcats, which thinks standin' 'roun' an' lettin' him get away is all yore expected to do."

He mopped his sweat-beaded brow.

"Dang me, Cochita, gal, I'm plumb tickled I was here in time to help yuh escape. Had a hunch I'd be needed an' I shore been coverin' some tall ground with this bronc a' mine."

The punchers, already mounted, roared with laughter.

"Lotta help yuh was," Mowbry hurled at him. "Whaddaya capturin' ol' Pedro fer? Ain't a man got a right to walk acrost the flats any way he wants to?"

The cook was nonplussed.

"Say," he asked himself, "what did I capture him fer? I didn't want him. I wanted Vasquale. Aw, yuh go to the devil, will yuh?" he threw at Red as he eased his cramped legs over the horse and slid stiffly to the ground. "Reckon I've rid enough fer one day. I done my duty, though. Yuh fellers cotch Vasquale. I ain't got no more int'r'st in yore man hunt now I've rescued my little gal."

"Ride!" barked Dawson, breaking in on the monologue. "We're losin' time. Get Pedro!"

The posse flashed down the ravine, leaving the chef alone. That worthy cast an anxious glance at the cabin, then across the expanse of prairie over which the twilight dusk was settling.

"Reckon I better jine up with the gang," he groaned. "Ain't no place fer a man to be waitin' by his lonesome."

His great belly heaved with exertion as he clambered up again and turned the nose of his mount down the arroyo. The animal broke into a lumbering trot.

"Aw, Gawd!" he bawled. "Stop it! Whoa! Ain't yuh got no feelin' fer a feller? I tried to play yuh out. Yore

276

the hardest thing on four laigs. Do yuh hear me, yuh mullet-head? Whoa!"

Jiggling the mass of chafed and quivering flesh on its sharp backbone, hurling it aloof like a rubber ball at each stiff-legged step, the horse only trotted the faster in the wake of the posse.

A mile down the draw they found old Pedro stretched face upward on the ground, his body partly covering the packs. The burro was nibbling with unconcern beside him. Dismounting, the men approached cautiously, but the peon did not move. In vain Jack attempted to hold Cochita back, but she was at his elbow as they leaned over the wasted figure. A weary smile at sight of her played on the seamed face.

"*Muchacha*," came feebly from the withered lips. "Vasquale, he ees drive ol' Pedro, who ees all time afraid. *Madre de Dios!*"

The faltering voice ended in a gasp. A gleam of satisfaction flickered in the age-dimmed eyes.

"Vasquale, he say —"

The words were growing fainter. The peon was exerting every effort to control his sagging jaws.

"— he say Bevins an' Riley he ees not Chreestian. Cline he ees make fun of Virgin. Yore padre he ees try to keel ol' Pedro's God. Vasquale, he tell Pedro — then Pedro — he keel!"

He attempted to raise himself on his elbow but sank back weakly. The faded eyes fluttered and came to rest on Cochita's ashen face.

"Vasquale —"

The name was almost inaudible, coming in a choking sob.

"— back — at rancho — say — *pequena muchacha* — she steal Pedro's God. He — ees lie!"

The cracked lips skinned over the toothless gums. "Padre!"

The voice was but a sucking whisper.

"Ol' Pedro — he see — Vasquale push — leetle Cochita off cleef. *Buen Dios!* Thees leetle *muchacha* — good to ol' Pedro. She ees save! Vasquale — he pay! Tokee! Tokee! Tokee."

As though his last thought was of his one friend, the faint cry that tightened the nerves of the silent group, brought the burro trotting to its master's side. The trace of a smile played on the wrinkled face at sight of the inquisitive, flapping ears, then with a feeble groan the ancient body stiffened.

A sigh escaped Dawson. Tears trickled unheeded across the girl's cheeks.

"Jack," she whispered fearfully, snuggling close to him, "he's dead! Is Ramon?"

Drawing her closer, he nodded toward the cabin.

"Pedro killed him up yonder in the shack," he said hoarsely, attempting to soften his tone. "We didn't get here in time or we could have stopped him."

She looked at him bravely through the tears.

"It's — it's just as well," she choked. "The boys — would have — have —" She fought desperately to control her emotions.

"The boys would have hung him," grated Red, finishing her sentence.

"And it's what he deserved!" she added fiercely.

"The hull thing's cleared up," observed Dawson, glancing at Peters, who suddenly had found it necessary to tug at his latigo. "There's yore 'tokee' explained. Jack saw Pedro croak Vasquale, an' the pore ol' devil admitted the other killin's. But what —"

"Get back, Cochita!" Larimore's warning fell like a stroke, as the girl, to conceal the tears which she was fighting to check, took a step toward the body of the peon.

The roar of Jack's six-gun at her elbow brought her about, rigid with fright. The bullet kicked up a puff of dust at Pedro's side. Dawson sprang forward, clutching the hot barrel. Larimore tore it from his grasp.

"Jack!" screamed the girl. "What are you doing?"

"Have yuh gone plumb loco?" demanded the sheriff. "What's the idee a' shootin' a dead man? Gimme that gun!"

"Get out of the way!" Larimore shoved the officer aside.

The girl stood motionless, watching him. His face was drawn and bloodless. His gaze was riveted on the still form of Pedro. Unconsciously she recoiled from the fire blazing in his eyes.

"Cochita, stand still!" he pleaded through whitened lips. "For God's sake, don't move!"

A look of amazement crossed Peters' face as he strode to Larimore's side. Mowbry and the rest of the party closed in. It was evident that none of them understood the cowboy's sudden warning.

"Cochita!" Jack's voice was scarcely above a whisper. "I'm going to shoot! Don't move!"

She stared at him through eyes wide with terror, and made the slightest movement toward him. He leaped forward suddenly, seized her by the arm and shoved her roughly behind him.

"This has gone far enough!" roared Dawson. "Drop —"

His voice was drowned in the blast of Jack's gun. The trembling girl buried her face in her hands. Peters whipped out his Colt.

"You got him!" he shouted. "Why didn't you tell us?"

"Tell you hell!" blazed Jack. "I was afraid Cochita'd jump right into it. There's what did your killings, Dawson!"

He stood, wiping the beads of perspiration from his brow. Cochita stifled a scream. Within two inches of where she had stood writhed a huge, orange-colored Gila monster.

Just topping the rim of the arroyo as the second shot broke the stillness, the cook's horse shied, pitching him headlong to the ground.

"Under cover, boys!" he squealed. "They got us cornered. Give 'em hell! Ever' man fer hisself!"

He climbed to his feet, slashing the air viciously with his knife. In spite of the seriousness of the occasion the punchers could not repress their smiles at sight of the bow-legged man cutting blindly at an unseen foe. Their laughter died quickly. Leaving the cook to engage his imaginary adversary, they turned back to Larimore, who had not moved.

The girl came timidly to his side.

"Forgive me, Jack," she said simply. "I couldn't understand why you didn't want me to move. It sounded so foolish. I thought —"

"Just what Dawson did," he supplied smilingly; "you thought I'd gone loco. I knew what was in those packs and had my eye peeled. I saw that Gila up yonder at the cliff and tried to get a crack at it, but the burro got away. It's what's been causin' those marks over the heart. The victims were choked with a bolo. Vasquale was the rustler leader; Pedro the killer."

"What did he wanna go to all this trouble fer?" questioned Dawson.

"Kept you guessing and getting nowhere, didn't it? Then he was a religious nut. He said before he died that he did those killings when Vasquale told him they was making fun of his God, didn't he? Looked like fetishism up at Riley's that night, but you wouldn't give me a chance to say."

He reached out quickly as the girl swayed dizzily. Clasping her in his arms, he supported her trembling body.

"Jack," she sobbed, "take me away. I can't stand any more!"

"We're going pronto, little pard," he whispered, stroking her hair tenderly. "Don't worry. It's all over now. We'll try and forget it and —"

He looked up, embarrassed, but the others were tiptoeing from sight in the dusk veiling the arroyo. "And just be happy."

"Jack," she crooned the name.

With a contented sigh, she buried her flaming face against his shoulder. He stood awkwardly as her arms crept about his neck, then squaring himself, he lifted her face and planted a kiss on her lips.

"Time to be ridin', Cochita, if we're goin' to get home afore midnight," the voice of the cook broke in on them gruffly. "They ain't got a bite to eat at the ranch 'ceptin' a little bacon an' they'll be needin' fresh bread in the mornin'. Cut out the courtin' an' le's travel."

Larimore flashed him a hateful look, then smiled as his eyes met those of the girl.

"Come on, Jack," she said, almost gaily, "let's go home."

"Heading home, little pard," he whispered hoarsely, squeezing her hand as they started for their ponies. He turned at the rim of the arroyo and looked back.

"Singing Lizard," he muttered, "you've sung your last tune."

W